Wearing

Pink

Pyjamas

by

Jane Dare

Copyright Jane Dare 2013

*For Michael, Kez & Beth
The happiest moments, the greatest successes.
The dazzling moments of joy that will burn brightly forever.*

This book is a work of fiction. Names, characters, places, and incidents are either a product of the author's imagination or are used fictitiously. Any resemblance to actual people living or dead, events, or locales is entirely coincidental.

'I do not wish women to have power over men; but over themselves.'
Mary Willstonecraft Shelly

'A woman is like a tea bag - you can't tell how strong she is until you put her in hot water.'

Eleanor Roosevelt

Prologue
December 2009

Birmingham, West Midlands

'Your life is immense and precious. What do you plan to do with it?'

Angela gestured around the dreary room as she spoke, to emphasise her point. It was a simple enough question but she wondered why she was bothering with such bored looking women. The years had brought different rooms in different countries, full of different faces, but somehow the problems always remained the same.

She hated how disheartened she'd become lately. This was supposed to be what she lived for, an obsession to right the world in her own small way. Perhaps, she pondered, it was simply the memories attached to this time of year that made her gloomy. She absently contemplated the olive green floor, worn down to resemble bare earth rather than carpet. The forlorn sight of it pulled her further away from the young women watching her until only the deep luscious aroma of coffee brewing reached her. As usual, and right on time, something deep in her core bucked her out of self pity to the job she was here to do. The stab of possibility and promise pierced Angela as she reflected on the journey that underpinned her own cosy existence.

'It's inevitable,' she resumed. 'You're young and you believe the world is out there, just waiting for *'you'* to happen. And it is. But don't think for one second you can just sit there and wait for a free ride to success.'

Angela paused and the ghost of a smile went out to her young audience. It broke her heart, to see all these girls, desperate to lift themselves out of the life they felt destined to lead. Where was it all still going wrong? But at the same time she felt buds of hope. Looking around the small community centre room she realised many of the faces were drinking her in. Even the gang hardened teenagers, who stared into space and feigned indifference were free to leave but, so far, had chosen to stay.

'I don't believe in fate,' she continued, with an edge of firmness lacing her voice. 'Only the one you make. So let this programme teach you how to take control of your lives and work towards being more than anyone has told you is possible.'

'But let's be clear here and use that word *'work'* again. Remember no one, and that includes me, is offering you a free ride. I've had role models in my life, many of them women, and their wisdom and experiences guided and inspired me to dream bigger than I should have dared, but nothing came without hard work. For me, or for them.'

Angela smoothed a manicured hand across the back of a battered chair. Keep it together Angie, she told herself. You've done this a hundred times.

'Some days you'll breeze through life.' The words came out before Angela had a chance to catch them and a haze fell as she remembered the first time she'd started this speech. So much celebration and too much heartbreak. She found herself unable to finish the sentence and quickly changed direction.

'But most times you won't. Accept that. Plan for that. Turn that round and you're half way there.'

Realising her voice was trailing away, Angela instantly pulled herself back to the present and said a little more insightfully than anyone could realise,

'What do you want to be remembered for?'

Angela saw some eyes roll. It saddened and angered her in equal measure, because it had never been more relevant than it was today. Women had spent decades laying the foundations for equality and freedom of choice with hard work and tenacity only to find a new underbelly of apathy, and celebrity seeping up and convincing these young women that effort and education are outdated and no longer required.

Settling herself on one of many ancient, comfortable

armchairs filling the small room, Angela knew she needed to look approachable to these young women. Her message was a tough one but it had to be delivered by someone authentic, someone these women could aspire to be. A woman they wanted to listen to, not some corporate fake talking a good game. She hoped she hadn't sounded full of text book crap. Angela always felt a weight of responsibility when she came to these gatherings. How could she look genuine and worthy of their trust? How could she convince a group of disengaged young women that they should dare to hope and dream of a more fulfilling life? How best to show them that it required work and determination and not a quest for fifteen minutes of fame or notoriety?

If she had all day she would tell them about where she started and about her dearest friends Kitty and Bee. She would remind them that life has both good and bad times. That the happiest moments, the greatest successes won't lessen the pain of loss. It still has to be endured. No, no she wouldn't she realised. She would start at the beginning, with *why* she met them and she would teach them that disappointment and loss will never dim those dazzling moments of joy. They will burn brightly forever. The story would have to start, with her own mother and with Jenny, two women who couldn't have been more different, but who fashioned a young girl into the woman Angela had become.

Chapter One
1983

Barnstone Near Nottingham

'I don't know why you're thinking about college and exams Angela. What happens when you leave school and get married? It will just have been a waste of time and money.'

Angela had heard those words in a variety of guises for the last year from her mother, Joan, and was starting to feel a very physical irritation that she had never once considered Angela had other choices.

Her father Robert had always worked hard and his modest wage was only lightly supplemented by Joan working evenings in a packing factory. Living in a very modest terraced house on the edge of the village, Joan would often tell people that they lived in the countryside and although Angela didn't speak up she would internally correct her mother's misplaced snobbery, and scoff that Joan seemed to equate their unexceptional lives with fulfilment.

'I know you're laughing at me young lady,' Joan would scold when they were alone. 'But we were the first in our family to have a mortgage. Your father has worked hard for you. You'll understand some day when you have children of your own.' When Joan spoke, Angela noticed that she often fluffed up her hair even though the home permed curls were immobile with hairspray.

It had been a very normal, uneventful upbringing. A house that was clean and neat, the smell of home cooked meat and gravy, nothing spicy and certainly never extravagant and, as Angela had come to realise by the time she reached sixteen, a virtual replica of her Grandmother's life. Angela tried, though often failed, not to hold this as a criticism. Her mother was happy with her life and it was the life Joan had planned, but it was that fact of the matter that defined Joan's view of Angela's future.

'Find yourself a nice boy Angela. There are two type of girls you know. The ones boys want to sleep with and the ones they want to marry.'

Angela was starting to experience real alarm and anxiety that her life was planned out to replay lives before and she would never live beyond the small village she'd grown up in.

'What about what I want Mum? What if I don't care what type of girl a boy wants?'

Joan would sniff, smooth down the apron covering her turtle neck jumper and trousers and walk away to busy herself with folding washing.

If Angela fell out with friends, and sulked about the house, Joan's advice was just as consistent.

'Don't let them upset you Angela, once you're married and have a family of your own you won't need friends.'

Angela didn't think less of her Mother for believing any of this was true. She decided it was just the way Joan and generations before her had been brought up. What did astound her was that no one in the family had broken the mould. It was impossible for Angela to comprehend and at her most frustrated she felt she'd grown up in a lie where women believed the world flat and they shouldn't dare venture to the edge.

Determined to prove she did have a choice, to herself as much as her Mother, Angela resolutely followed school with two years at college. Weekend working at the local supermarket paid for the forty minute bus journey twice a day and Angela was justly proud that she never once asked her parents for extra money.

'It still costs money to feed you young lady.' Joan's disapproval was barely hidden, but as time went by she pondered that college, or even the bus journey, were all suitable places to meet husbands. It wouldn't hurt to make less fuss, she decided, hoping college would become a suitable means to an end.

Although college had been a daunting prospect initially for Angela there had never been a doubt in her mind that it was necessary and easily achievable. University, however, seemed imposing and too terrifying a prospect.

'I'm not sure I want to go to University Mum,' she confided. 'I think I can get a good job in town without it.' Lack of belief in her own ability was paralysing and colossal and Angela couldn't bring herself to admit it to anyone.

'I don't think University is for the likes of us Angela,' her mother concluded with the authority of relief. 'Don't put yourself out there to be trodden on.'

This conclusion only served to madden and exasperate Angela to the point where the desire to succeed pushed her at eighteen to apply for jobs in nearby Nottingham. She reasoned that the journey each day would be no longer than she was used to already and if she wanted to get anywhere in life, she had to get away from the village.

'A nice little secretary job sounds lovely,' Joan conceded.

'Mum, I'm getting six thousand a year already,' Angela argued, desperate to show her mother this was more than a time filler before she settled down to looking after a husband. 'And who knows where it could lead.'

Joan could only watch and pray that her daughter didn't fall. She wasn't stupid, she knew ranting at Angela was just pushing her further away, but her desperation for things to be as they had always been was so deeply rooted it was impossible for her to imagine Angela's growing ambition as anything but alien, eccentric and doomed.

*

You often hear people say that their life would have been very different if they hadn't met a particular person. A person who touches your life in a way, good or bad, that never leaves you. For Angela, that was Jenny. Jenny was everything Angela wanted to be with the same intensity that Joan was everything Angela planned to avoid.

Angela couldn't put an age on Jenny. She decided Jenny was probably the same age as her mother, perhaps older. She was the most elegant, chic woman Angela had ever seen, so much so that when Angela described her she could smell 'Miss Dior' as palpably as if Jenny was stood in front of her. She wore a full face of make up, but it was always immaculate and understated, never racy or lewd and she framed it with shoulder length, glossy, super straight chestnut hair. Each day her skirt would stop at the knee and show off her slender legs, always in nude coloured tights and never in anything but heeled shoes always darker than the shade on her legs. Regardless of whether she was wearing a blouse or a jumper, you could always detect the shape of her slender frame, but never in a suggestive or improper way that would be less than professional for work. The whole ensemble was always completed with a stylish jacket; not always the same colour as the skirt, but always co-ordinating.

Quietly worshipping her, and diligently following her lead, Angela decided from the first week she worked alongside Jenny that she wanted to be her.

Jenny had a manner about her that was composed and serene. She could organise and manage everyone meticulously and Angela never caught her looking remotely stressed or under pressure as she ordered their daily lives for them. Angela, young and unsophisticated, made lots of the simple mistakes you would naturally make fresh out of college.

'That's OK Angela, come and sit with me and I'll show you some tricks of the trade.'

Jenny's voice would always glide reassuringly over to Angela.

'Thank you Jenny. I really don't want to mess up.'

'And you won't. Have a little faith in yourself. We all have to start somewhere. Come on, we'll do it together.'

Working at desks next to each other, Jenny guided and taught Angela through the next two years. It became Angela's obsession to soak up everything Jenny did and said, and how she did it and how she said it. On rare occasions she showed confidence and panache, but through the early months she relished the security of keeping quiet and learning from Jenny's experience.

Angela felt honoured as their work relationship evolved into friendship, and during some of the dinners they shared together, Angela knew that Jenny enjoyed her tales of the latest boyfriend or night club as much as she enjoyed hearing Jenny's stories of countries she had visited and men she had fallen in love with.

Being with Jenny, or rather, wanting to be Jenny was the final inspiration Angela needed to spread her wings. She knew what had been right for her mother and her grandmother would never make her happy.

'What do you think Jenny? Do you think I should apply for a promotion? What if I'm not good enough?' Just because Jenny was strong and successful didn't mean she would be, she agonised to herself.

'I can't believe you are even asking me that,' Jenny replied playfully. 'You'll always meet people that believe you're practising witchcraft, but that's their problem. Don't make it yours.'

Still only twenty, Angela applied for a job as senior secretary in the London office. Hugely unwilling to believe in her own potential, and not practised at brazen pretending, she dithered when she was offered the role.

'What is it with you girls,' sneered one of the senior partners. 'You make such a fuss about wanting equal money and thinking you should be taken seriously. It's all we have to listen to these days, and then, when it comes to making a decision you can't cope. Your lot will never make progress you know. This is ridiculous.

You should quit while you're ahead.'

Angela burnt. She was rooted to the chair in the office staring at the chipped edge of the wooden table while picking at the thread it had pulled on her skirt. After mumbling that she just needed five minutes she fled from the room forcing her back straight and her head high. She wanted to sob with humiliation but her anger at her own indecision crushed and smothered the burning in her chest.

Jenny was determined Angela would stay empowered.

'Forget him Angela. Ignore the comment and take the job. He won't be the last and you can't let him defeat you. You can't let any of them defeat you. Fight back.'

Joan, secretly proud of her daughter's spirit, tried not to sound negative when Angela told her she was leaving Barnstone.

'No one in our family has ever lived so far away from home.'

Any trace of pride as Joan spoke was trampled by concern, and Angela detected neither as she replied matter of factly.

'Your beginnings don't dictate where you go Mum.'

Joan couldn't get close to understanding her daughter's choices and she noted with sadness, and in silence, that her visible unrest would only serve to push them further apart.

Chapter 2
October 1987

Palmers Green, London

'Hi. You must be Ange? Come on in,' asserted a confident voice, before the door was even fully open.

It was a decidedly chilly evening, the muted light fading fast, as is inevitable in autumnal England. Whereas the curb had been an array of gold and red leaves discarded by the trees, Angela noted that the steps approaching this front door were swept and painted rather than ignored by the young residents, who Angela had assumed would have neither the time or the inclination to clear them away.

Bee held the door open wide and Angela took a deep breath and smiled as she stepped into what she hoped would become her new home.

'God, it feels cold out there,' gushed Bee, as she ushered Angela further into the hall and shut the door with a sharp flick of one hand.

No wonder she felt cold. Bee was dressed in a short sports skirt and vest top, her bare legs strong and toned, not skinny. She was striking, tall and athletic, not what you would call immediately beautiful, with not quite tanned skin, more freckly really and long sandy curls pulled up high into a no nonsense pony tail.

'Hi. Yes, I'm Angela.' Smiling, she extended her hand as she would have done at work. It still felt odd for her to do that but she wanted to give the impression that she was professional and destined for greatness even when she actually felt overwhelmed and completely out of her depth. She had already decided she liked the way Bee had abbreviated her name, it made her feel like a different person.

'Thanks for inviting me over to look round Bee. This place looks lovely already and believe me, I have seen some nightmares this week.'

'Well it's nice to meet you Ange, come into the kitchen. Shall we have a glass of wine?'

Unsure if Bee's words were suggestions or commands, Angela quickly followed her along the hallway past the living room. Having a quick peek around she was impressed, but not surprised, that it looked remarkably tidy and organised. One of the young chaps who worked in the post room at the office had told her about Bee. He and Bee played together at a badminton club in Islington and he knew she was looking for a third house mate to share the rent with.

'Make yourself at home,' called Bee, as she rummaged in a drawer for a bottle opener.

The kitchen was much bigger than Angela's kitchen at home, and had trendy additions like a tall glass spaghetti jar on the side, and a wooden wine rack full of bottles. A large pine table inhabited the middle of the room surrounded by four not quite matching pine chairs, each with a flowery pad tied to its seat. Angela was loving it already; a ready made future full of choice and independence.

'So when do you officially move to the London office Ange? You don't mind Californian wine do you?'

Mind! Angela smiled shyly to herself. She knew nothing about wine. She knew nothing much about alcohol actually, other than drinking Babycham or Snowball at Christmas and the odd dry Martini and lemonade. Jenny would always drink a sweet sherry before a meal and she had quite enjoyed that, but no way was she any kind of expert. A smile spread to her eyes as she remembered when she was sixteen being able to have a glass of Liebfraumilch with the Sunday roast and her head spinning while trying to revise in the afternoons for 'O' levels. The smile wilted slightly as she suddenly suspected her life was about ten years behind everyone else's.

'One of my favourites,' she fibbed as she took the glass. 'I transfer properly in two weeks. I have this week off to find somewhere to live and next week to move. John said you had a room available now, and to be honest, I was relieved. I would rather live with other women and someone, well you know, recommended.' She stopped talking, aware she was rambling and took a sip of the wine. It was cold and not as sweet as the wine she had drunk before but she liked it.

Bee, who had been rummaging absently in her bag, came and sat down at the table. She took a huge gulp of wine and said very casually, 'John and I have known each for about four years now, nice bloke, we play as partner's at the club,' she motioned to her attire. 'No idea what he's doing with his life other than spending his parent's money. Certainly doesn't look like he plans to leave home.' Bee took another swig and smirked, 'I suppose I'm being a bit of a hypocrite though, I only live here because my parents are paying the mortgage. I couldn't afford it myself, but at least I have a decent job and can afford to pay them rent, well some of the rent.' She smiled as she gestured towards Angela in what Angela assumed was her way of saying she needed help with the rent. 'I was just there this afternoon, at the badminton club, having a doubles game with Dad. We didn't win and he was in a really grumpy mood when I left him, he's so competitive. Do you play?'

Angela always considered what to say whenever asked this question. 'I like exercise,' she started brightly, trying to sound decisive and confident. 'I'm not really one for team sports though, didn't do much of it at school I guess. I love to swim and at home a group of us used to go to aerobics twice a week.' She hoped this made her sound like a sociable safe bet for a house mate. She had no idea why she never participated in team sports, but suspected it was same subtle stereotyping that had been at play during her childhood reinforcing that women need not be competitive, it wasn't their role in life. It had certainly left a fear of failure that paralysed her from trying and a tendency to gravitate towards activities that required you to rely on yourself rather than play a role in a bigger team.

Bee seemed to buy it. Her smile was bright and she took another large mouthful of wine, jumped up and headed for the hallway.

'Come on, come and have a look round. I really hope you like it here, you could move in whenever you want as the room is empty.'

Liking the house was an understatement. As Angela followed Bee around the house she knew this would be a place to call home. It was old, probably Victorian, with charming sash windows and handsome fireplaces in every room, but it was simple and unpretentious now due to its modern colour scheme and the fact that two twenty some things on the bottom of their career ladder lived here. There were two bedrooms upstairs and a large bathroom which presumably had once been another bedroom. Angela would also have free use of the kitchen and living room. The dining room downstairs was now being used as a third bedroom, although, Caroline, the girl who lived in the house with Bee, wasn't in right now.

'Kitty, that's what everyone calls her. Her parents live close by so she pops off to bible study every week with them.' Bee's nose wrinkled slightly as she said it. 'They are a nice couple, her Dad is a doctor,' she corrected herself quickly aware she sounded critical. 'Kitty is a sweetie and likes to go with them just because she always has.' Bee chuckled slightly. 'Kitty is lovely, really kind and gentle. She's not as religious as they are and she doesn't shove it at you or anything, but … she is also gorgeous to look at, and quite enjoys the attention that brings.' Bee pondered on this as she said it. 'She seems to take it in her stride, that they're all queuing up to drool over her when we go out,' she added dryly. 'I guess it's the way it has always been for Kitty.'

Angela noted Bee sounded very matter of fact, but wondered if there was a tiny edge of disapproval.

Tour over, Bee poured herself another glass of wine, topped Angela's first glass up and discussions moved on to how much the room would cost each week and a date Angela could move in. During the following week in fact, which was perfect and Angela relaxed visibly when she realised it had all gone smoothly. She wasn't sure what had her more excited, the fact that she had done this herself, taken the initiative, made her own decision, relied on herself and succeeded or that she was about to start living the life of an independent woman. She had a career, albeit still new, a place of her own in London and the world really was there for the proverbial taking. Already knowing a few of the people in the London office would make her first day there less daunting and Bee was really excited about introducing Angela to her friends the following Friday, once she felt officially moved in. Bee already had plans for some of her friends from the badminton club to come over and had decided that as soon as Angela left she would write a note for Kitty, in case they missed each other in the morning, to tell her the good news and to make sure she would be around next Friday, for what Angela now detected was becoming a party in Bee's busy head.

As Angela walked back to the train station she could have been flying. She took in a huge breath of air until there was a delicious pain at the top of her chest and her head felt dizzy. As she released the breathe she shivered slightly. An hour or more had passed and the air was definitely frostier now but it was excitement that she was struggling to control. She was so proud of herself at that precise moment that she wanted to suspend it in time, to re-live over and over, especially as she knew there would be times she would need the affirmation. It didn't give her any satisfaction knowing herself so well.

During the train journey home Angela allowed herself to enjoy the exhilaration of anticipation for the week ahead, ignoring the guilt she could already feel emerging from the pit of her stomach. She knew when she got home she would have to restrain her delight. Desperately wanting her mother to share her success and tell her how proud she was, Angela knew Joan didn't identify with the woman she wanted to be and had never shared the same ambitions. Telling her mother she had found a perfect and respectable place to live would make Angela feel like a naughty schoolgirl.

The train moved steadily onward and with each city light that gradually tapered into the night, Angela felt a fragment of courage flicker out. Eventually she closed her eyes, refusing to watch and searched for peace from the turmoil searing inside her head.

*

Being torn was becoming exhausting. Angela loved her mother and hated to disappoint her, and that's exactly how Joan looked when Angela told her; let down and dissatisfied. At twenty you can have no comprehension of how it feels for a mother when her child leaves home. Add to this your child leaving to live in a different town, to start a life you would not have chosen for her, a life you don't believe is the right path. They were emotions Angela could not even hope to fathom and Joan didn't try and disguise them for her benefit.

'I know this is what you want Angela, and your Dad and I will be here when you need us. Your room is always there when you want to come back.' Joan had doomed Angela's dream before it had even begun.

Anxious and unsure, she met with Jenny the next day. Jenny had picked a quiet corner of an otherwise flamboyant bar hoping to push the point that Angela needed young and vibrant. Angela, so deep in her whirlpool of angst, hardly noticed the location. She was scared of hurting her mother and letting her down by not giving her what she wanted, but more scared of not doing this. Not taking the chance to make the most of her life. It made no sense to Angela that her family wouldn't validate this decision for her and send her off joyfully. It wasn't as if they would never see her again. Jenny could see the turmoil and spoke carefully and kindly, but she never took her hands from Angela's and she didn't drop her gaze. She locked her eyes on a face packed with tears and distress and as she spoke Angela wondered which of them she was really talking about.

'I won't tell you what to do, but you have worked hard for two years, and got yourself a sound reputation. Strong enough that they agreed to transfer you to London, into a better role with more money. If you love it as much as I think you do, if you are really happy, then you have to think about yourself. You have to follow this dream and do what's best for you. So what if it doesn't work out, at least you won't be left wondering. Sometimes there's no right or wrong, just a decision to be made, and no one else in this life will truly look out for you Angela.'

Jenny paused and waited for a reply that didn't come. She could read in Angela's face that she understood but, as yet, she was not ready to voice the acknowledgement. To voice it would make it final.

'Don't try and live someone else's dream,' continued Jenny. 'You might do it for a year, maybe longer, but think about waking up tomorrow and twenty years had passed. Would you still be happy then or would you be bitter and resentful?'

Jenny was eloquent, almost rehearsed and it was easy to get lost in her words and start to fly. At home in the darkness, hours later, Angela listened to her mother and father argue about what was best for her and she sought comfort and clarity mulling over Jenny's words until the light poked through the curtains and Jenny's was the only voice she could hear.

The following week Angela moved to London. With Jenny's blessing and even her father's, but not her mother's.

She felt disloyal and anxious and then angry that those feelings were suffocating the excitement and pride that were struggling to be celebrated. It was a familiar turmoil and chaos in her heart but as Angela unpacked the next chapter of her life she became aware of a unfamiliar composure soaking through, and she knew for certain, the decision was made and there was no turning back.

*

'Open the door Bee...Freezing out here.'

Angela sat up abruptly in the unfamiliar bed and took a second to remember where she was. It was silent in the house and her room was shrouded in a murky stillness. There was no way it was morning yet.

'Beeee, come on. Let us in. Got no key,' the voice bellowed and shivered at the same time.

There was nothing to see out of the window, even the street light was vague hiding behind the dawn mist. Then Angela heard voices in the hallway downstairs so guessed that Bee had heard the commotion and gone to open the front door.

'For god's sake Paul, tell me you didn't get her in this state? You know what she's like after a few drinks. Help me get her up.' Angela could hear Bee's assertive voice, breathy and hushed.

'No. I did not. Why am I getting the blame? That's charming. She's your friend and I'm the one getting dragged out of bed at four in the morning to bring her home.' The man's voice seemed to find humour in the irony of the situation. 'I expect she called me because she knows how judgemental you are Bee.'

Bee laughed out loud at this, 'She called you darling brother because she knows you always come running.'

'I am still here you know,' whined a new voice, 'Help me up you two, I need to get to a sink.'

Feeling like a spare part and knowing it must have been obvious she was awake, Angela started down the stairs and called out.

'Can I help?'

Her gaze was immediately drawn to the sprawled body on the floor, not least because of the comedy of the situation. Now sitting upright, one leg out front and the other bent obscurely behind her, a mass of blonde hair moved round to reveal red lips and huge eyes with the messy remnants of a good night out around them. A small hand wiggled from side to side at Angela in a child like way.

'Hello, you must be Ange? Do I look a mess? I'm so embarrassed. Lost my key. Bee I need the sink, going to be sick.'

'Meet Kitty,' said Bee raising her eyebrows and being slightly theatrical.

Doing her best to suppress a smile, Angela moved from the bottom of the stairs and started to help move the blonde heap towards her bedroom. The scent of alcohol grew stronger as Angela bent nearer to Kitty's face. Pure, intense almost antiseptic. Even in her current dishevelled state Angela could see why men would follow Kitty around. Her hair, although rumpled now, had probably started the evening as cascading curls down to the middle of her back. The puffy panda look obscured large brown eyes and smooth flawless skin. Kitty was definitely mesmerising to look at and Angela wondered about the morals of the men Kitty was hanging around with. Did none of them feel the need to get her home safely?

'Nice to meet you Angela, I'm Bee's brother,' rasped Paul in a voice still full of humour due to the fact he was attempting to arrange Kitty on top of her bed and trying to untie her arms from his neck. Angela noted that this was the first person she'd met since moving in a couple of days ago who had used her full name. Not that she minded the abbreviations, in fact it suited her new life, but despite the humour in his voice Paul seemed more modest than his sister and her friends. His blue eyes twinkled with kindness from under a mop of sandy hair that looked capable of curling untamed, if left unattended for too long. He was handsome Angela decided, not jaw dropping gorgeous but definitely very fine looking.

'Paul, can you go and find a bowl or a bucket we can put by the bed? I think you're enjoying all this cuddling a little too much.' Bee took control again and didn't look up to see the mock offended look Paul gave her before he mooched out of Kitty's room in search of a suitable receptacle.

'Your brother is a sweetie Bee, I do love him,' Kitty had her eyes closed now and was mumbling. Angela felt sorry for her, as she imagined how her head would feel in the morning. Kitty forced her eyes open one last time and looked around the room for Angela.

'I'm Caroline. Did I tell you that? Call me Kitty, everyone does.' Her face looked pinched and then with one great effort she turned her head away and curled into a ball.

'Hmm, yes he's a sweetie all right.' Bee was fussing over Kitty making sure she had some covers over her to comfort her when the inevitable chill set in.

'Problem is she doesn't really love him. She loves the fact that he runs to her every whim. He's been besotted with her since she moved in and she can't do any wrong in his eyes. They are good friends, but I know which one will end up with the broken heart.'

Just at that moment Paul walked back in with a large glass mixing bowl.

'Best I could find,' he advised.

Angela wasn't sure if he'd heard Bee's whispered assessment or not.

'Look at her now,' he mused, 'Who would have thought something so small and dainty could make so much noise and mess.'

Then turning to Bee he continued, 'I've no idea why she called me to go and get her and as much as I would love to stay and chat, it would be nice to get some sleep before work in four hours.' His voice was gentle and if he hadn't been so tired his eyes would have sparkled with yet more humour.

Paul was nearly at the door when Bee suddenly followed, 'Paul,' she whispered lightly. Angela moved from Kitty's room and shut the door quietly. Bee hugged her brother, 'Thank you for bringing her home. I hope she remembers in the morning what a love you are.'

Paul smiled down at Bee and, as he turned to leave,

raised his hand to say goodbye to Angela.

'Nice to meet you,' he said smiling warmly.

Bee shut and locked the door behind him. She turned and gestured to the room where kitty lay gently snoring. 'There we are then,' she said with a feint smile, 'that's the three of us.'

The following morning

Angela didn't expect to see Kitty during breakfast the next day and she welcomed Bee's suggestion that she accompany Angela into the city to shop for clothes. The brief time she had spent in the London office had shown her she needed to update her wardrobe. Dress for the job you want, she reminded herself. It was also a good idea, Angela decided, as Bee had been frantically cleaning the bathroom and kitchen and tidying the front room since seven, and Angela was finding it hard to convince her not to start the vacuum cleaner. Kitty's door remained closed. As Angela quietly finished a tidy up in her room and took measurements for some new curtains, to match the daisy covered bed spread she'd ordered from a department store in Oxford Street, she wondered how Kitty was feeling and hoped her head wouldn't throb too much when she finally surfaced.

'I am a bit of a clean freak,' Bee admitted while they sat in the kitchen with a mug of tea each. 'Everything has to be in the right place, drives me mad when people are messy or things get spilt.'

Angela noticed admiringly that Bee was not making an apology here, more of a declaration which Angela had to accept.

'Watch me tomorrow. After we've had a house full of people. I'll probably be at it all day.' Bee smiled and Angela thought she looked positively excited about the prospect of the clean up.

'One day I am going to make the perfect housewife.' Bee was laughing at herself. Angela broke into a huge grin. She liked Bee enormously already and respected her for being self-assured and direct without being rude or aggressive.

'Rather you than me,' toasted Angela with her mug, knowing that she had no intention of being anyone's perfect housewife.

*

Kitty heard the door close and pulled the covers back from her head as the voices walked down the road and disappeared. She had wanted them to leave so desperately all morning and now they had, she felt so alone a whimper of despair came through her parched lips. The lipstick had worn away, and her lips now looked raw and swollen. Her eyes were bloodshot and tender and they ached when she tried to keep them open. Hot tears had burnt through her pillow and now the damp cotton was making her cheek sore. She lay huddled up in her bed, reasoning with herself to re-live the events of the previous evening. Her preferred choice would be to lay there for as long as it took for the world to stop. It didn't happen, it wasn't real, everything in the world and everyone in the world was just as they had always been before last night. Nothing had changed. But the discolouration on her arms, the blouse hanging from her chest and the welt appearing on her neck where she'd been held down, exposed her life as having turned into an abhorrent nightmare.

Time moved slowly for Kitty and she became grateful at least that no one was coming in to check on her, or offer tea. She wondered if it would be possible just to lay here, live here, never leaving, but each time her mind settled on this she became painfully aware that at some point she would have to get up. The weight of this conclusion was more onerous and profound each time. Kitty didn't know how she would bear the nausea of confusion any longer.

In the end it was the practical, persistent force of nature to use the bathroom that lured Kitty from her room and up the stairs. She crept through the house with her coat and scarf pulled tightly around her. No one had noticed the real state she was in last night and she hadn't removed the coat since. She had no idea what she was going to do if someone walked into the house now. In fact, she had no idea what she was going to do beyond the next five minutes. Every step banged inside her head and every breath she took filled her nostrils with revolting smells of life. When she got back down to the bottom of the stairs she was shivering and trembling, her arms and legs self governing. Thoughts came sputtering into Kitty's consciousness. *A friend of dad's...known him for years...what changed...what happened...did I do something to...my fault...can't be...who will believe me....can't tell anyone...A friend of dad's.* Words spun round, over and over, lost in chaos and contorted into a mass of hysterical shouting; deafening and defeating. Kitty slumped at the bottom of the stairs and cried out for help. If there was an exit point inside her head from this misery it was lost to her.

She had no idea how long she lay there crying out to the empty hallway, or how long it took for the voice shouting on the other side to reach her.

'Open the door'

'Can you get to the Door?'

'Open the door Kitty. It's Paul'

'You have to open this door... Kitty? Kitty! Open the door...Now!'

Reeling and stumbling over to the door, Kitty lent on it and pressed her cheek to the glass.

'Paul, I don't know what to do, I can't...I can't think...I can't let you in. You can't see me.' she sobbed the words out.

Pressing his own face against the other side of the door,

Paul pleaded gently, 'Kitty, please just open the door.'

A minute passed and then the door cracked open just enough for Paul to gently push against it and ease himself swiftly through the small gap he had created.

Kitty was unsure if she fell into Paul or if he scooped her into his arms, but with the momentary relief of someone trustworthy to soak up her despair, she latched on tightly and a new flood of quiet weeping overtook her.

For the next hour Paul sat on the floor with Kitty in his arms just where they had fallen. The cold terracotta tiles numbed him and his back ached but he didn't want to move her. Arms wrapped tight around Kitty, he rocked her quietly and slowly, every once in a while staring in horror at her face as he moved strands of tear drenched hair away from the bruising. Kitty sunk into the sheltered comfort. Keeping her eyes closed so she couldn't see Paul's face, she gradually slowed her breathing to intermittent sobs and gasps for air, scraping up the courage to speak.

It was hard for Paul to understand everything Kitty mumbled and sobbed, but he got an adequate enough picture to feel a pure rage building inside his stomach.

'He offered me a lift home...known him for years...Dad's friend...what did I do wrong?...is it my fault Paul?...thought he was our friend...I wandered for hours afterwards...drank...Paul, he hit me when I said No...hit me...he hurt me...held me down...bit me...I kicked him...screamed...he'd pulled into lay by...must be something I did...why would he suddenly do that?...called me names...said I was asking for it...he hit me Paul...he pushed my arms down really hard...he touched me...I said No, Paul, I said No...he hit me...he said I was asking for it...Is that what people think of me Paul?...I said No...how did this happen?...must be my fault...Is this my fault?...don't tell anyone, please Paul, you can't tell anyone.'

Even when the words were no longer coming from Kitty's mouth, they were still spiralling downward, never ending to the pit of her stomach and inside she started silently screaming.

Pure fury continued to burn and climb from somewhere deep inside Paul, but the heartbreak of seeing Kitty so broken, so defeated kept him focussed on the immediate dilemma. Kitty needed protection and peace and Bee had invited enough people over this evening to fill two houses over.

Stroking her hair gently Paul spoke as carefully and slowly as he could.

'Kitty, this is not your fault, this is truly not your fault,' and then after several more minutes of holding her tightly, 'Would it be OK if I pick you up and move you to the sofa? I need to get you warm.'

Kitty kept her eyes firmly closed and nodded slightly. She didn't know what she would see in his eyes if she looked at him. Shame? loathing?

With Kitty on the sofa, wrapped in a blanket from her bed, Paul felt lost as to how to move forward. He needed more facts, but he didn't want to cause more distress. Kitty finally seemed to be calm, but as the cushions enveloped her she looked crumpled and hollow.

He decided to sit close by and take her hands softly, just so she had a connection with him.

'Kitty do you want me to call a doctor? How badly hurt are you? I can only see your face.'

Kitty shook her head and let out a stifled sob, 'Just my arms...and my neck...he held me down...my legs hurt.' Kitty shivered a deep sickening shudder as she remembered his hands between her legs.

Paul soothed her gently, and deliberately kept his voice low and calm. He was terrified of the answer to the question he wasn't sure he wanted to ask.

'Did he...did he..?

The reply was almost inaudible, and Kitty thought she might vomit.

'No. He tried. He was against my skin, against me...but no...I bit him and he jumped away.'

Kitty shook, another deep cold quake, as she remembered with revulsion the texture and taste of skin in her mouth. She retreated further under the blanket.

Noticeable relief escaped Paul as Kitty spoke and then immediate guilt. He closed his eyes. Kitty was there, damaged and abused. True, far worse could have happened, but despite that, here was a clever kind hearted young woman now violated and broken.

'Do you want me to call your parents?'

'*No.* Promise me Paul. They can't know, don't tell them.' Kitty pleaded.

'Kitty, you haven't done anything wrong. A crime has been committed against you. You need to know you're not alone, let us help you. We can all take care of you...I will take care of you.'

Minutes passed in silence before Paul spoke again. 'It wasn't your fault Kitty, you have to know that?'

More silence, more minutes.

'Let me help you.'

It was barely a whisper but, for the first time, Kitty opened her eyes staring into nothing. Paul was shocked at how swollen they looked, the warmth and sparkle snatched away.

'Will you stay with me Paul, at least until Bee gets home?'

It was the first time she had looked at him since he'd found her. Paul smiled at her sweetness, did she really think he was going to leave her alone? He squeezed her hand lightly.

'I won't leave you.'

*

When Paul heard the front door open he reassured Kitty he wouldn't be long and slipped out to the hallway to intercept Angela and Bee before they saw Kitty.

Kitty was aware of Paul's voice, low and calm and could make out gasps from the two women as he spoke. The stone floor in the hallway did nothing to soak up sound, although Kitty supposed the red oriental rug might mask the sound of impending footsteps. Either way, she knew with renewed nausea what Paul was telling them and closed her eyes to contemplate her continuing nightmare.

It was Bee that Kitty saw first when she opened her eyes. She came crashing through the door and caught Kitty up into her arms.

'Oh my God. Oh my God, Kitty what the hell. I wish you'd told me last night. I wouldn't have left you this morning. Oh my God. How could someone do this to you? We need to call the police, he won't get away with this. You need to see a doctor.' The words kept tumbling from Bee, kind but commanding and insistent.

'No, Bee. No doctors. No police,' Kitty repeated with every plea from Bee.

Paul fidgeted at the door and Bee sensed he might be about to return to the room and pull her away from Kitty. Determined her message would not be diminished she bent forward slowly and kissed Kitty softly on the forehead. 'I'll get some warm water and cotton wool to soothe your face,' she suggested.

'Thank you Bee, yes please, I want to be clean,' admitted Kitty. Bee felt a stab of fury as she looked at the lost child Kitty had suddenly become.

Paul followed Bee up the stairs.

'Bee, you need to calm down a bit, you have no idea what state I found her in earlier. She is on the edge and you pushing her like that isn't helping!' Paul objected strongly to Bee but tried to keep his voice low so Kitty wouldn't hear them.

'Calm down! You want me to *calm down*?' Bee emphasised the words as she swung round on Paul.

'You're lucky I'm not round her Dad's house now demanding to know where this man lives. It's an outrage. No, it's more than an outrage, I don't even have a word to describe what this is. How dare he judge her and decide he can take what he wants. He needs to pay for what he's done. He tried to rape her Paul. *Rape Her*!
'

The volume in Bee's voice was escalating beyond her control.

'Her neck Paul, did you see her neck? *It's purple*. I want to scream Paul. How dare he, how dare he!'

Bee's anger was frenzied barbed wire crumpled up and piercing the inside of her head.

'Bee this isn't helping Kitty. We need to go at her speed. We need to listen to her, show her she isn't alone. You're not the only one that's angry here, but it's not about us.' Paul's voice was measured but insistent and formidable. He moved his face closer to his sisters to try and get her to focus on him.

Bee didn't respond immediately, so Paul grabbed the opportunity to continue to reason with her, 'Kitty thinks this is her fault you know. We need to give her some time to realise a crime has taken place. Being a good friend to her is what she needs right now, and we should start by cancelling the party tonight.'

Bee shot a glance up at Paul, 'Oh my God, the party.' She placed her hands over her head as she remembered their plans, all so ridiculous now. 'Yes, tonight. I'll...I'll go and make some phone calls, make an excuse. That's the last thing Kitty needs right now, a house full of people.'

Annoyed her brother was right, but equally determined not to let this go, Bee set off with her purpose to collect the toiletries she needed for Kitty's face and to come up with some suitable excuse for cancelling the planned evening.

Meanwhile downstairs Angela had slipped into the front room. For the second time since she'd met Kitty she felt like she should be doing something other than standing around like a nosey neighbour.

'Can I get you anything?' Angela asked carefully.

Kitty shook her head. She eased herself to a sitting position on the sofa but didn't meet Angela's gaze.

'What must you think of me?' whispered Kitty. 'Look at the state of me, what a mess.'

Angela had heard that self-deprecation so many times from herself, albeit in different circumstances, that she had to stop herself from rushing to Kitty's side and drowning her in statements of reassurance that would sound hollow and most probably patronising coming from a virtual stranger.

'Do you want me to sit with you while you wait for Bee and Paul?' Angela asked, again carefully. There was every reason to assume that Kitty would rather Angela not be there, looking at her. Kitty nodded, and just the merest hint of upturn could be seen at edges of her mouth, almost definitely out of politeness as her eyes held no evidence of joy.

It was uncomfortably quiet in the room and if Angela could hear Bee roaring upstairs then Angela was sure

Kitty could too. Whilst it was surely good to know your friends cared and had your best interests at heart, Angela wondered if talking to someone you didn't know might be less daunting and she was reminded of Jenny and how easy it had always been to talk to her. Angela sat quietly for a little longer staring absently at the expertly arranged flowers on the window sill and the book case piled neatly with records. Everything was ordered, except when she looked at Kitty, and then nothing really was.

'I'm so sorry this happened to you Kitty,' she tested. When no sobbing broke out she decided to keep talking.

'You didn't bring this on yourself and you need to start telling yourself that over and over. Eventually you'll believe it's true.'

Kitty raised her head for the first time to meet Angela's gaze.

'Why shouldn't you be strong and beautiful, that doesn't give him the right to judge you. No one has the right to take anything from you without your permission. Don't give him the satisfaction of beating you down, or changing you. He committed a crime, not you Kitty.'

Angela could hardly believe herself. She couldn't stop talking. She sounded like Jenny and she could feel energy in her words. They held such force that it became really important to Angela that this young woman in front of her healed and came back stronger. A woman she hardly knew mattered to her.

'Don't let him win.' Angela felt a confident power in her own words and the painful stirring of a sob in her chest.

She lent forward and put her hand gently on top of Kitty's.

'Right now you probably don't know who you are because he took that from you.'

The pain in Angela's chest increased and the words trembled.

'Bee and Paul will take care of you. You know that don't you?'

Kitty continued to watch her and Angela was sure she saw just a flicker of warmth returned in Kitty's gaze.

'And one day you'll be back, stronger. I know it.' Angela willed the burning in her throat to stop and hoped she sounded convincing.

'Thank you Ange,' murmured Kitty. 'Are you always this wise?'

Angela smiled. 'Sorry, am I spouting at you like a self help book?'

Kitty turned her own hand over and squeezed Angela's.

'It's OK to be afraid,' murmured Angela as she finally forced down, although not altogether successfully, the persistent sob. 'We just have to find some courage.'

Chapter 3

1987 Christmas & New Year at Ivy Cottage

Taking care of Kitty consumed them all over the next few weeks. The physical effects of the attack, left to the natural resources of the human body, had healed leaving no scars. There was, however, a deeper more bewildering process of healing required to deal with the emotional effect on Kitty and no one was underestimating this. Kitty was adamant she didn't want to go to the police and insisted she couldn't tell her parents about the attack as they had left for a Christmas retreat with a group from their church. They would be gone for at least three weeks and it was clear Kitty was relieved she couldn't tell them. This worried both Angela and Bee, as whilst it would have been an easy option for them all if Kitty tried to get on with life and ignore the assault she'd suffered, they could see that by pushing her feelings away and ignoring them, the more insistent they were becoming. Kitty was not herself. She was becoming unable to cope with even the simplest of tasks. Bee commented to Angela that it was not normal for Kitty to stay home and live in her tracksuit. With an ever growing queue of admirers, she had previously spent most evenings out dancing or at the cinema, with the exception of the nights she accompanied her parents to church meetings. Unaccustomed to sitting still, Bee busied herself every evening after work with cooking and cleaning. Kitty's room had never been so fresh and the house was constantly filled with deep, comforting aromas that meant cake, hot chocolate and cookies were on offer.

'Bee, these are delicious,' Angela remarked one evening, as they tucked into Bee's chocolate chip filled cakes, 'We will be huge by Christmas. You should stop.'

'But I love baking,' Bee responded breezily. 'I'm a bit rubbish at that touchy feely stuff, so looking after you all this way... well it's, you know, my way.'

'Bee, you're wonderful. I feel very loved, by both of you,' acknowledged Kitty, smiling gently at Bee and rubbing Angela's arm. 'But I do wish you'd stop fussing.'

Angela had been rushing home every day after work to spend her evenings by Kitty's side. She hadn't known the old kitty but the young woman she was getting to know was warm and sweet and in her brighter moments, amusing and teasing. It also suited her to spend the evenings with Kitty, as there was such a lot to learn and read with her new job. Angela was happy to spend time sitting next to Kitty, making lists for the next day to get herself organised and ahead of the game. When Angela was working, Kitty watched television or flicked through one of Bee's magazines. It was becoming a comfortable, quiet ritual. Often they chatted, sometimes the discussion came round to Kitty's attack, and Angela hoped she was doing the right thing encouraging Kitty to talk about it. She occasionally saw flickers of anger from Kitty towards her attacker, but mainly she saw repulsion and humiliation, like the time Kitty had described the moment she'd felt him pulling at her clothes, his sweaty rough hands moving across her skin. Kitty had looked sick to her very core and Angela had pondered on where this fragile young woman would find the toughness she would need to get through this.

Without trying to make himself too obvious or a complete nuisance, Paul popped in most days around tea time. If he was alone he would almost certainly complement Bee on whatever she was cooking, and manoeuvre himself an invitation to stay and eat. Afterwards he would settle himself on the sofa next to Kitty, never pushing her to discuss her ordeal or make decisions about telling anyone else.

'He just wants her to move at her own pace,' Angela would offer to Bee, when they shared quiet words in the kitchen.

'Hmm, what my brother wants is for Kitty to fall in love with him,' argued Bee.

The one thing Bee and Angela did agree on was that Kitty would need to get out of the house soon and face the world, or risk becoming fixed in a bubble of detached existence.

On one or two occasions since Kitty's attack, Paul arrived with his house mate, James, in tow. He and Paul played at the badminton club twice a week and popping in on the way home would have been a natural occurrence when everything was normal. At the beginning of December Bee insisted to Paul and James that they resume being normal for everyone's sake.

'Hi James, how was the game?' Bee called. She was standing over the cooker and didn't turn round.

'I don't want to talk about it,' grumbled Paul, answering on James behalf and plopping down next to Angela at the kitchen table to put his head on his arms. Angela smiled widely at Paul and briefly noted to herself that she had not yet met James.

'Sore loser,' laughed a loud voice from the hallway.

Angela turned her head and watched James saunter in. His approach was like an eclipse; a subtle darkening, a change in the air and an inexplicable feeling of tension. Despite feeling slightly off balance, Angela extended her smile towards him expecting him to come over and introduce himself, but although he looked right back at her, he said nothing. In fact, he walked into the kitchen, past Angela and started to help himself to a beer from the fridge.

'James, this is Ange our new house mate.' Bee turned purposefully around to enforce the introduction.

'Yeah, Paul mentioned someone new had moved in. Hello.' James answered Bee, without turning his head towards Angela, thereby continuing to completely ignore her gaze.

This gave Angela time to take in his lean lines and the muscular legs showing from under his shorts. Her gaze travelled up. His dark hair was cropped and accentuated his cheek bones and sharp chin. She wasn't sure how he would look clean and showered, but there was something about the way he stood tall in rumpled t-shirt and badminton shorts that convinced her he was careless and arrogant.

James turned suddenly, startling Angela, and smirked at her in a way that didn't reach his eyes. Pale, pale green, against his latte skin. But so conceited. The way James surveyed Angela made her feel over dressed in her navy skirt suit and heels, and she felt an overwhelming urge to slink away. Even though he was the only one in the room looking at her, she felt likes all eyes were on her. She hated it when men made her feel uncomfortable, or was it that she hated the fact she was letting him make her feel that way.

'It's nice to meet you.' Angela offered her hand, trying to regain her composure. There was no way she would let this man know how intimidated she felt.

James paused, seemed to deliberately note Angela's hand and then lifted his head to meet and lock on to her gaze. His stare pinned her to the spot. Angela was losing herself in at least three shades of muted but self-important green, and an unspoken challenge was set as to who would break away first. Only when Angela started to lower her hand in defeat did James bring his forward and catch it swiftly. The sudden movement made her jump and she knew a small gasp escaped her lips when their hands touched. This seemed to satisfy James and he released her hand, her gaze and finished the encounter with another smirk. Angela, mortified, and reddening was sure she heard him chuckle. His eyes might be charming, but the rest of him was most definitely not.

'So Bee, when you up for a game next?' asked James, looking completely comfortable and still half smirking at Angela, but turning his attention to Bee. 'Your brother sucks and I need more of a challenge,' he added, guaranteeing a laugh from Bee and a moan from Paul.

'Help me out, they're ganging up on me,' sighed Paul taking Angela's hand in mock despair.

'So, is it easy to teach someone badminton? I seem to be the only one around here who doesn't play.' Angela, trying to recover quickly, smiled and spoke confidently, willing the burning flush she felt on her face to dissolve and determined to match the self-assured James.

'Um, I teach actually. I have a class of under ten's you can join if you like.'

Angela felt the burning make a hasty return. Was James mocking her? Or was he being serious? Without waiting to hear what she had to say, he strolled over to the cooker and started to stir the supper Bee was cooking on the hob. Angela used the opportunity to excuse herself, to go and change her clothes. She fought the desire to run out of the kitchen. Breathing steadily and willing herself to be stylish and graceful, the walk from the kitchen, down the hall and up the stairs took a thousand years. She didn't see James turn round and watch her slender frame walking away, whilst he continued to absently stir supper.

Bee gave him a playful slap on the arm. 'Behave James,' she scolded warmly.

Angela was conscious of James glancing at her all through supper. She was sat with Bee, Kitty and Paul at the table and James, at his own insistence and a lack of any more chairs, was leaning against the side eating sausage and bean casserole from a breakfast bowl. It was the perfect position to see everyone at the table, even though they couldn't all see him. The meal proceeded with idle banter and much taunting of Paul for his badminton loss that evening. James didn't address Angela directly again, even though he seemed very at ease with Paul and Bee. Kitty was quiet as she ate and although James did not initiate conversations with her, it was clear they knew each other well and James was respectful and actually very sweet to her. Angela spent supper desperately trying, and failing, to think of a witty or clever way to engage with James on her terms. By the end of the meal she was feeling foolish for bothering.

Later, after Paul and James had left, she asked Kitty and Bee if she had done something to offend James.

'Oh god no,' re-assured Kitty. 'He's always like that. Actually I think he's quite shy, and not good at small talk, but very funny once you get to know him.'

'Hmm, you sure about shy?' countered Bee clearly amused. 'He seems to have a stream of girls from what Paul tells me. He's never short of attention from the ladies,' she emphasised her words for added humour.

Angela wasn't sure she wanted to get to know him. She was meeting enough bigged up, arrogant men at work at the moment and getting very good at putting on a poised, self-reliant front to get her through exchanges that two years ago would have had her trembling in her heels. The last thing she needed was James mocking her. It was time she stopped looking for confidence and strength outside herself. As she lay in bed that night she found herself thinking about James and how foolish he made her feel. She resolved that he wouldn't do that again, his opinion could hold no power over her unless she let it.

*

As the evenings drew in ever closer, there was no light left outside by four in the afternoon. The ground was becoming hard as iron and the air started to cut into Angela's cheeks as she walked down the road each evening from the tube station. At the end of the first week in December, Angela came home to find Bee singing along with Christmas songs.

'Ange, in here, come and see,' greeted Bee calling in an excited tone when she heard the front door open.

Bee was balancing precariously on a bedroom stool, reaching up to place a toy reindeer at the top of a Christmas tree covered in multi-coloured fairy lights, and candy canes.

'Thank god you're home Ange, she's been a woman possessed all afternoon.' Kitty was in good spirits and didn't really seem to mind that Bee had taken the afternoon off work to fuss over her and more to the point, taken the opportunity to get Christmas under way. Kitty hadn't been back to work since the attack and no one had yet broached the subject with her. She had got used to solitude during the day. The children at the infant school in Chingford where Kitty taught had sent messages and handmade cards which Bee had displayed around the front room and kitchen. Kitty appreciated this from Bee of all people, as she could only imagine how torn Bee would have been as each clean line and spotless surface was replaced with squiggly, enchanting, randomness.

'Wow, you've been busy. It looks very twinkly and homely in here.' Angela smiled and ran her hands along the mantle piece which was now holding a long, thick piece of faux ivy, tangled very deliberately with lights and pine cones.

'I can't wait for Christmas,' Bee enthused almost singing. 'One day I would love to have an old house with really high ceilings and a massive tall tree in the hallway. We would take the kids out to play in the snow and sing carols and then sit by a real fire in our dressing gowns toasting crumpets and drinking hot chocolate.'

'Got it all planned out I see,' Angela smiled kindly, admiring once again the conviction in Bee's voice.

'Sounds like Christmas for the Victorians to me,' Kitty interjected, teasing gently, 'but the hot chocolate and crumpets does sound good.'

'Oh be quiet you two. Mr Right is out there somewhere for me, with truckloads of money and a company car,' insisted Bee smiling at her friends. 'Anyway now I've said it, I like the idea of crumpets and chocolate too, so I'm off to the kitchen. Paul will be here in a minute, says he has an invitation for us.' Bee's voice trailed off towards the end of her sentence as she was already busy looking for a saucepan.

Not long after, the three of them were settled in the front room slurping chocolate and gushing about how lovely warm butter was. When Paul arrived the delicious smell wafted over him almost immediately. 'Am I too late to eat?' he wailed.

Settling himself next to Kitty, as he always did, Paul took the napkin from her lap and handed it to her pointing at the chocolate foam on her lip.

'Can't take you anywhere,' he laughed as he sat back. She smiled gratefully and shifted back slightly to make sure there was enough room for Paul next to her. Bee observed later to Angela that Paul probably wouldn't have minded being squashed there.

'So what's the big invite?' Bee nagged. 'You sounded very excited on the phone.'

'Well, how would you like to be away for New Year?' Paul announced. 'All of us of course,' he added looking round at Kitty and Angela.

'Mum and Dad told me they're planning to go down to Dorset, to the cottage, for Christmas and want us to go with them,' he nodded to Bee, 'But they plan to come back home for New Year. They've got a party to go to, but they said we could stay on there if we liked and invite friends over to stay. So how bout it?'

Angela wondered just how much money Bee and Paul's family had. They had their family home near Epping Forest, this house which they all paid rent on and now a cottage.

Bee looked immediately excited, 'Oh, I love it at the cottage, let's all go...please... It will be wonderful. We can get wrapped up and walk on the beach, and up along the cliff. And the little shops in Lyme Regis are such fun to mooch round. Kitty say you'll come, I won't go unless you come with us.'

Kitty receded into the sofa slightly. 'I don't know,' she

whispered looking anxiously at Paul, 'I would spoil it for everyone. Why don't you all go? I'll be fine here.' She could feel a small panic rising in her chest at the thought of leaving the house.

'Kitty, this is exactly what you need,' argued Angela gently. 'You can't stay in forever and this is the perfect opportunity to get out of the house and still be surrounded by friends. Besides, I don't think you should be here alone, you need someone close by in case...well just in case.'

Angela was unyielding but soothing as she spoke and she moved close to Kitty. She wasn't sure if Bee knew, but she had been in the house twice now when Kitty had suffered a panic attack. She knew Kitty would rather pretend they hadn't happened but, having seen her struggle to breathe, there was no way Angela wanted Kitty to be alone until they were sure she could control the uninvited dizziness and sickness.

'Of course you're coming,' Paul told Kitty. He looked genuinely hurt that she would consider staying behind and the idea of being in Dorset without Kitty was not anywhere near as appealing as the holiday he had been imagining all day. 'I don't plan to go without you,' he added fixing a deep blue stare.

Bee sighed and raised her eyebrows. Perhaps inviting her was just the cover Paul needed for getting Kitty to go away with him. She certainly didn't believe her brother would take advantage of their currently broken friend, but Kitty was becoming very reliant on Paul and he was doing nothing to discourage that. In fact he seemed to have taken on his new role as protector with relish.

'You'll come too won't you Ange?' Bee interrupted her brother's silent staring.

Going on holiday with her new friends sounded wonderfully exciting, but Angela knew she would have to go home for the Christmas holidays. She had only managed to get back twice since she had moved to London. That had been exhausting, not only in terms of juggling work and travel, but also the emotional wash and spin cycle with her mother.

'I'm expected home,' she replied forlornly. 'My parents will never speak to me again if I don't go home for Christmas,' and then added quickly, 'I would've loved to though. It sounds perfect.'

'What about New Year though?' Paul insisted. 'Can't you spend Christmas with them and then come down for New Year with us?'

Everyone looked at Angela expectantly. She had gone out with friends on New Years Eve for several years now opting out of staying in with her parents, so she could reasonably see how this was a natural extension. She was an adult after all. She needed to get a grip on the guilt. It wasn't as if she was proposing to run naked around Trafalgar Square.

Kitty pulled her from her guilt trip. 'If all of you are

going, I'll come,' she offered, while looking directly at Angela.

'OK, deal,' squealed Angela in agreement.

'Oh My God, it's gonna be such fun,' shrieked Bee as she skipped off to get a pad and a pen to start making lists to organise everyone.

*

Looking forward to meeting up with Bee, Kitty, and Paul for New Year had kept Angela focussed and calm through Christmas with her parents. She'd planned four days at home as she wanted to meet up with old friends in Barnstone and Nottingham and, in particular, make time to see Jenny. Now it was over, she huddled against the breeze running through the train while it worked its way city by city towards the Southern coastline. She smiled, thinking of Jenny. It had been wonderful to see her and Jenny had looked so proud and gratified as Angela talked about her first two months in London. For the first time Angela had felt more like Jenny's equal.

'Oh for goodness sake, take me off that pedestal,' she had laughed, when Angela told her all the times she'd used Jenny's recited wit and wisdom to help her through the day.

'You have to come and visit for the weekend,' Angela had pleaded. 'Everyone has heard so much about you and I know Kitty would gain so much from meeting you.'

'I promise I will, in the new year. I could come and see you at the office and then get a nice hotel on expenses,' Jenny had smiled. 'A nice expensive one in central London,' she'd added winking.

What she had said next brought tears to Angela's eyes. Angela turned her head, to lean on the cold glass pane of the train window, turning the words over in her head. 'Have you taken a look in the mirror lately my darling girl? I remember a timid teenager, with a dream but no confidence sitting at the desk next to me, and now...well now, I see a young woman, who made that dream a goal and worked damn hard. You did it Angela.'

Jenny had touched her face with all the love of a mother.

'And now you're there, take a look even further forward. Don't stop. Never stop, if it's what you want.'

Jenny had welled up as she spoke and Angela had felt compelled to wrap her arms around her friend, to seal the moment, to show Jenny she was still the same girl who needed her just as much as she always had.

The time spent with Jenny had been so wildly different to the time spent with her mother, and that, plus the conductor calling for new tickets, brought Angela sharply back to her surroundings. She sighed heavily and blew her nose. She had resolutely decided on the way home just before Christmas that she would deliberately talk about her new friends, the places she had been, the work she was doing. In fact, she would talk about everything that was important and real about her life right now, so her parents would see how happy she was, and surely then they would feel happy for her. Of course she would be interested in catching up with local news and gossip, she didn't want to come across as selfish or too absorbed in her own life. Yes, she'd decided, that would be a good balance. Joan though, had decided on a plan of her own.

'As no one has seen you much the last couple of months, we thought we'd better have some people over Christmas night,' had been the first of many digs Angela detected when she'd arrived on Christmas Eve. Christmas Day had been uneventful in itself and followed the same pattern it had for years with eating and watching television. Angela wondered if Bee, Paul and Kitty had played board games or gone out walking and then felt immediately guilty for belittling the Christmas day she'd been having since as far back as she could remember. On Christmas evening, and over the next two days, she had been ambushed as a succession of relatives came and went. Sometimes they had addressed their remarks directly to Angela and sometimes when she had visibly switched off, the discussions carried on in the room as if she wasn't there. All of them may as well have been primed and prepared by Joan and Joan herself was not even bothering to be subtle when she spoke.

'Sit down and show me the new baby pictures.' 'Oh Angela look at these. Isn't she just the loveliest baby? I don't suppose I'll be a grandmother for a while, if ever.' 'Look how lovely she looks. I remember I always dressed you in pink. Just the way it should be for a girl.' And then to Angela's cousin, 'Yes, I want to hear all about the wedding plans. I would love to have a wedding to plan, but sadly...' And to an Aunt, 'Yes you'd think she would have got it out of her system now wouldn't you.' 'Nearly twenty-one and no plan for her life.' Even one of the neighbours was dragged in. 'She doesn't want to live around here, we're not good enough for her any more.'

So many times Angela had willed herself to get up and leave, but she held back. Flouncing out would just fuel the fire, that she didn't know what she was doing, had no structure, had no plan. Eventually Angela had given up protesting and defending her job and her desire to live her own life. She'd just counted down the time before she could leave.

'It's not right you flouncing around in London you know, you need to have a stable home.'

Joan had stood in the bedroom doorway as Angela packed her bag ready to escape to the station and on to Dorset. She had just picked up an old photograph frame and was thinking of packing it; the caustic tone of Joan's voice made her jump.

It was the morning of December twenty eight and Angela really wanted to get to the cottage before nightfall so she would have this evening and a full four days with her friends. Tired of listening and not being listened to since she'd arrived, Angela had felt ready to break. 'What is that supposed to mean?' she'd sighed, biting down on her lip and running her fingers over the little girl in the photograph dressed in pink pyjamas. She'd then taken a deep breath to calm herself and push down the pool of anger whirling up through her chest.

'Well, I mean you're asking for it aren't you? What do you think is going to happen when you waltz around town dressed up to the nines, full of attitude. Look at that other girl, what's her name? Kitty. That's going to happen to you sooner or later if you keep this up. It's a man's world and you can't change that. High heels and a suit won't make anyone think you're important young lady. Doesn't make you anything more than you are. You should settle down. It was good enough for me and your grandmother. And I hope you don't have men coming in and out of that house, what must the neighbours think? I expect your friend Jenny is encouraging all this, she struts about from what I've heard dressed like lady muck. And this girl, Kitty, I don't expect she thinks any of this is her fault...'

'Have you quite finished?' Angela had roared, cutting Joan's speech dead, her eyes screwed up in anger, tears spilling down burning cheeks.

'Why can't you just be proud of me! You've never once told me you're proud of me! I'm sick of waiting for your approval. I'm never going to be what you want me to be. I like my life. I'm good at my job. I don't want to get married and have babies, I want something different. Why is that so hard for you to understand? Why is that so wrong?'

Angela had spat the words out, anger suppressed from the last four years finally exposed and free. Her fist had been been clamped so tight she'd felt a cramp coursing its way up her arm.

'If you can't accept me for who I am and what I want, I won't bother coming home at all.'

Joan had jolted at the volume and venom of Angela's voice. They had stood then and stared at each other for what seemed like an age, anger and hurt swallowing Angela's view of her crumpled mother. Angela's heart had been thumping against her ribs, a million furious thoughts had raced from her brain towards her throat which closed up with a dry nausea. After several attempts to open her mouth and say something...anything, Angela felt crushed and overwhelmed. She'd realised nothing she wanted to say at that point would help or heal the situation. Tossing the frame on the bed, she had picked up her bags and fled from the house.

Angela only realised she had fallen asleep when she heard the guard calling that they were approaching her station. She sat upright with a small gasp. She was the only person in her carriage now, which was a relief after she checked her face in her handbag mirror. She quickly took out a wipe and smoothed away the tear stains and wandering mascara.

'That will have to do,' she muttered to herself deciding there would be plenty of time to reapply make up when she got to the cottage. Besides, she was desperate to lock the memory of her argument with her mother away, at least until it was less raw and damaging.

Axley Station looked fairly small and only a few people were milling about when Angela got off her train. Paul had said he would drive up from the cottage to collect her as it was roughly a ten mile journey to reach Fairmouth. She ran her fingers through her dark glossy hair and looked around for a familiar face.

'Almost didn't recognise you. You look normal,' said a voice immediately behind her.

Angela swung round, almost falling. Shock gripped her as she found her face only inches away from James, and he was looking down at her as if he found her falling thoroughly entertaining. What was he doing here? No one had told her he was coming as well. Could this day get any worse? With an enormous sigh Angela blew some hair from her face but didn't say anything. She was tired, hungry and feeling really strained. There was no way she was going to find anything witty or clever to say to this man right now and in that split second she decided not to bother trying.

James inhaled the pretty violet smell around Angela and the fact he liked it annoyed him intensely. 'You can let go if you want, I don't think you'll topple over.'

He had that same mocking tone from the last time they'd met. Angela, acutely aware of how close they still were, couldn't breathe. Looking down she realised she was in fact gripping James' arm for support. It felt strong and perfectly sculptured through his sweatshirt. Angela immediately reddened and released him.

'You made me jump, I...I didn't see you there. I didn't know you were coming too.' Angela mumbled looking down, refusing to get trapped in his icy stare. Once again she felt foolish in his company. He would probably delight in telling everyone that she had fallen at his feet, she thought crossly to herself.

'Yep, here I am,' said James, and then noting the annoyance in Angela's tone he added, 'If that's OK with your majesty. After all, I did know them first.' He was smirking again but to Angela's relief he was no longer staring at her.

'The car's just outside, shall we go?' James put out his hand, offering to take a bag for Angela. He had already half turned to walk away.

Feeling slightly ashamed of her manners, Angela gave James one of her bags and thanked him quietly. Moreover, it suddenly occurred to her that James was here, meeting her, and presumably he hadn't been forced to do that. She walked quickly behind him, trying to keep up as he headed out to the car which was parked just outside the station in the waiting area.

The car journey to the cottage was awkward. Angela stared straight ahead at the road and wondered if she should start a conversation. James, stole several glances at his passenger and decided he liked Angela's natural look. Her hair fell in loose, unstructured waves and moved freely onto her face when she looked down. He'd noticed at the station that she wore less make up and a few tiny freckles were sprinkled casually across her nose. She was very pretty, he decided. Just a shame she was so prickly.

Useless at small talk, James shifted uncomfortably in the drivers seat willing the journey to be over. He'd offered to pick Angela up as a favour for Paul, who was at this moment out walking with Kitty along the Jurassic cliff framing Berry Bay. James wasn't familiar with making any effort to get women to talk to him. In fact, he was happily resigned to the fact that they normally instigated and led most conversations.

'So, um, did you see your parents over Christmas or have you been here with Bee and Paul?'

Angela decided the silence was deafening and couldn't stand it any more. She'd noticed James shift in his seat, so she knew she wasn't alone with the tension. They had just stopped at traffic lights. She ran her fingers through her hair to pull it from her face and turned her head towards James as she spoke. Their eyes locked. A smooth, intense shiver went through Angela before his gaze wandered down her nose and onto her mouth. She could feel her heart wallop her ribs as she forced herself to breathe out. An exquisite almost painful silence hung between them. James broke away first as the lights changed to green, the car behind having given them a prompt horn blast. Angela saw his angular jaw line tense before he replied.

'Just my Mum. She lives in Camden. I came down here late yesterday.' James answered very matter of factly. He gripped the steering wheel and stared ahead wondering why Angela was so curt. She was nothing like the floaty, flirty girls he usually met. It was an altogether new experience for him to have anyone meet his gaze like that, almost challenging him.

Angela wondered if she should ask more or stay quiet. A quick glance at James showed his eyes fixed on the road and he looked deep in thought, so she bit her lip apprehensively and then ventured, 'Do you get on well? You and your Mum I mean.'

James kept his eyes on the road, but ran one hand backwards and forwards across his cropped dark hair. A small smile played at the corner of his mouth and made a deep, rugged furrow up to his nose. Angela looked away quickly, conscious she was following the line back down to his mouth. James, for his part, wasn't sure how much to divulge about his life but decided as she'd asked he might as well be honest. He hadn't had the luxurious upbringing Bee and Paul had, but he was really proud of his Mum.

'My Mum's an amazing woman,' he replied, 'It's been just me and her since I was five.'

There was something in the loyal, honourable way he spoke that floored Angela and she remained quiet.

'I guess women hope men will change.'

Another pause.

'But they don't. We got by just fine without him.'

The same small smile teased again at his mouth.

'She's such a gentle woman, has such grace and kindness, but I know it was tougher than she made it seem.'

He paused and then added quietly, 'She loved him and he let her down.'

James finished by flashing a look at Angela to see her reaction. He was astonished and annoyed that he'd said so much to her. He found Angela already staring and caught her in an pale endless wave. She could see a son's love shining so brightly green that she felt like an intruder. Feeling her own eyes brim with tears she pulled in a deep breath, pulling them back and clamping them down. She couldn't remember the last time she had said anything beautiful about Joan. James looked away, the moment too penetrating. The way Angela had looked at him unnerved him. It was as if she had crept too far in, seen the very essence of him without his permission. No-one had done that before and he preferred it that way.

Both were grateful when minutes later James pulled off the road and announced, 'Here we are.'

Ivy Cottage stood comfortably in its surroundings, whitewashed but grubby, with Ivy gripping to the areas where the brickwork was exposed. It looked quite narrow at the front, but Angela could see it extended back making it actually a fairly large building, perhaps even two buildings originally. As they were on the side of a hill, the picture was framed flawlessly by the cliffs and beyond that the English Channel, frothy and wild.

'Oh my god,' Angela whispered, her gaze fixed on the cottage and the picturesque setting, 'Beautiful...just beautiful.'

James turned his head and studied Angela. She didn't notice him looking. He didn't reply.

*

The hamlet of Berry Bay is less than one mile south of Fairmouth. Part of the Jurassic Coast, the area is filled with sandstone cottages, some of them with thatched roofs, making it the perfect example of a quaint old English village. In the 18th century, the coast between Berry Bay and Whistlers Bay was the territory of a gang of smugglers. The gang had used the high jagged cliffs as their lookout post.

Paul had convinced Kitty to wrap up and take a walk with him on the long shelving pebble beach. The day was clear and cold, but not yet icy or windy. They had, in fact, been out all afternoon, weaving a path up over the old rock face, and down along the beach, stopping often along the way to wonder at the jagged and unforgiving cliffs and watch the water racing fierce and unleashed towards their feet.

Kitty had enjoyed listening to Paul's stories of smuggling. She thought the place was full of passion and romance, rather than being harsh or inhospitable. She felt safe and warm with Paul. It reminded her of normal when she was with him, as if she could see a path back to herself, and she trusted that he would be with her on each step if she needed him.

'Look at these marks,' Paul exclaimed, running over to where the bottom of the cliff face met the pebbles. 'We should bring everyone down here and look for fossils. You can see here where something has come out of the cliff. Coastal erosion you see and soft clay, there are tons of fossils and stuff on this beach.'

Kitty smiled as she watched Paul's boyish spring to the cliff and back and then his foraging. She laughed and playfully pushed him when he chased her with a handful of dry crispy weed, that the sea had spat out earlier that day.

'Paul, I think I'm ready,' she said without thinking, quietly but resolutely.

Paul moved closer to Kitty and swept away a strand of pale hair obscuring her face.

She leaned her cheek onto Paul's hand and smiled. She had no idea what she would have done without him recently, or Bee or Angela for that matter. They had held on to her strength for her when she had felt too ruined to keep it.

'In the new year, I want to tell my parents. I want them to know what happened. I can't keep hiding from them, and I can't move forward until I tell them. Angie is right, small steps. I don't expect to make this go away in an instant, but I have to move forward. I actually started getting angry the other day when I thought about him, and Bee thought that was a good thing. But I don't want to be angry, I just want to be happy again.'

Paul hadn't moved. His feelings for Kitty had grown to the point where he would do anything for her, and he was relieved and glad she felt ready to take a step forward, but in spite of this relief he was knocked off balance as he realised how disappointed he was that she'd been referring to talking to her parents when she'd said she was ready. For one fleeting ridiculous second he had thought she was talking about their relationship. He concentrated hard, to get a grip on his emotions and get back to what Kitty was telling him.

'I sometimes see it again in my mind. It plays out over and over. I didn't tell you. I didn't want you to worry.' Kitty gently rubbed Paul's arm. 'I have to remind myself the worst is over, that it happened in the past and he can't hurt me again. Angie keeps reminding me that I'm in the here and now, I got through it and even though it's vile to remember, the memory can never be as vile as the attack.' Kitty smiled gently. 'I repeat what they tell me over and over to myself. They always sound so wise,' she mused.

After a pause Kitty took Paul's hand in her own. Paul's stomach flipped, he ached to kiss her, but knowing he couldn't, he didn't dare to move.

'I need you Paul. I can't do this without you. Lots of brave words you see, but I need you to keep me strong. Will you come with me? Will you be there when I talk to them? Please.'

Paul smiled tenderly at Kitty and then lent forward slowly and touched her forehead with his lips, lightly enough so as not to startle her, but compelling enough to let her know she could depend on him. Her hair smelt of coconut and he lingered there willing her to lift her face to his.

'Of course Kitty, whatever you need, I'm here for you.' He answered softly letting his lips touch her skin again as he spoke. He felt ashamed that while she was reaching out for support and strength, he was thinking about how soft her skin felt under his lips.

'Thank you Paul, I don't deserve you. Bee and I love you so much.' Kitty sighed and she wrapped her arms around him.

Paul held her close, 'I love you too,' he murmured over her head, barely audible against the early evening waves crashing up onto land.

By five in the afternoon, the dark had swallowed the view from the cottage completely and icy shards were coming in from the channel. Kitty and Paul entered the cottage to find James listening to music, lounging on the floor. He had cushions scattered everywhere.

'There's a sofa you know,' Paul laughed and playfully kicked James foot as he stepped over him. 'You're making the place look messy.'

'I'm keeping out the way. Suggest you get down here too and keep a low profile,' James replied in a mock, fairly loud whisper. 'When we got back from the station, we found your sister making eyes at some old bloke who lives across the road, something to do with the boiler packing up and apparently he knows all about it.'

'Ah, so you remembered to pick Ange up from the station. Where is she?' Paul was on his way out to find Bee, so wasn't really listening to James any more.

'Yeah she's about somewhere. Don't think she was too impressed it was me at the station.'

'What? Don't be daft, she hardly knows you. What makes you say that?' Paul replied absently, not really waiting for an answer. James just shrugged. He had already closed his eyes and started drumming on his legs with two bread sticks.

*

'Bob, thank you so much,' gushed Bee, 'I know you offered to look after the place when Mum and Dad weren't here, but I bet you didn't really want to be dragged out at Christmas did you?'

Bee lent back against the dresser in the kitchen trying to make herself look relaxed and in control, even though she was wearing her mother's apron and had flour up her arms and in her hair.

'Really not a problem,' Bob assured her. 'You need to be warm down here at Christmas, it can get very chilly. You should be fine now, but don't be a stranger, come and bang on the door if you need me again.'

Bob smiled at Bee, and she wished she looked more glamorous at that precise moment and less homely. Bob's clothes looked very expensive, even his watch was very elegant and definitely designer. He was impeccably groomed and looked every inch the accomplished business man that Bee's parents had described.

'Would you like to stay for a drink with all of us?' Bee asked hopefully. She was aware of James lolling about on the floor in the next room so didn't think her offer would be particularly appealing.

'Perhaps another time?' Bob ventured. 'I'm meeting some friends for supper tonight at the Church Inn.'

He noticed Bee looked genuinely disappointed and he didn't want to appear rude. Even though he really did have friends to meet this evening, he had assumed that Bee's invitation was just good manners. After all, he was at least twenty years older than all of them and he didn't imagine they would want to socialise with him.

'Tell you what, let's not say 'another time', and then never get round to it, how about we make a firm date now? You and your friends meet me for a drink at the Smugglers Rest tomorrow evening?'

Bee ran her fingers absently through her hair and flour scattered between them both. Bob laughed and waved his hand about to clear the air.

'Yes, definitely. That would be great,' Bee agreed quickly. 'First one is on me though, to thank you for fixing the heating.'

Bob made for the back door. 'I'll see myself out, you stay here in the warm,' he insisted.
'Bye.' Bee replied, making an excited mental note to shower and wash her hair before they met again.
'Bye,' smiled Bob in an easy, even tone as he closed the door behind him.

'Got a date?' James and Paul now appeared from behind the door to the hallway and teased Bee in unison.

'Don't be ridiculous,' Bee retorted, smoothing her hair again with floury hands. 'He's a friend of Mum and

Dad, and a very helpful one, thank god. You'll both be grateful tonight when you're warm and cosy in here. Anyway, that so called date was for all of us, not just me.'

Bee went back to the kitchen table and resumed making the apple pie she had been half way through when the boiler had clunked loudly and died.

'And. He is not that old,' Bee continued, while the boys just stood and smirked at her. 'He can only be early forties, maybe mid-forties at the oldest. He is no where near mum and dad's age.'

'He's nearer their age than yours,' argued Paul, but he was laughing and had picked a piece of sliced apple out of the bowl, dipped it in sugar and popped it into his mouth.

Bee tapped his hand to reprimand him. 'Stop that. And there is nothing wrong with having friends the same age as one's parents is there?' she half asked, half lectured whilst smiling.

Paul flicked some sugar up at Bee, as if to have the last word, grinned and then snatched another piece of apple, threw it at James, who tipped his head back and caught it in his mouth.

At exactly the same time, Angela walked into the kitchen. James, caught off balance by seeing movement in the corner of his eye, stumbled slightly. He unconsciously reached out to the door frame to steady himself and Angela simultaneously put her hand out to stop him falling into her. As their hands connected both of them stopped breathing and Paul and Bee dissolved from their view. James straightened up, refusing to look up at Angela as he passed inches from her face. Her skin felt smooth under his fingers and he was so close to her he could feel the warmth coming from her body. As he passed her neck the perfume of violets hit his senses. Her neck was damp where she had recently sprayed the fragrance and he watched her throat move as he lingered there.

'Sorry,' he mumbled, 'I didn't see you there.'

He felt foolish and completely unnerved. Normally he was calm and unruffled around women, but she was making him feel like a bumbling idiot.

Angela took a huge, faltering breath in, and prompted herself to breathe out as her skin burnt from James touch.

'Well I guess that makes us even today,' she muttered as James released her hand. And then they looked at each other. Pale green eyes locked on blue, like bulls ready for conflict. Coming here was a mistake thought Angela. James clearly loathed her and right at this moment the feeling was undeniably mutual. As if Christmas hadn't been bad enough, now she had committed herself to more mocking and inadequacy.

Paul broke the tension.

'When will tea be ready Bee? I'm starving,' he requested nudging Bee with his hand willing her to look at James and Angela, and deftly stealing another piece of apple.

*

Time seemed to move too swiftly for them all at the cottage. Kitty felt safe with Paul and wished they could hide there forever. Paul was vowing to himself that he would be the friend that Kitty needed, even if she never returned his growing feelings for her. He hoped that would be enough for him. Bee enjoyed every second of flouncing around her friends like a hen, baking and clearing up for them. It was miles away from her job in a payroll department and she longed for the day she could give it up and be a home maker. She suspected people thought her old fashioned and not helpful to the female cause, but in Bee's mind she was the most driven person she knew so that made it their problem. Angela was grateful she could be herself around her new friends and felt a guilty relief that she was miles away from her own family. She managed to avoid being on her own with James and that seemed to suit them both, but it had not gone unnoticed to both Paul and Bee that James seemed slightly uneasy and a little more hesitant than usual to wallow with them in playful banter and teasing.

Bee was upstairs getting ready to meet Bob for the second time. The others were lounging around the sitting room discussing if they should go out with Bee or leave her to it. The tall tree Bee had decorated when she'd first arrived on Christmas Eve was standing proudly in the corner, twinkling silently. James was on the floor looking into the unlit fire place, his long legs stretched out towards the chair where Angela had curled her legs up to avoid touching him.

'Can we make a fire in this Paul?' he asked casually, already picking up pieces of wood lying on the hearth.

'Always the boy scout,' laughed Paul. 'Help yourself, it's all set up for a real fire.'

'Nothing wrong with that,' James retorted throwing the matches at Paul. 'Would have made a real man of you my friend. Come and help me.'

'Were you really a scout James?' asked Kitty laughing at Paul's attempt to get up as she pushed him gently off the sofa on to his knees.

'Yes, I really was,' answered James as he built the base of the fire.

'And he's a youth leader now,' added Paul, 'It's a great talking point with the ladies.'

James threw a look at Paul, as if requesting him to stop talking, but he didn't look that offended by the statement.

'It can be real character building stuff. Gives you drive and determination, a sense of accomplishment from an early age.'

James continued to look at the fire he was building. 'Don't forget some of these lads have no father figure in their lives. What they do with the club seems fun now, but it's more than that, much more.'

James hadn't looked at anyone in particular but the depth and integrity clear in his voice as he spoke, held the entire room.

'Plus the girls do love it when you tell them,' Paul whispered under his breath and received a cushion blow to his head from both James and then Kitty.

Angela, careful not to seek out James attention or look remotely impressed that he worked with children in his spare time, simply looked down and sipped her tea.

'Oh come on people, why aren't any of you ready to go out?' nagged Bee when she saw the group lounging around.

'Oh Bee, James just lit the fire and it's all warm and cosy in here,' pleaded Kitty.

'We came last time,' added James with a whine, making everyone laugh except Angela, who bit her lip to suppress the unwanted grin pulling at her mouth.

'Why don't you go on your own anyway, as I really don't think he intended us all to turn up again. He was just being polite,' added Paul who was already settling himself back on the sofa next to Kitty.

Angela was about to tell Bee that she would go and keep her company. She'd decided she needed to get away from James laying on the floor looking mysterious and sultry and annoyingly arrogant, but Bee cut them all dead.

'Fine, going on my own then. See you all later.' And she stomped off without another word shutting the front door with a little more force than was necessary.

'Want me to go after her?' James asked Paul. 'I shouldn't tease her so much.'

'No, she'll calm down quickly, she always does. She won't sulk. Mind you she may not cook for us for the rest of the trip.' Paul smiled, not looking the least bit bothered that his sister had flounced off.

'I'm sure she'll be safe and have a really nice time,' added Kitty. 'She seems quite taken with him and your parents consider him a good friend don't they?'

She took a sharp intake of breath as she finished her sentence. The irony of what Kitty had just said was not lost on anyone in the room, least of all Kitty herself. Paul sensing the fresh wave of misery sweeping over her, touched her lightly on the shoulder. Angela, at a loss to know the best course of action; say something, or wait for the moment to pass, looked around the room helplessly. Her darting eyes were caught and held frozen by James piercing stare.

'When it's dark enough, we can see the stars,' he

muttered and moved his gaze with a single blink from Angela to Kitty and Paul and then out of the window towards the cold night. Kitty and Paul didn't really notice James random comment but Angela pondered on whether this objectionable arrogant man actually had more to offer than he made visible.

*

'All visitors to Fairmouth should visit St Peter's church, it's beautiful,' remarked Bob as they strolled through the chilly, still evening. In the distance they could hear church bells chiming 'O little town of Bethlehem' and 'Hark the Herald Angels Sing'. Bee found herself feeling a nostalgia that didn't quite fit for someone of only twenty three. She smiled to herself, realising it was more of a longing for how every Christmas should be.

Bob had an air of authority about him when he walked and he was very attentive to Bee, showing impeccable manners and introducing her to everyone who stopped to say hello to him. Bee felt deliciously special and valuable and not at all as if she was out walking with someone old enough to be her father.

As they walked down to The Smugglers Rest, Bee learnt more about the two antique businesses Bob owned. One was just down the road and the other in Brighton. Growing up in Fairmouth, within two foster homes, Bob knew many of the local community and had become heavily involved over the years in local issues and politics. He had a gravitas about him that enthralled Bee. She was mesmerised that a man from such humble beginnings had worked himself tenaciously into a position of money and authority. She was thoroughly enjoying walking by his side.

'Smugglers Rest,' announced Bob as he held the door open for Bee to enter first. 'I didn't tell you last time, but this was originally a smugglers haunt as you can probably guess by the name. A lot of the original buildings have been destroyed by the sea, which I'm told, is still eating the coast on average three feet a year.' Bob relayed the facts smiling, self-effacing and charming. Bee beamed at him, completely beguiled. In the distance the feint chimes of 'O come all ye faithful' were enchanting enough to pull Bee from her reverie and she hesitated at the door looking back out into the captivating darkness. The outside terraces and seats on the cliff would provide the perfect opportunity to enjoy the tranquillity and views offered by the rugged, immense coastline now bewitched by fairy lights and a glowing moon.

'Or we could sit outside?' Bob suggested watching Bee look out to the water. 'Mad I know on a cold night like this, and we can't see the cliff that well, but we can hear the sea. Listen to that, so strong and unrelenting, wonderful and dangerous in the dark.'

Bee smiled. This was all perfect. The view, the night, Bob. All perfect.

*

It was New Year's Eve and Berry Bay was a flurry of activity. The Smuggler's Rest had propped its doors open and the sounds of people singing and shouting were intertwining and sailing out to the water's edge before being swallowed by foamy, wild waves. Children ran along the dark beach, laughing and clamouring for attention as their parents repeatedly told them to stay away from the water. The moon was clear and proud throwing a magnificent spotlight across the sea, which ignored everybody as it always did, continuing to breath with experienced rhythm. Bee was torn between the lure of the coloured lights, happy voices, the promise of a party or simply staring at the resilient cliffs, shaped by thousands of years of steady effort from mother nature who, even now, worked tirelessly at their feet.

'Penny for them? Oh and where's the old fella?' Paul had come out of the pub to fetch Bee.

'Um, oh, he went to Brighton this morning. He had to get the shop ready for the start of the year. Anyway, don't look at me like that, I'm not thinking about him. We had some perfectly nice evenings, but for all I know, we will never meet again. We didn't make any plans to meet. We're not dating.'

'Don't stand here getting cold then, come up to the pub and have a drink. I can't stay down here long as Kitty is up there on her own. Well, not completely on her own obviously. Angela is there getting chatted up by the bar man, and James is, well James is being James. There are at least three women trying to get his attention. Anyway, I want to get back.'

Bee turned to face her brother. 'Paul, what's going on between you two? It's obvious to everyone that you are head over heels. Does she feel the same way?'

'Nothing is going on. We were friends before and we're even better friends now. What's wrong with her needing me?'

Paul looked out to sea deciding to deflect his sister's questions.

'Nothing is wrong with that Paul. Just be careful. Please. You were friends before and it was fine. Nice and light and normal, but now, well it's just that now you seem to be more than friends, but not 'together'. She is relying on you and you are getting used to it. You're encouraging it Paul. What happens when she gets stronger and doesn't rely on you so much? How are you going to feel? You've put your life on hold for her and I don't know if she feels the same way about you. I worry that you are setting yourself up for a fall.'

'Thanks. That's charming. Why do you assume I'm doing this for my own personal gain? All men are the same are they Bee?' snapped Paul, affronted but continuing to deflect Bee. After all, if Kitty were to fall in love with him as a consequence, he wouldn't be complaining.

'No, that's not what I meant Paul. I love you, that's all, and I care so much for Kitty. If you two were together it would be perfect. But you're not and I just want you to be careful. She is so vulnerable still and if circumstances had been different, if she hadn't been attacked, I can't help wondering if you two would have got quite this close.'

'Once again, thanks', mumbled Paul staring out to sea. Normally he laughed at his sister's straight forward manner but right now he didn't want to face the obvious.

After a minute Bee broke the silence.

'Come on. I can see Kitty on the terrace waving at us, let's go and have that drink.' Bee linked her arm in Paul's and steered him towards the Inn, aware she had hurt his feelings but not willing to retract anything she had said or let it cloud the rest of their evening.

*

Inside The Smuggler's Rest the countdown began. Angela, tiring of the noise and the drivel coming from the man behind the bar, slipped over to the door while he was serving a customer. Before she moved out onto the terrace she looked over to where James was standing with a blonde. Wearing little more than high heeled sandals and a belt, the blonde was staring up into his face, her sweet chaste expression at complete odds with the volume of make up she was wearing. She was talking animatedly to James. Well, more *at* him than to him Angela noted because James seemed busy drinking from a beer bottle and looking around the room at frequent intervals. The blonde didn't seem to notice his lack of interest, she just needed to keep him there long enough to kiss him as the crowd continued the count down to the new year. Angela rolled her eyes, pulled her long glossy hair off her face, and quietly walked out and onto the higher terrace which looked out directly to where the moon was still taking centre stage,. She watched its quiet elegance, serenaded by the wild pulse of the water below. Angela could hear the cheers as the new year was welcomed in but it was merely background noise for her and the ancient sea cliffs.

Inside, James made his way through the crowd to Paul and Kitty, stopping constantly as each of the girls he had met that evening delayed him with kisses and questions about where they could contact him. It was like walking through treacle. His mind wandered to Angela and how wishing her a happy new year might be an opportunity to catch a glimpse of her being less frosty but, typically, it appeared she had left.

Kitty wrapped her arms around Paul's middle and hugged him as the new year came in.

'Thank you for everything Paul, I would be lost without you,' she whispered to him and kissed him lightly on the lips. Paul, still smarting from Bee's words, just smiled gently and wrapped his arm around Kitty resting his chin on the top of her head. He looked across the room and saw Bee chatting to the locals. She raised her glass and smiled kindly at Paul.

Outside, Angela stared into the blackness, deepest where the moon couldn't reach, and thought about the journey she had made in the last two years. She couldn't turn back now, there was so much she loved about her job and her life in London, and it was just beginning for her. She had a potential promotion next year if she worked hard and that was all she wanted at the moment. That and to be talking to Joan. Angela sighed. How was she ever going to reconcile her life? She shivered as she entered the new year alone.

Chapter 4

June 1988

City of London, South Bank

'You certainly have an excellent track record Angela and come highly recommended by all who work with you, but why would I give you a position in management and not one of the new young chaps just in from completing a degree? After all, they've been trained for this sort of thing and expect to get on the career ladder.'

Angela sat at one end of a long office desk, facing her senior manager and the manager from Personnel. Her own manager, who supported her without exception, was a man who believed in the best person getting the job regardless of age or gender but his boss, now staring smugly at Angela, was anti-women in any position of management. In fact, rumour had it, he had been heard to say that a woman's place was in the bedroom and the kitchen and not necessarily the same woman. It wouldn't be the first time she'd come up against dinosaurs but it scraped away at her still malleable confidence. She wondered if this would ever become less of a battle. She thought about Jenny, and reminded herself to stay calm and professional, play his game.

Making direct eye contact, Angela didn't smile, but retained a pleasant, composed aura.
'I can understand that question. This company makes a large investment each year in courting and bringing in the best from universities. However, with me you have proven ability and experience. I would be managing a group of women who do exactly the job I have been doing now for three years. I know all the management team, how the business works, what the business needs, in fact, there would be no break in continuity of service, no new relationships to build, no time needed to invest in my training. From where I sit the only thing I lack is a piece of paper that says I attended university.'

Angela's heart was pounding. She was shocked at the clarity and strength of her argument. Had she really said that? She looked away for a moment towards the personnel manager, more for respite than to seek his reaction. She needed to take a breath and not give away her nerves.

'Hmm but even so, these chaps have always come in with an expectation that they will go straight into management positions, not sure how they will feel if they find themselves working for someone they consider not as well educated.'

The now slightly red face behind the desk was taunting her. He clearly did not appreciate Angela sticking up for herself.

Outrage brewed in Angela. He knew damn well how good she was at her job but had the audacity to sit there and belittle her for not going to university. She shifted in her chair wanting to run away from the visible confrontation. Despite herself, she sat up very straight, buttoning her jacket and placing her hands in her lap. She could hear the echo inside her head, 'fight back'. She turned again to look at the personnel manager, this time directly fixing her attention on him.

'There's no reason why anyone coming into the company, should be made aware of my educational background surely? I always believed one of our principles was that once you're here and delivering excellent service, your school record is not relevant. It's what you've done here that's important. That's what you measure us against. Am I wrong?'

No one had interrupted Angela, so she took a deep breath and reached her conclusion.

'I see tremendous value if you promote me, in terms of motivating others and showing active support for equal rights amongst the staff. After all, we don't have that many women in management right now and it's becoming sorely obvious.'

Why was she having to state the obvious in front of personnel? Why was she having to fight so hard for this when she was more than qualified? Could that ill mannered man at the end of the table see her hands were trembling? Had she gone too far in starting to openly criticise the management team? Angela needn't have worried. The personnel manager started to nod in agreement after she finished speaking and he shifted uneasily about in his seat. She knew he was thinking about how it would look if the best person for the job was turned down because she was a woman who didn't have a degree. Angela felt quietly proud of herself but at the same time she was devastated at the turn the discussion had taken.

The craggy faced executive in his crumpled suit wasn't quite finished yet though. Clearly feeling outnumbered and out of his depth having this young woman challenge a belief system that had worked for him for forty years he taunted triumphantly, 'How old are you though, must be time for a baby soon, then where will that leave us? All that investment, wasted. That's the problem with giving a woman a man's job to do.'

Angela's eyes opened in horror. She couldn't believe the savage tone of his voice. Speechless she looked to the personnel manager for a clue on how to respond and found he'd jumped round anxiously in his chair to whisper frantically in the now purple ear attached to the craggy face. Angry words stuck dryly to Angela's mouth, still open in shock. She'd encountered snide remarks simply because she was a woman since she'd started here, she even suspected that in the lofty offices the male executives covertly plotted ways to maintain the status quo, but never had she encountered a childish outburst like this.

'I'm sorry Angela, would you disregard that question and accept our apologies?' The personnel manager was looking clearly mortified, and actually as outraged as Angela.

Deciding to take higher ground and end the interview while she had the upper hand, Angela responded with not very well concealed sarcasm.

'I hear it's entirely possible to give birth and have a job these days.' She spoke evenly and slowly looking directly at the stony faced executive, controlling her anger with good grace. 'I'm sure our female prime minister would agree with me. However for your record, I am not married and have no intentions of starting a family now or in the future.'

Angela promptly got up from her seat, thanked both men for their time and exited the meeting room looking composed and serene. Inside she was boiling over with anger and humiliation. How she would have liked to jump across that table and slap the craggy face full on. How could he get away with being so disrespectful? He hadn't even apologised, someone else had done that for him. She wanted to turn round, go back to the room and scream at him. Instead she walked straight out of the building, down the concrete steps, putting distance between herself and work. If they wanted her in the next hour they would just have to wait.

Chingford, London

Around the same time, Kitty was settling her children down on the rug at the front of the class for story time. It was the last activity of the school day and Kitty's favourite. She had been back at work now since February and no one in the staff room would ever know or guess she'd been the victim of an assault. Being with the children was the time she found easiest and most enjoyable and Kitty was careful to block any negativity that could spoil those short precious hours for her each day. Despite her brave words over the new year she had still to tell her parents about the attack. She was seeing them regularly at their home but had made excuses as to why she couldn't go to their study group any longer, or attend their church. Her parents were not impressed with her story that she was busy with a work colleague who attended another church. They decided that any man worth this much of their daughter's attention would surely have been brought over to meet them by now. As Kitty scanned the three rows of children sitting neatly and waiting expectantly for her to start reading, she felt dizzy for the first time in weeks. Her parents were coming over tonight and she had vowed to herself this would be the night she would tell them. She just needed to ground herself now and keep herself in the present. She couldn't lose her nerve this time. Kitty looked around the room again, noticing the colours of the children's school jumpers. She needed to focus and breathe. Paul and Angela would tell her to focus. Focus on something real and right now. They were red, the jumpers, but based on number of washes and probably the number of children they had been worn by, Kitty now noticed that some were a brighter red than others. She pushed her feet to the floor and willed herself to open the book and focus on the words. She took several slow deep breaths, this was her safe place, she couldn't lose it.

*

City of London, South Bank

By seven in the evening, Angela was starting to wish she had left the office with everyone else. She could see the early evening bustle down below, from her glass tower beside the River Thames. The day had drifted to a warm evening and everyone was looking relaxed and pleased to be out strolling by the river. If she didn't get a phone call from her boss in the next ten minutes, Angela decided she would leave. There wasn't anything urgent she needed to finish here, but she really wanted to know the outcome of the interview before the weekend. Angela was sure the old man would dig his heels in and not want her promoted and conversely she was starting to imagine how awful it would be working for him if she did get it. Perhaps it was for the best. She sighed and thought about how her mum would say *told you so.* Angela stared out of the window again and absently looked for women who might be out walking with their daughter's. She felt ashamed that she hadn't spoken to her mother now for six months. Initially she hadn't wanted to call or visit, still outraged at her mother's words, and then she had been fearful of calling knowing that her mother would be cross with her for not getting in contact. It became harder to contemplate and easier to leave alone as each week went by, and then the weeks had turned to months and now Angela couldn't see how she could just suddenly turn up or call. It was never going to be the same between them was it? Not after six months of ignoring each other. Or is that what families were supposed to do? Just move on and pretend it never happened. Angela exhaled heavily and considered with a new wave of irritation that her mother could have called her, but she hadn't, not so much as a message left at work or at the house. The phone rang on her desk, abruptly ending her wallowing.

'Hello Mark, about time too, please, please put me out of my misery,' Angela instructed smiling into the phone nervously. 'I can't tell you how awful that interview was.'

'Hello. Is that Miss Angela Duncan?'

'Um, yes. Yes it is, sorry I was expecting someone else. Yes, this is Angela Duncan.'

'Miss Duncan, my name is Dr Anthony Thompson from the University Hospital, Nottingham. Can you confirm that your mother is Mrs Joan Duncan?'

Angela felt a jolt of dread and her stomach lurched

over.

'Yes. Why? What's happened?' she stammered, feeling nausea crawling into her mouth.

'I'm sorry Miss Duncan. I have some bad news. Your mother had a major heart attack at home earlier this afternoon. I'm afraid she did not regain consciousness. I'm very sorry, your mother passed away at five o'clock this afternoon.'

*

Palmers Green, London

By eight, that same evening, Kitty and her parents had finished eating. Bee had offered to make a pasta dish as a quick supper and Kitty's parents had been delighted to accept on the condition that Paul and Bee also ate with them and their daughter. It was nice, they decided, to see Kitty still so close to Paul and Bee rather than this new man she seemed to be hanging around with. They had discussed on the way over bringing up the subject tonight and trying to convince Kitty to re-join them at their church.

After the meal, Bee made herself scarce on the pretence that she had to tidy the kitchen, having ushered everyone to the front room, telling them she would bring coffee through shortly. She looked knowingly at Kitty and then smiled with gentle encouragement as she left the room. Kitty smiled weakly back at her.

'We thought we might meet this new young man of yours this evening Caroline. Have you met him Paul?' Kitty's father was straight to the point. His tone matched the proud manner he walked across the room and Kitty noted that he was dressed very smartly in a grey suit. She distracted herself wondering if he had worked late today.

Paul looked at Kitty for help. He had no idea what Kitty's father was talking about.

'Actually Dad, that's something I want to tell you about. I should have told you before Christmas but, well, I ... couldn't.' Kitty sat down. There was no turning back now and she was terrified. She knew her parents would be horrified by the attack and equally horrified that she hadn't told them before, as they had no doubt been socialising with her attacker while she had been veering between torment and misery. Paul sat down next to her and took her hand in support.

Kitty's parents sank into separate chairs as Kitty re-lived the lift home she'd accepted from Charles Dunbar, curate and close friend of her parents. She left out the gorier details for her own sake as much as theirs, and didn't make eye contact with either of them apart from when she heard a gasp from her mother. She knew they would feel desperate for her and shocked to their very core, so, when she had finished telling them she sat quietly looking at her lap waiting for them to surface from the revelation. She hoped they wouldn't feel too guilty that this man was their friend, after all, none of them could have predicted what he was capable of.

'Just so you know Mr and Mrs Garrett, we've been taking good care of Kitty. Please don't think she has been completely alone all this time.' Paul broke the silence. He knew it was a lot for them to take in but he was slightly unnerved by the atmosphere and the lack of movement in the room.

Kitty's father made no attempt to move to her side. Looking at the taut lines of his face, Paul couldn't make out what he might have been thinking.

After another moments silence, Kitty was starting to look even more fragile. Paul could see tears flooding her eyes and her face tensing as she fought to hold them back. He held her hand in both of his now and stared over at Kitty's mother, who remained stationary in the chair looking horrified at her husband rather than coming over to comfort Kitty which, he assumed, would have been a mother's natural instinct in this situation. She looked caged, like an animal unsure of what their next move should be.

'And you haven't been to the police you say?' questioned her father, abruptly and rather too formally for Paul's liking.

Kitty shook her head and then looked down quickly as tears escaped cascading down her cheeks.

'I think we should though Mr Garrett, don't you agree?' Paul was getting impatient and angry now. 'He can't be allowed to go unpunished, we all agree on that don't we?' Paul stared backwards and forwards between the two parents willing them to come over to where Kitty was visibly shrinking and looking lost.

Finally, her father came over to where Kitty sat, quietly sobbing. He bent down and took her hands. She looked into his face and he wiped her cheek with this thumb and moved some hair from her eyes. She smiled faintly and held on to the sob that was consuming her. If he would hold her now, she knew she could bear it all.

'Caroline. Darling,' he began, 'You do know Charles Dunbar is one of the most influential and popular men at the church don't you?'

Paul's eyes narrowed and Kitty nodded helplessly.

'That's why she needs your support Mr Garrett,' interrupted Paul suspiciously.

Her father ignored him.

'Even if it really happened that way, I'm not sure you have enough evidence to push it forward. A family man of his standing and reputation will simply deny it ever happened. What proof do you have?'

'Hold on a minute,' Paul tried to interrupt again.

'It will be stressful and devastating to us all to have to go through that darling. I know it was awful, but you look fine and no harm done really.'

'W..What?'

'I think we should keep this between ourselves and not make a fuss. Better for us all in the long run.'

Kitty's father put his hand up without looking at Paul, to silence him from interrupting again.

'He is very influential, he could make it very awkward for us all.'

He finished by wrapping his arms around Kitty and patting her back.

'You're such a good girl Caroline.'

'No. You can't...,' Paul mumbled disbelieving. His brain was having trouble understanding what had just happened, but his anger had already erupted.

'What the hell are you saying? That you don't intend to do anything? Are you going to let some low life get away with this?' Paul pleaded and looked round at Kitty's mother who had risen from her chair looking suddenly frail and desolate.

Kitty didn't move, didn't speak. A chill shuddered through her shoulders, trembled uncontrollably and spread down her body. A slow, methodical spray of ice. She started to feel all the threads that held her together unravel. Her mind swirled and everyone's voices became a incomprehensible blur.

'Did you not listen to anything she just said to you?'

Bee charged in to the room. She had caught the end of her friend speaking and watched the poker-faced reaction of Kitty's parents. How could they be so impassive? How could any parent not want to kill someone that hurt their child?

'She was nearly raped. Raped! Which bit of that don't you get?'

Her voice was bellowing across the room as if spreading a toxin.

'Stressful and devastating for you. For you! What about Kitty? This isn't about you!'

Kitty still didn't move or speak, she took a deep breathe as if to re-start her heart and several tears splashed down her cheeks. Inside her, the threads continued to silently unravel. Part of her wanted to fall into the security that her father offered, get away from this brutal misery but mostly Kitty knew that if she let go now she would lose herself completely. She could already feel herself tumbling over and over, towards darkness with no idea where she was heading.

'You should calm down young lady, I just mean that we need to look at the bigger picture here.'

'The bigger picture? How dare you. Your daughter... your daughter needs you right now. That's all you need to know. That's the only picture you need to see. The one there in front of you. How can you not focus on her right now?'

She continued to bellow, her anger escalating.

'She got away from a man who was going to rape her. Rape her!'

Bee wanted to keep shouting the words until they sunk into his clearly impenetrable head.

'We're going to go now darling,' Mr Garrett was ignoring Bee and looking to Kitty.

'We love you and we'll see you Sunday for dinner. Don't come back to church if you don't want to, but at least think about what I've said. I know it's difficult right now but no good will come from making a fuss. You're young, you'll forget and you can't let this ruin your life.'

Paul and Bee continued to look horrified. He may as well have said, 'there, there, never mind.'

Kitty stared at her parents, standing side by side and mourned for her life before this evening.

'Oh yeah, it's difficult all right. Difficult to see who the biggest monster is right now. The man who nearly raped your little girl, or the man calling himself her Dad.'

For once Paul let his sister rant and scream. He echoed it all but couldn't take his eyes off Kitty, who was staring at her parents with no discernible emotion in her eyes. It was as if Kitty had left her own body. She was only vaguely aware of the words spoken by her father before he left. Those same threads that held her together also tethered her to her parents, and one by one with each step they took further away, those threads snapped and recoiled. If it's possible for a heart to truly break then Kitty felt the searing pain of hers being ripped from her chest when she heard the latch of the front door open. She felt the icy, absolute realisation that they were walking away.

'See you in Church Sunday,' screamed Bee in one last outburst, 'I might just come along and meet Mr Dunbar for myself.'

She slammed the front door so forcefully, it bounced against the frame and sprang back open again.

Chapter 5

September 1988

Palmers Green, London

Bee watched the neighbours cat bravely stalking a blackbird as the early morning sun kissed the window sill. She sipped at her coffee and sighed. She was dreading the winter this year. Kitty and Angela were so hard to reach at the moment and the time of year she usually loved for its potential fun and celebration wasn't holding much promise. The bright morning outside at least held the possibility of warmth for today and she cheered slightly. She turned as she heard the front door close quietly.

'Kitty? Have you just got home?' Bee quietly took in Kitty's tousled hair and the dark shading under her wide startled eyes.

'Just had another wonderful night,' came the defiant

reply. 'We went clubbing and met some nice chaps from Croydon. Went to a house party with them after the club closed,' Kitty revealed in a sing song voice.

'I thought you were going out with Paul and James? Were they with you all night too?' Bee asked in a concerned but even voice. Kitty seemed to be out at parties all the time now. This in itself was not a cause for concern, after all, Kitty had always been gregarious, but the marked change in her behaviour since she told her father about her assault was a real worry. She'd transformed, but not back into the confident, poised girl she had been, but into something altogether more desperate and unrestrained.

'Most of the time we stuck together,' Kitty lied as she flicked the kettle on for coffee and then checked to see if there was any wine left in the open bottle on the side.

'God Kitty. What are you doing? You need to be careful,' warned Bee, struggling now not to sound over protective and judgemental. 'Did you even know the person having the party?'

Kitty laughed, a hollow sound with no depth.

'Do you know what Bee, I've been careful all my life. Ever since I can remember I was a good girl. I did what I was told at home, I was respectful to my elders and everyone else around me for that matter. Do you know the worst thing I ever did growing up was cut the toes off a pair of socks I was wearing. I was five.' Kitty's voice took on a harder edge as she wound herself up ready to uncoil at a seconds notice on anyone in her way. 'I played by all the rules. I did well at school, never had a detention, became a teacher, turned out nice,' she started to mock herself, 'But where did that get me Bee? When it mattered, where did that get me?'

'Kitty. It made you a beautiful, charming person, that's where it got you. Someone we all love.' Bee had interrupted Kitty and Kitty stopped staring into nothing and was now looking intensely at Bee.

'But it didn't make me important enough, or believable enough, to love me when I needed it most. Just love me. Not worry about reputation, or what others will say. Just to know that the single most important thing, right that second, just for that second... is me.' Kitty's voice trailed off and she dropped her gaze to the floor, struck by the total misery that governed her.

Bee felt a new flash of anger at Kitty's father hurl itself at her insides. Paul had talked her down from turning up at Kitty's parents house so many times over the last two months. She could not bear the injustice of that evening for much longer and she was fearful that doing nothing was only causing her to nurture and feed the frenzy. She wished Kitty would get angry and fight back, but instead she seemed to have absorbed the pain and was allowing it to dictate to her. She went over to Kitty and grabbed her shoulders a little more forcefully than she'd intended.

'Listen to me. Your father doesn't deserve you. He had something precious and he made a choice not to protect it. That was the wrong choice Kitty. It wasn't because you weren't important enough, or what happened to you wasn't bad enough. You don't have to be grateful for his love or his attention, you deserve better than what he gave you. You are right, when it mattered the most he let you down.'

Bee stroked Kitty's arms, desperate not to cause a fresh flood of tears but feeling an unfamiliar need to hold on to her in the absence of anyone else.

'All our lives we can wait for that one moment, one defining moment, when we get to do something that proves beyond any doubt to someone that they're precious to us. And he didn't see that moment Kitty. Not because of anything you are or you did, but just because h*e* was too blind. Too concerned with the world around him and how it views him. His problem Kitty, his weakness, not yours.'

'Don't you see though Bee? There is no moving on from that,' Kitty whispered, looking right into Bee's eyes, 'A Daddy who doesn't protect his little girl when she reached out for him. I won't ever believe he loves me again, even if he tells me over and over, and I don't know know to live with that.'

Looking into Kitty's eyes Bee saw heartbreaking absence. They were looking at each other but Kitty was somewhere else, tangled in a futile labyrinth.

*

As the light became muted earlier each day and the chill started to follow Bee and Angela into the house each evening after work, they saw less and less of Kitty. She would finish her school day by four and be home and out again by the time Bee and Angela returned. She was still spending time with Paul but even he couldn't keep up with her social life during the week and would have to concede defeat and get home to bed, leaving Kitty to socialise her way into the early hours of the morning.

'Now will you let me talk to her parents Paul?'

It was the middle of October and Bee was in the front room commenting to Paul and James that Kitty had not been in all week and, in fact, Bee wasn't even sure Kitty was sleeping in her room any more.

'I have to agree with Bee, we should do something,' observed James, although he was watching the TV and didn't make eye contact with either of them.

'She came over the other night and I could tell she had taken more than alcohol,' admitted Paul. 'She seems to be hanging around with a bunch of losers.'

'It's just going to get worse,' insisted Bee. 'I don't think she comes home some nights and I know she doesn't have a steady boyfriend. I don't know where she's sleeping or who with. God knows where this is all heading, and I know I sound like an old fogey but...'

'She's looking for attention,' interrupted James, 'Searching for love in empty places.' He swung his legs off the sofa to sit up and give them his attention. Both Paul and Bee turned to face James, their expressions rapt with mild astonishment at the insight.

'Mum's fostering a little girl at the moment. Holly,' explained James. 'She's five, and her mother is still only eighteen. Holly's mum was raped at thirteen. From what I gather from the social workers the mother goes out partying, drinking, sleeping around. Holly was used to stepping over drugs on a daily basis by the time social services got involved.'

James got up and hovered just inside the room. No one else had spoken.

'They say it's a reaction to being violated then abandoned. The social workers I mean. No support when she needed it. Now she wants to shock people, get them to notice her. The more people push her away, the more shocking she thinks she needs to be.'

James stopped. He'd said too much.

'But really she wants to be loved?' asked Paul distractedly.

'All the men. If there are men, well I guess it's easy to confuse sex with love.'

Bee continued to stare at James, astounded.

Paul sank into a chair and looked defeated. 'I would have loved her,' he whispered more to himself than anyone else.

'Don't sit there and feel sorry for yourself,' lectured Bee firmly. 'That's not going to help her. This isn't about you, or you and her, this is about her and her father and the fact that he is a useless excuse for a man.'

That was it Bee decided. She was going to forge ahead with her plan to talk to Kitty's father or even get to Charles Dunbar.

James passed Paul, gently patting his shoulder.

'Drink?' he asked.

Angela, who had been on her way to the front room dived back into the kitchen.

'Hi,' said James awkwardly to Angela. She wondered how and why his demeanour could change so quickly.

'Um, Hi,' she replied, only glancing quickly over her shoulder as she made herself busy filling the kettle with water.

James and Angela had not spent any time alone together, certainly not since Joan had died. This was not deliberate on anyone's part, just a consequence of the others always being there when James was over and Angela spending more time in Nottingham with her father. But here they were now, alone in the kitchen and Angela was convinced she had James eyes boring a warm hole into her back. She turned abruptly.

'What does everyone in there want to drink?' she asked cheerfully and forced the corners of her mouth up. James, caught out at the speed she'd turned, dropped his gaze instantly to the floor.

'Um, er, Paul and I will have a beer...um think Bee will have coffee, please,' he added the *please* quietly on the end making an effort to be polite. He wondered why Angela was always so snooty with him.

Angela turned away to make the coffee and an awkward silence prevailed in the kitchen. James didn't leave and Angela wasn't sure why he was still stood there. He hated the way Angela frustrated him and made him unsure of himself, but he knew she'd been going through a really tough time and he found himself caring about how she was feeling.

'How have you been Angie?' James decided to venture, but quickly opened the fridge door and reached for a bottle of beer, relieved that he could hide behind it for a few seconds.

When he looked back, Angela was staring at him. He had never used her name when speaking directly to her. Ever. Hearing it now, and in such a sensitive almost tender tone, left her catching her breath. James, ran his hand back and forth across his head, unsure of how to take his eyes from hers. They looked full of tears and it shocked him to realise he wanted to reach out to her.

'Up and down,' Angela replied slowly, still looking into

James eyes. 'Thank you by the way. Thank you for the flower arrangement you and your mum sent for the funeral. It was beautiful. That was really very kind,' she finished, remembering how touched she had been that all of her friends had sent flowers to the little church in Barnstone.

James offered Angela a feint smile and took his beer over to the table. She realised he wasn't leaving and turned back to the coffee to regroup her thoughts.

'Why did you choose giant daisies and white roses?' she asked, without turning back to him. She didn't want James to see the tear working its way down her cheek.

'I've seen you come home with daisies for your room. I know you like them. And I asked Bee what flowers your mum liked.' James felt uncomfortable. He had never bought flowers for a woman before. He hadn't ever needed to and more to the point, he hadn't ever wanted to.

Angela closed her eyes and lent against the sink. She'd never thought of James as thoughtful or considerate and the revelation that he'd made that effort for her, coupled with the grief she felt whenever she thought about Joan utterly overwhelmed her. James watched her head drop and her shoulders start to shake.

'Angie, I'm sorry I …' Angela cut James off mid sentence, rushing from the room with a gasping sob. He stayed rooted by his chair unsure what to do next. Normally when a woman stormed off it was a relief to

James and at his instigation. Even if he did go after her, what would he say? How would he behave? This was completely uncharted water for him. He heard the front door slam. Ignoring the conflict in his head, he pushed the chair back and ran out into the bitter night after her.

*

Angela had disappeared in the darkness so quickly it took James several minutes to catch her up. Not wanting to startle her he called ahead when she came into view, 'Angie. Wait.'

She didn't stop.

'Please, Angie. Wait.'

Hearing James use her name over and over made Angela bewildered. As if they were connected somehow. They had never been what you would call friends. Certainly they shared and got involved with discussions in the group and went to places altogether, but they didn't have what anyone would call their own relationship. In the absence of any other appropriate response to James calling her and asking her to stop, she just kept going. Anguish had taken over. She had no idea what she was doing, striding about in the cold with no coat on. Drizzling rain was flattening her hair around her face, which was starting to sting and throb from fresh hot tears turning quickly to a cold sticky mess around her mouth and chin. If she had just run upstairs to her room, this would be over. Why was he following her? Then James caught her arm. She whirled round and screamed at him, 'Leave me alone,' but found herself pulled against his body. She fell against him without a struggle. His hand was on her back, fingers spread as if to catch as much of her as possible. She felt his other hand holding her head against his chest. He felt warm but damp from the drizzle and she could feel his heart thumping against her cheek. The enclosure made her feel sheltered but strangely alive. She allowed his breath to warm her forehead. She shivered and the tremble worked its way down her back like cascading silk. James closed his eyes as he inhaled sweet feint violets.

'I'm sorry, I shouldn't have mentioned it,' he whispered into her skin, his lips brushing her forehead as he spoke.

He held her a little more tightly. His lips were damp from the rain and the intimacy made Angela want to push herself even closer to James body and break away at the same time. She struggled to remember why she was there.

'Why are *you* sorry?' Angela replied sadly after a long pause. Then she added with detached calm, 'It's my fault she's dead.'

*

An hour later James and Angela had found refuge from

the rain in a small family run café on the high street. There were teenagers wandering in for chips, but in the main the place stayed quiet enough that they could nestle uninterrupted in a corner booth right at the back. James had ordered hot drinks and apple pie for them both. His mum always made him apple pie when he was upset as a child. Angela had smiled sadly at this, huddled opposite him with her hands tucked inside the long arms of his leather jacket.

'I hadn't spoken to my mum for nearly six months,' explained Angela quietly, knowing that James was waiting for an explanation and, oddly, wanting to talk to him. She hadn't told anyone how she felt since Joan had died, saying it out loud would have validated her feelings and she was secretly terrified someone would agree with her. Why she had picked James she had no idea. Perhaps it was just timing she told herself. Or perhaps she didn't care as much what James thought of her.

'The last time I spoke to her, I was so vile. Terrible things were said, and I shouted at her. I can't take that back. I can't tell her I loved her. She died thinking I didn't care. She died thinking I was selfish. That I thought I was better than her. I think she worked herself up into such a state that she had the heart attack. I did that to her. I could have called any time after that argument and tried to sort things out, but I left it because it was easier for me. My feelings were hurt and I was angry, so I suppose I thought I was justified in not calling. I could have been the bigger person and called first couldn't I?'

Angela played with her food.

'But I didn't. Now she's dead. How do you live with that?'

Angela looked at James. She was half waiting for an answer. Having convinced herself that Joan's death was down to her the only way she could stay sane was to search for a way to live with herself and what she had done. It wasn't an option to try and believe it wasn't her fault.

'Dad thinks I'm to blame too, I can see it on his face.'

James shifted in his seat, not sure if he wanted to comfort Angela or shake her. But he didn't speak.

'Oh he hasn't said it out loud, but I know he's thinking it. He hasn't said it *wasn't* my fault, none of them have. I could see it on all their faces at the funeral. All Dad will say is that she was taking a nap on the sofa. That's all he'll say. He doesn't say anything when I cry. So I know he thinks I'm to blame.'

James was willing himself to speak now but Angela took the silence as agreement.

'Anyway, it doesn't matter what he thinks because I know it's my fault and I hate myself. That's enough.'

Angela sank her head onto her hands. She felt exhausted as if she had talked for hours and she couldn't look at James any more.

James felt the now familiar flutter of panic and exhilaration as he watched Angela. It would be so easy to reach across now and take her hand. It would be just as easy to open his mouth and say completely the wrong thing. For a few crowded seconds James wanted her and wanted to be somewhere else simultaneously. He took a deep breath.

'She could have had heart problems for all you know. There are a thousand different reasons why someone has a heart attack.'

'Yes and one of those reasons could be me,' argued Angela. Her eyes were swollen and her nose red. James had never seen her look vulnerable.

'She didn't suffer Angie. We're all gonna die one day, and at least she was spared pain. I hope I go quickly. It would have been worse to watch her suffer wouldn't it?'

Angela pushed her pie around the plate. 'I suppose so,' she whispered, 'but at least I would have been prepared. I would have been able to tell her how much I loved her and say I was sorry.' Fresh quiet tears spilled towards the plate.

'You could write to her,' ventured James, trying to sound more positive.

Angela looked up quizzically.

'It's something that social workers get the foster kids to do. Even if the kids know the parent can't see the letter. Sometimes they just write a letter to themselves,' he continued carefully, wondering why he was so intent on getting involved. 'They tell their side of the story. Write about what's happened to them, how they're feeling, all the things they wish they could say to that parent.'

Angela was staring at him. He felt the heat.

'I'm not saying it will be any kind of solution for how you feel but it might help a little. At least you could say all the things you can't tell anyone else. You can at least get it all out and into some sort of order from your head. Might at least help you move a small step forward.'

He was aware he was rambling, but in the absence of anything else except Angela's eyes he felt out of control. The way Angela looked at him always threw him off balance. It was the same as new year. When their eyes met they were somehow allied and it was as disconcerting now as it had been then.

Angela managed a slight smile of thanks. It was the first time she had opened up to anyone and James was listening, rather than just looking as if he felt sorry for her like everyone else seemed to. It occurred to her then, that she had just spilt her darkest admission to a man who had done nothing to earn it.

'One other thing I can do,' she quietly announced, 'Is not take the promotion I've been given. My manager offered to stay in the job until I felt up to the challenge, but I'm going to turn them down and move back to my old job in Nottingham. Mum didn't want me trying to be something I wasn't. She was right...look what happened.'

'You got offered the promotion?' James asked, slightly taken aback.

'Yes. But it's not important now.'

'Of course it's important. You can't throw away everything you've worked for,' snapped James. True, he didn't much like Angela lording it about in her suit and heels but he knew how hard she'd worked to get this far.

'Look what it caused though. Mum would still be here if I hadn't moved away.' Angela spoke calmly, but emotions were escalating again and she wanted to run away from the confrontation. Who did he think he was giving out advice?

James was aghast. 'Even if you did cause her death, *which you did not*,' he emphasised, 'how does not taking the promotion help matters? It won't bring her back and if it was important enough for you before, then surely it should be even more important now. If you let all your hard work go to waste then... all I'm saying is... I think you're cutting off your nose to spite your face. You're a fool if you turn it down if you want my opinion.' He lectured just a little more loudly than he intended. The waitress looked across at him and smiled sweetly trying to catch his attention for the tenth time. Angela looked from James to the waitress and then back to James.

'Perhaps, James, I don't want your opinion,' she smarted and stormed out of the café still wearing his jacket.

**Chapter 6
April 1989**

Palmers Green, London

The last six months had been relatively uneventful, or at least that's how it seemed to Bee. Admittedly, after spending Christmas with her parents at the cottage in Dorset, she had been feeling very upbeat and quite lost in her own thoughts. Meeting Bob again was the reason for this optimistic outlook and the knowledge that he was due to spend time in London over the next few months to set up a new shop, was keeping Bee positively radiant. She loved how accomplished Bob was, how successful in business. Learning he had built his success from nothing, no money, no real parents, just a loving foster home, made him all the more attractive to Bee. It shone through in the way he spoke to people and in his impeccable manners and equally impeccable appearance. Just being by his side made Bee feel elevated and elegant. She liked the way she dressed when she knew she might see Bob. She liked the way she felt in his company, the way he treated her. It may have been old fashioned to some people but Bee loved the chivalry and romance of it. Essentially, she really liked Bob. So, although she had no idea where their relationship was heading, or even if it was heading anywhere at all, she'd not hesitated when he'd called last week and invited her to the theatre. Most of the men her age wouldn't dream of going to the theatre and she was so desperate to ensure Bob was equally impressed, she'd blown a large sum of money having her hair done and purchasing an entire outfit.

'Wow, who are you and what have you done with my sister?' laughed Paul, when Bee swept nervously into the kitchen to tell everyone she was going out.

'Oh God, how do I look? Tell me the truth Paul, is it too much?' asked an unusually nervous Bee, ignoring her brother's teasing.

'You look beautiful Bee, take no notice of anything these two say,' interrupted Angela and she gave Paul a playful shove and shot a furtive glance over to James, who had just whistled at Bee.

'Thank you Ange. I hope I won't be too cold. I mean, I know it's Spring but it's still chilly in the evenings. God, I wonder where Kitty has got to again, not seen her since Wednesday.' Bee, wanting everything to be perfect, was babbling more to herself than Angela.

'So, should we expect you back this evening?' wondered James, with a sly smile playing on his lips. 'Mind you, at least he knows it's not a school night,' he added, as a direct reference to their age difference, attracting a loud burst of laughter from Paul.

Bee looked hopelessly at Angela.

'Come on Bee, let's wait in the other room, and ignore the little boys,' encouraged Angela, smiling as she jumped down from the work counter. James watched the angle of her hips as she moved and the way her hair fell onto her face and decided, not for the first time, that she looked so much more tranquil and untroubled in over sized shirts than her structured, correct suits. Angela caught his gaze and blushed a little. Lately she had started to enjoy the clandestine attention and on more than one occasion she had found herself teasing James to generate a reaction, particularly if his attention was not immediately forthcoming. Ever since she had stormed out on James at the café it had become an unspoken competition between them, which neither would openly acknowledge and both were becoming addicted to. A game, teetering nervously between the flutter of anticipation and a panic of mistrust.

Angela had taken the promotion to her first management position, albeit not until after she had spent Christmas with her father. She had relived her encounter with James over and over for weeks and it had pained her to accept that he was right. She then had to confront the fact that she was not only being stubborn about the job but also about taking James advice. Typically, it had been Jenny who had pulled her together.

'So do you plan to just stop living?' she had asked over dinner, just before Angela had gone home for

Christmas. 'I think your James makes a good point, even if you don't want to hear it. Life won't just stand still and you won't be the same person ever again, but you have a choice. You either make it part of you and move forward or you... well I don't know what the alternative is, but I guess it's kind of do or die.'

Jenny had spoken kindly but resolutely and Angela was so amused by her reference to James as 'your', that she was completely unprepared for the admission Jenny had then made.

'I married, once, many years ago. It didn't last. I couldn't take his drinking, but no man ever came close in my mind, before or after him.' Jenny had smiled fondly as she remembered, and then her voice wavered, 'He died ten years ago. Drank himself to death. Not a day goes by when I don't think about what I could have done to help him. I used to torture myself on why I wasn't enough to stop him drinking. When he died the obvious thing to do was blame myself.'

Angela was memorised, rooted to the chair, staring at this strong woman who she had always seen as self-assured, now looking vulnerable and raw.

'But you have to move beyond your circumstances. Like I said, do or die. You can't not live your life Angela.'

With a quick check in her compact and an almost visible shudder, Angela had watched a familiar veil envelop Jenny and when she spoke again it was unyielding and resolute.

'But you can't pretend it hasn't happened either. If you ignore something like this it festers, turns toxic, eats away at your life. You have to find a way to acknowledge it, make it part of you, live with yourself. So that's why I agree with James, take the promotion. You can never make life the way it was, but you can celebrate your mother's life by living yours properly.'

By the time Angela had returned to London in the New Year she'd found herself feeling a slight excitement about the coming months. She still felt crushing guilt and she had no idea how she could reconcile her last angry words to her mother with her untimely death but she did at least concede that she wanted to find a way to move forward. She loved her job and she wanted that promotion. She had taken James advice and written the letter to Joan. She'd cried endlessly while she was writing and found the overwhelming exhaustion cathartic. Not knowing what to do with the finished sheets of paper, she had sealed them in an envelope and hidden the letter away at the back of her bedside table drawer. Now four months into her new role at work, she couldn't imagine her life any other way. She had several younger girls under her direct nurturing management. Angela pondered on the irony that they looked up to her, even though some days she still barely held it together, but her most fulfilling moments were not on the business practices but listening to them talk about their lives, their aspirations and their hurdles. She didn't claim to solve their problems but she knew she helped and she started to gain strength each time they turned to her for support.

Once Bee had left for the evening, Angela strolled back to the kitchen to find James and Paul where she'd left them, but now devouring a curry that Bee had cooked yesterday.

'You two are so lucky you have Bee,' Angela teased them. 'Goodness knows what you'll do when she has children of her own to replace you two.'

'If she gets together with Bob, kids might not be on the cards at his age,' laughed Paul. 'So I think we're pretty safe for now.'

'If she does, you'll have to look after us Angie,' added James, as he took another mouthful.

'There is zero chance of that. I don't plan to have children and I don't plan to lumber myself with you two either,' insisted Angela in amusement, getting a plate out ready to rescue the last helping of food for herself.

'I don't even have time for a boyfriend,' she stated absently, as she sat down across from Paul and James.

She looked up at Paul, who had stuffed a large piece of chicken into his mouth. She'd been meaning to ask a favour of him.

'I don't suppose you're free on the tenth of June are you Paul? I have a dinner dance for work. I have to go, I'm one of the management team, but I don't have anyone to take. I could go on my own but it would be nicer to have someone to alleviate the boredom of listening to the senior managers talking about themselves all night. Free food and drink.' She added the last bit in the hope of making the night sound less tedious.

Paul considered this for a moment while he chewed the chicken.

'Hmm, actually, that's Mum and Dad's wedding anniversary. I better not book anything up just yet until I find out if they want us over.' And then without much of a pause he added, 'James mate, you'll go won't you? You're never one to turn down the chance to meet beautiful women and get free food. Angie will be busy chatting up the boss for her next promotion, so you'll have loads of free time to ..erm mingle.'

Angela looked at James who did not return her gaze. She felt a familiar heat start to rise up her throat and into her cheeks. The idea was not completely awful but how humiliating that she was sat here waiting for James to answer.

'I resent that!' argued James, grinning and stealing a large piece of chicken from Paul's plate.

'Did you know that James is often in Jubilee Park on a Saturday morning trying to meet women? He uses the pretence of little Holly to attract sympathy.'

Paul was openly laughing at James now and the two were lost in their own little world, happily goading each other. Angela was barely listening, lost between the idea that James might go to the dinner dance and an annoyance that Paul was ridiculing her for being ambitious.

She was saved from any further torture when the phone rang and she excused herself to answer it. Her thoughts danced disordered and tangled. Why did she like the idea of James coming to the dinner dance? That Paul thought she was power hungry irritated her. Was she disappointed that James hadn't even looked at her when the suggestion to go out had been made? Why was she so mortified at his arrogance that, whilst he hadn't declined the offer, he had actually ignored the suggestion completely.

*

The following day was a Saturday and the bright sun was trying hard to warm the otherwise chilly morning. There was a crisp fragrance to the air that tempted happiness. Angela was heading to the tube station having decided to take a trip into town. If she had to attend the dinner dance she might as well look her best and seeing Bee looking so dazzling last night had inspired Angela to plan something bold and audacious. She was still feeling slightly affronted about James as she walked. Weeks of surreptitious looks and almost flirtation had left her with an expectation of his attention. If this was a game then she didn't feel she was winning it right now.

Mulling over the discussion in the kitchen Angela

seamlessly changed her route and headed towards Jubilee Park. After all, it was on her way and the day was so clear and light it would be a shame not to see the ducks and the spring flowers. Of course, she insisted to herself, if what Paul had said was true and she happened to see James, she would be friendly and not in the least judgemental about his somewhat underhand method of meeting women.

When Angela reached the children's play area she found herself scanning the swings a little too fervently and she had to admit to herself, she wanted to find him there.

And there he was.

Dressed in a thick sweatshirt, scarf, jeans and trainers, James was pushing a little girl in a swing and singing a song about the alphabet.

Angela could hear her screaming, 'Again Jamesy, again,' every time he reached the end.

There were other women in the play area but James was giving the little girl his undivided attention. This made Angela feel strangely benevolent towards him and simultaneously stirred an unwelcome feeling of desire, which she quickly covered when James looked up and saw her watching them. He bent and whispered something to the little girl, who immediately smiled and lifted her arms up to enable James to take her out of the swing. She ran over to Angela eagerly and stood staring up at her.

'Hello your Angie aren't you? I'm Holly, wanna have ice cream with me and Jamesy?'

The little face that looked up at Angela had enormous caramel eyes that were far to big for her currently dinky round face. As she spoke the long black ringlets surrounding her flawless skin bobbed about excitedly. She had a look of such openness and expectation on her face, there was nothing Angela could say except, Yes. Looking at her made Angela want to smile and when she did she was rewarded with an enormous grin back including one gap which the little girl quickly pushed her tongue into, just because she could.

Angela looked up from Holly to see James sauntering idly towards them. She knew part of her wanted to run away from him screaming Fire! But the rest of her was increasingly drawn forward, to see how close she could get without burning.

'Hi Angie, I see you've met the gorgeous Holly,' smiled James, as he swept Holly up from the ground and onto his shoulders. Angela noted that he seemed so natural with the girl and not at all fazed by her seeing them together. Holly giggled as James pretended he was going to drop her several times on the way up. Once up on his shoulders, Holly rubbed James head back and forth with her hand the way she had often seen James doing. It made her wonder what his head felt like. Was it soft like velvet or would it tingle against her hand?

'So ice-creams all round then?' James voice rippled

slowly over her thoughts.

'Um,' mumbled Angela, trying to remember what she was doing.

'Pleassseee Angie,' wailed Holly gently, her eyes seeming to grow even bigger.

'Yes, I'd love that Holly,' replied Angela, smiling up at the little girl now pulling James ears as if she was riding a horse.

Not long after they'd finished their ice creams, Holly ran off to play on the slide.

'So Paul was right then?' teased Angela. 'You really do come here on a Saturday to meet women.'

James turned his body to face Angela and put one foot up on the bench, his bent knee creating a barrier between them.

'Why would that matter to you?' he asked grinning. 'Jealous?'

'No!' shrieked Angela. 'Just curious,' she added desperately, wishing she hadn't said anything and feeling his stare mocking her.

After an awkward pause James sighed. 'Actually I come here to give Mum a chance to get things done in her house. Holly isn't the only child that Mum looks after. Saturday mornings I do a lot of taking and fetching to various clubs and stuff but Holly doesn't do any clubs at the moment, so we come to the park before I pick everyone up.'

Angela was stunned. She should say something. She couldn't not acknowledge what she'd just heard, but was totally unprepared.

'Oh, um, that's, well that's really nice.' Really nice? had she really just said that she thought to herself, how completely under whelming.

'Bit of a shock though isn't it?' James questioned. 'Me, being really nice.'

Angela wasn't sure if he was teasing her, but she sensed a melancholy in his voice which was unfamiliar. She felt she should apologise, although she was not quite sure what for. She turned to look at James. He was already staring at her and probably had been for the last minute. She bit her lip at the power of his expression and the intensity she saw in his eyes. Her heart started to thump wildly at her ribs. James continued to stare at Angela, ignoring the spiralling panic in his stomach but acutely aware the silence and distance between them was growing smaller with every passing second.

'By the way,' he said curtly and Angela jumped slightly when his voice broke the intense atmosphere. 'I meant to say last night and didn't get the chance. If you still need someone to escort you in June. I'm free. I mean, if you want me to.' He stumbled over his words and was fully aware of how feeble he sounded. He spoke to women all the time, and now his confidence had fled when he needed it most.

'Well if you're sure it's no trouble,' replied Angela in barely a whisper. Why couldn't she just say yes she reprimanded herself. Imagine yourself at work she told herself, be assertive.

'It's no trouble,' James mumbled, wondering what he would say next if Angela turned his offer down.

'OK. Yes. Thank you.' replied Angela, managing an awkward smile as she felt a queasy mix of exhilaration and fear rise into her throat.

A short time later she was strolling towards the tube station. The need to get a stunning outfit for the dinner dance was now an imperative. She realised with shock that she was daydreaming about how she would look on James arm. The evening had suddenly migrated from a corporate duty to be endured, into a thrilling night out that she could hardly wait for. She was staring so avidly at her day dream that she almost missed the huddled figure in the band stand.

The long, blonde curls were unmistakeable.

 'Kitty? Kitty, oh my god. You look frozen.'

Angela sat down quickly next to the heap nestled on the bench and wrapped her arms around her.

'Have you been here all night? Please tell me you haven't,' pleaded Angela softly and she kissed the top of Kitty's head gently.

'No,' replied Kitty absently without looking up. 'I haven't been here all night.'

Angela pulled Kitty closer and held her. She had no idea what to say or how to help, so for the next five minutes Angela allowed the silence to be as still and peaceful as silence should be.

'I was picked up by the police last night Angie.'

The words tore at the peace like tissue. Angela's stomach seemed to sink and she didn't dare speak, wondering what horror Kitty was about to tell her. When Kitty finally spoke she was calm, but there was a steady edge to her voice which made Angela sit up a little straighter.

'Can you imagine how humiliating that is?' She was looking directly at Angela now and Angela felt like Kitty was waiting for a response rather than musing to herself. She shook her head slowly and stroked Kitty's hair tenderly, fearful that she looked judgemental.

'They thought I was touting for business!' Kitty would have laughed if she hadn't felt so disgusted. 'But then why wouldn't they think that? I was wandering the streets at stupid o'clock dressed like a hooker and smelling of booze. I wasn't just drunk either. I was on a different planet.' Kitty paused and sighed heavily.

Angela struggled for something to say, anything to say, but Kitty wasn't finished.

'What happened to me? I was a star student at school. I was a prefect. I got a degree. I love my job. How long till they sack me? I'm hurtling head first for the rubbish heap and I don't know how I got here.'

It was awful enough knowing the truth, but hearing herself say it out loud nearly killed Kitty. She wondered who she was now. She didn't recognise herself and it was the worst feeling she had ever experienced. This, she decided, was much worse than the attack. Now she was lost. Finally and utterly lost.

'What happened with the police?' Angela interrupted. She needed to stop Kitty wallowing and also find out how much trouble she was actually in.

'They took me to a women's shelter,' replied Kitty. 'I told them I had no where to go for the night. I couldn't come home in that state, not via a police escort anyway. Bee would have a fit and she would tell Paul.' She paused and then whispered, 'Paul. There was a time when I thought Paul and I could get together, but why would he want me now? Look at the state of me Angie, I am just a filthy mess.'

Angela stroked Kitty's hair again and searched for words.

'Do you know I met women at the shelter who had the courage to run from violence and drugs and all sorts of unsafe situations, but me, I'm just the girl who wants to have a good time. I put myself in danger for the hell of it. I disgust myself.' Kitty looked straight into Angela's eyes, barely three inches away from her own and pleaded without words.

'I don't want to be this any more,' she said finally in the barest, most heartbreaking whisper Angela had ever heard. 'I want to wake up and feel beautiful'.

Angela pulled Kitty close again and thought carefully before she spoke.
'Then do something about it Kitty. You can fix this. This isn't who you really are. Let us back in. Let us help you.'

'You know sometimes I think I have a demon inside me,' muttered Kitty once again staring, but Angela saw signs of life deep behind her eyes for the first time in months.

'It's like I'm stuck and Charles Dunbar has all the power. He's there pushing in, leering at me. When I do block it, I just see my Dad's face and I can't think or breathe. It's easier to let them suffocate me. I'm becoming so confused. I don't think I'll ever know the way back.'

Hot tears of anger sped down Angela's face, following the lines of tears spilled listening to Kitty's misery. She decided her first action would be to take Kitty back to the house and surround her with people that love her. Her next action she knew with certainty would be far less benevolent and, for that, she needed Bee.

*

'Oh my god Ange, you look gorgeous,' gushed Bee staring at the reflection in the full length mirror.

The night of the dinner dance had arrived quicker than Angela had anticipated and she was struggling to conceal her nerves. She wished she had Bee's confident calm and was envious of how truly elegant Bee looked in the little black dress edged in lace at the hem.

'Seems like Bob is always about these days? Must be getting serious?'

Bee smiled coyly and re checked the mirror again.

'He's taking me out to dinner tonight. I hope I'm not over dressed. Bob has some business associates that also eat at this particular restaurant and he thinks we might run into them. I want to make sure I don't let him down.' If there was a note of worry or anxiety in Bee's voice, it went undetected by Angela.

'You don't think this red is too much do you Bee?'

Angela was now wondering if she should have gone for basic elegant rather than the plunging silk dress which hugged her figure. She eyed the fabric flaring out under her hips and cascading down towards her ankles where four inch spiked heeled sandals could be seen completing her daring ensemble.

'God no. You look fantastic. You spend too much time in suits if you want my opinion. You need to lighten up and learn brazen.' Bee was looking at Angela with a slightly more serious expression than Angela could fathom.

'Wear your hair up though, it will make you more chic,' instructed Bee and she pulled Angela down onto a stool and started to pin her hair up.

'Bet those old codgers you work with will have heart failure when they see you,' smiled Bee, 'And, I think even James is going to have his work cut out keeping the competition away.'

'I think it's me that will need to keep hold of James,' blushed Angela. 'The girls in the office can't wait to meet him. He will think he's died and gone to girl heaven,' she added, wondering just what James would say when he saw her.

'Are you mad Ange? Oh my god, you really have no idea about men. You are far too serious for your age. He won't be able to take his eyes off you.' Bee laughed and then turned more serious. 'Don't drink too much tonight though, we need to be alert and ready for tomorrow remember.'

Angela sighed but nodded resolutely, to acknowledge Bee and the plans they had been making.

Charles Dunbar and his wife had been out of town for the last few weeks, or at least that's what they were being told. Having returned earlier in the week, Bee and Angela were planning to pay him a visit tomorrow. They had discussed going straight to the police or even turning up at his church to confront him but they decided a private chat with him might persuade him to confess to the police, or at least give him warning that Kitty planned to go to the police. Kitty had not yet agreed to this but Bee and Angela were adamant they would move forward with some kind of action to find justice, however small, for Kitty.

Kitty herself had been quiet but resolute since her escort by the police. She and Paul had resumed their old routine of spending free time together and the others were heartened when they occasionally heard laughter and banter coming from the front room. Paul kept her diary full. No one was under any illusion that Kitty was finding life easy, and with all of them taking turns to be with her and reminding her constantly to take one day at a time, she might have felt she was slowly swapping one crutch for another, but at least this one came at a more than acceptable cost.

Everyone jumped at the loud knock on the door.

Paul and Kitty, who were watching a film in the front room, rushed to the hallway to watch the proceedings, as if swapping one form of entertainment for another. Bee checked herself in the mirror one last time and then swept down the stairs to open the door. Angela followed gingerly behind, conscious of the high heels and the low cut of the dress while she navigated herself.

'Bee, you look lovely, as always,' said Bob as he kissed Bee full on the lips. Bee breathed in the now familiar scent of lemon and bergamot and stroked the weathered but impeccably groomed face.

Kitty looked at Paul and raised her eyebrows, realising she had a lot of catching up to do.

'Wow and who is this gorgeous creation? Is that you Miss Duncan? I might be taking out the wrong lady tonight.'

Bee gasped in mock horror and wrapped her arms around Bob while beaming at Angela.

'She looks amazing doesn't she? Wait 'till James sees her.'

'Why thank you Sir, but I think your card is already full,' replied Angela to Bob, returning his attempt at chivalry and smiling broadly at both him and Bee.

She didn't notice movement on the path behind Bob. She didn't hear the intake of breath as she swept into view across the threshold. James halted and stood behind Bob completely lost for words. He wished he could stay hidden and look at Angela, unseen, with no one to read his deepest thoughts. He felt a foolish lurch of panic as he desperately scrabbled for something to say. He would have given his soul to the devil at that moment to make this feeling of helplessness and desire disappear.

'Well James, don't you scrub up well,' observed Bee teasingly, reaching behind Bob and pulling James' arm. She dragged him into the house forcing him to surface from his unwanted reverie.

'Look who I found on the doorstep Ange. Will this waif and stray do for a date tonight?'

Angela had never seen James in a suit let alone a tuxedo. The smart, formal lines of the cloth triggered thoughts of the hard chiselled lines beneath and the monotone of the colours detonated an urge to seek out his pale green eyes. She felt a thrilling mixture of panic and excitement in her belly that carved its way indulgently down her legs.

'Ready to go?' James asked quickly, deliberately only looking only at Angela, who smiled and walked carefully towards him.

James offered Angela his hand which drew coy noises of approval from Bee and Kitty. He ran his gaze seductively down Angela as she moved towards him. She felt his eyes devour her, assessing her from head to toe. A hot ache shivered through her. She wondered if a kiss from him would have felt less intimate at that moment. James hand felt hot. Burning Hot. She held it tightly and their eyes screamed to each other.

'Nice dress,' muttered James to Angela, before realising

that the group assembled in the hallway were all staring and smirking.

The taxi ride to the Grosvenor Hotel on Park Lane was quiet as both James and Angela contemplated what had just happened. Neither knew what to say. Their relationship had just evolved in the space of five minutes, without words and it was obvious they were both aware of how the other felt. The time for game playing might be over and this made both of them feel unsteady and foolishly inexperienced.

Heads turned when they entered the bar for drinks before dinner. Angela noticed many of the girls eyeing James approvingly and she wondered if maybe she had read the signs wrongly and she would, after all, have to make an effort to keep him by her side tonight. She also noticed many of the older more senior managers in the room cast their eyes up and down her body and for the first time that evening she wished she was wearing something less alluring. She needed a drink, before the courage to pull this evening off with borrowed confidence disintegrated.

The constant flow of champagne over the next few hours helped James and Angela generate an unconscious decision to make the most of the evening and they slipped into a stream of easy conversation. Throughout the evening Angela ensured she retained a certain level of professionalism and introduced James eloquently to every girl that came over to admire him. James was polite and interested in each of them, but he swiftly turned down every invitation to dance or leave

Angela's side. As far as he was concerned this was a double win, as he felt more out of his depth than he ever had, and it really was no loss to stand with Angela. She amused him by surreptitiously pointing out and telling him tales of the office leeches and the senior male bullies, who felt a woman's place was anywhere but the boardroom. James, in return, entertained her with stories of some of the less salubrious characters from his neighbourhood who, for a small sum of money, could break their legs. As they danced that evening Angela saw they were not all that different. She admired James for how seriously he'd worked on his apprenticeship when he left school and his aspirations, building his own business through hard work. It was not unlike her own efforts starting at the bottom of the company and she allowed herself a moment of silent congratulation. Neither of them belonged in this ball room, trussed up and drinking champagne, yet here they were.

When the taxi pulled up outside Angela's around two in the morning, James got out first and held the door open for her.

'Well thank you Sir, that's very chivalrous,' teased Angela and she took his hand not for the first time tonight. It felt warm and safe now but still held the thrill of anticipation, as if it could unexpectedly burn her.

'I'll just be a minute,' James told the driver and he lifted Angela's hand to his mouth and pressed his lips against it. The kiss froze between them as skin touched skin.

'I'll walk you to your door.' James smiled as he reluctantly moved his mouth. Angela could see the smile reaching deep into his eyes.

His lips were a darker shade of caramel to his skin and the presence of her hand near his face, against the firm flesh of his mouth made Angela shiver. Was that all he would do? Just kiss her hand she wondered. She also wondered how bold she would be after all the champagne and deliberately took an enticing step closer to him, as if to test him.

'Do you want to come in?' Angela stopped at the door and didn't take out her key.

'Not sure that's a good idea Angie. We've both had a lot to drink,' replied James and immediately regretted it when he saw hurt cross Angela's face.

'Wait.. Please. Don't think I don't want to. I do...I mean...Oh god I'm making a mess of this.'

Never in his adult life had he felt so awkward near a woman. He was so aware of her breathing, if he moved just a fraction their bodies would touch. Angela swayed slightly against the weight of all that wasn't being said and caught her breath rapidly as she felt James pull her body against his with one arm and move the fingers of his free hand into her hair. She was only aware of his face hovering dangerously over hers for a fraction of a second before she felt his mouth tease at her bottom lip. Angela's body sank against him causing James to pull her tighter. She could feel him pressing against the flimsy fabric of her dress. He moved his hand deeper into her hair and the kiss she was now returning became more passionate and desperate. James moved his hand slowly from her hair to trace down the back of her neck and onto her throat. She felt her body give way as his hand travelled down and his mouth covered her.

'Come inside,' she pleaded breathlessly as she gently bit his lip.

James breathing became quicker as he pushed their bodies up against the front door.

They were startled into springing apart when the door opened abruptly.

'Don't mind me,' said Bob smiling, 'I just need to get past, early morning tomorrow.'

'Um. Actually. I'm sorry. I need to go.' James was looking at the floor and rubbing his hair. 'I have some things I need to take care of.'

James sounded distant, almost angry and before Angela had a chance to stop him, he had flown down the steps, hurled money at the taxi driver and disappeared on foot into the night.

*

Heatherington Village Nr Epping, Essex

Angela hadn't needed to wake the following morning, she'd barely slept. She'd played the whole evening over and over in her mind. It was perfect. So what had gone wrong? Why had James disappeared like that, without saying a word? She had watched as a bright June morning had stroked away the darkness and the early warmth of the day had seeped through her curtains. Now sitting in Bee's car travelling through Epping Forest she tried desperately to focus on Kitty.

'You're quiet this morning Ange,' Bee said lightly, 'Good night? Heavy night?'

'Good, thank you,' Angela replied, which was not at all a lie. 'Just tired.'

'So, what happened? Spill. God you looked good together Ange. Tell me something happened between you two.'

'No, nothing happened,' Angela lied. 'We had a good time, a really good time actually,' she added with a hint of sadness, 'But there's nothing more to it than that. He's not my type.'

The small village of Heatherington sits next to Epping Forest, which lies north-east of the centre of London. It wasn't difficult to locate the house sitting about half a mile from the village square.

'Do you know what we're going to say to this man Bee? I mean, we don't really expect him to just admit it and turn himself in do we?' Angela was starting to feel nervous.

'Probably not, but we can't just sit by any more. We agreed. Kitty needs to see people on her side. We're not afraid of Charles Dunbar. Her father looked positively terrified of confronting him.' Bee was her usual feisty, confident self, which calmed Angela but also terrified her at this precise moment.

'Maybe just making him aware we know what he did will put the frighteners on him, make him panic if he thinks we're going to the police.' Angela was trying to convince herself. 'And judging by the houses round here I doubt he will want the neighbours to know what he's been up to.'

Angela raised her eyebrows as they slowed down and stopped. The house they were sitting outside was gated, high black wrought iron gates to be exact. Beyond the gates was a wide gravel drive giving way to it's centrepiece, a mock Tudor fronted house with wide bay windows on either side of the heavy front door. Above that were enough windows to suggest at least three large bedrooms just at the front of the house.

'Hmm,' agreed Bee, the sight of the house Charles Dunbar lived in clearly irritating her.

A woman in her mid-fifties opened the front door. She

had hair that was clearly styled regularly by a hairdresser, coiffured and held in place with spray. Her eyebrows, the same dark brown as her hair, were sculptured into arches. Her make up was a little too perfect, particularly for a weekend morning. Even her lips were painted bright red. Perhaps she had guests thought Angela. Why would anyone look like that on a Sunday morning? She was wearing a long dress shaped like a kaftan with winged sleeves and swirling patterns of cream, brown and black. To Bee she looked just like the housewives her mother played bridge with; wealthy, privileged and in most cases completely clueless of what goes on outside their own social circle.

'Hello. Are you Mrs Dunbar?' asked Bee politely.

'Yes dear, can I help you?' replied Mrs Dunbar, with an unmistakeable deliberate haughtiness.

'Actually it's Charles Dunbar we're looking for. Is he in? We need to see him please.'

'I'm afraid that won't be possible. My husband is out of town,' she replied and both Angela and Bee noticed her shift her weight back slightly from the door, as if she believed the conversation over.

'It's very important that we speak to him Mrs Dunbar, about a friend of ours. Kitty Garrett. I'm sure you know her parents?' Bee's voice had lost some of its congeniality and patience.

'Yes, very dear friends of ours. I have no idea why you would want to talk to my husband about their daughter though. Silly girl. I heard she's getting into all sorts of trouble these days. Some children are so ungrateful. Makes us glad it's just the two of us.'

Bee eyed Charles Dunbar's wife suspiciously.

'You know don't you?' she accused loudly and took a step into the house, so the door couldn't be closed.

'Bee,' objected Angela. 'What are you doing?'

'I think she knows and she's protecting him.'

Mrs Dunbar stood tall, and pressed her lips together in defiance.

'I really have no idea what you are talking about young lady, and I suggest you leave my house now before I call the police.'

'Please do.' Bee responded raising her voice and moving closer. 'Do that. Call the police and that will save us the job when we get home. Kitty plans to press charges you know. Everyone will know. Everyone. Your husband, hiding behind his big house, his grand wife, is nothing more than a vile piece of scum. Would you really want to protect him and allow him to ruin more lives? What if he actually rapes the next one or is it just Kitty particularly that he took a fancy to?'

Angela stood horrified as Bee's voice grew louder and more purposeful. This wasn't what she had expected to happen. Bee was rolling down a hill at a hundred miles an hour with no brakes. Months of suppressed anger spilling like acid. Mrs Dunbar looked equally horrified but Angela noted her eyes darting from one place to another, her brain trying to get one step ahead of the train wreck hurtling towards her.

'He bit her. Did you know that? He ripped her clothes and forced his hands....'

Mrs Dunbar whimpered and lost her balance slightly.

'Bee!' shouted Angela. 'Stop it!'

'He would have raped her,' shouted Bee. 'Raped Her.'

She couldn't stop the anger rising and bursting out of her, it was picking up speed with every word she said until even she became aware it was spewing unedited out of her mouth.

Then there was silence. Heavy, cold and tinged with a feeling of nausea. Mrs Dunbar's veneer cracked and she looked every inch an exhausted, broken woman as she sank down on a chair in the entrance hall.

'No. I didn't know about Kitty,' she mumbled finally, 'But I had a sense of dread when you asked to see Charles.' Bending down in the chair, her head falling forward, Mrs Dunbar began to cry quietly to herself, completely alone. She seemed not to notice or care that Angela and Bee were still in her hallway.

'Let me go and find you something to drink,' said Angela kindly. She knew there was more Mrs Dunbar could tell them and, although she didn't understand why, she felt a fraction of compassion for this woman who was married to a monster.

With her face now looking dishevelled and absent, Mrs Dunbar gazed around her hallway as if wanting the girls to appreciate the décor.

'Do you know I have spent hundreds, probably thousands decorating my home, and myself, just to make myself enough for him,' she murmured helplessly.

Angela had discreetly shut the front door on her way back from the kitchen. She was holding a glass containing gin with just a small amount of tonic. The bottles had been easy to find in the kitchen.

'But how he feels inside, what he wants, has never matched what he saw on the outside of others. What he craves as normal, most of us would be appalled at. I didn't know of course when I married him, and when I did start to find pictures and later video cassettes, I told myself all men probably did it and it was normal. I decided to let him have his fantasies.'

She stopped to take a gulp from the glass, but didn't look up. Bee and Angela glanced at each other, a shocking realisation flooding them that Charles Dunbar might have a history.

'He became more disconnected though, and the images he wanted to look at became worse. He hid them from me, and his drinking. I wasn't enough for him. I couldn't satisfy his, his lust for the obscene and the untouchable.'

She paused to drink again and cry quietly as if his shame was hers to bear.

'That became his reality, the pornography, behind our closed doors. The gap between my expectation of love and marriage and his reality became wider as the years passed.'

Angela and Bee were speechless as a putrid silence crept over the three of them.

'Why did you stay?' Angela heard herself saying out loud.

Mrs Dunbar seemed to rally. 'Because my dear, I was brought up to believe marriage was for life and it was not my place to leave.' She looked up for the first time but spoke like she had been betrayed by the rule book. 'And no one knew except me, so it didn't hurt anyone.

He was successful at work and kept that side of his life to himself. I could pretend to everyone that we were normal. That he was normal.'

She took another large gulp of gin.

'But then came the humiliation of finding out he was spying on girls. In cars and on benches, anywhere he thought he would see naked flesh or catch people in the act. Through windows was one of his favourites. Hoping to catch young women undressing.'

Mrs Dunbar looked frail and exhausted.

'I started to follow him you see, caught him in the act a few times. She looked defeated now, and disgusted as the words twisted her red lips. She fiddled with the glass as if she might throw it across the hallway, but years of self preservation stopped her.

'Would you like another drink?' offered Angela but Mrs Dunbar shook her head and looked around the hallway at nothing in particular. She stared around at the pretend world she had created to hide in.

'I had affairs in the end you know. I was so angry with him and I knew there was no hope of my life changing. I used to dream I would leave and find happiness, but deep down I knew I would never have the courage. Where would I have gone? I had no money of my own, no job, no skills, nothing. Not a jot of independent thought,' she scoffed at herself.

'Sometimes I even hoped he would get caught and I

would be rid of him. I wondered if experts would come up with some rational reason for his behaviour or if people would simply think I just wasn't a good wife.'

She paused and sighed deeply, and then after a few seconds, in a very quiet almost whisper she said, 'Then there was an attack one evening, on a teenage girl from our church,' another pause and then, 'She was blindfolded, bound and raped.'

Both Angela and Bee gasped audibly. Mrs Dunbar didn't want to stop now. She had never said any of this to anyone but she knew if she stopped now she'd never speak out again. It didn't matter to her that the young women in front of her were strangers. The consequences no longer held her prisoner. The words needed to come out. She had roused a half-tamed demon that she now needed to expel from within herself.

'He swore to me it wasn't him. He told me looking at them was enough. I don't know if I believed him or not, but I'd sunk so low that those words calmed me. Stalking girls and watching them in private acts was an acceptable evil. I was sickened and desperate and wanted to believe him, but I convinced him to move anyway. It was easy to do. A well respected business man and active church member, with his loyal loving wife, who wouldn't want us in their neighbourhood?'

'And now?' asked Bee, 'Are you going to protect him

again? You know this isn't going to stop and that's two attacks that you know of. Who knows how many more there may have been. You surely can't be thinking of protecting this man any more?'

Bee was business like and unswerving. She had come here to get this into the open and she was not changing her objective, no matter how ruined this woman looked slumped on the chair.

'Mrs Dunbar, you do have choices,' countered Angela, 'I know you think you have nothing without him, but the world has moved on. You don't have to cover for him any more.' Angela was trying a different tactic, smarting at the idea that this abominable man seemed not only to feel excused for his wicked, depraved activities, but that his wife was carrying all the guilt and seemed prepared to trade her health and sanity, while he remained a respected member of the community.

Charles Dunbar's wife stared into space again and swayed gently as she hugged herself. She looked so hopeless and alone. Minutes seemed to pass in a silence saturated with expectation. It was Angela that eventually went over and gently touched her shoulder, the need to show some solidarity with this defeated woman overwhelming her. It was as if this one small act of kindness roused Mrs Dunbar back to a reality she could no longer avoid.

Finally she whispered, 'I'll do whatever needs to be done.'

There was no anger in her voice, just defeat and shame.

Chapter 7

July 14th 1989

London Evening Standard

Local Executive found Dead at village home may be linked to sex attacks

A 50 year old man was found hanged in his garage earlier today, in the quiet village of Heatherington near Epping, Essex.

Charles Dunbar, an executive at a major pharmaceutical company in the City, died early this morning and reports confirm the cause of death as suicide. It is believed that Mr Dunbar's body was discovered by his wife, who was asleep in bed at the time of death.

In a bizarre twist, it would appear that the Police received information yesterday from an anonymous source linking Mr Dunbar to a string of sexual offences over the last ten years and in particular to a vicious sex attack four years ago in Leadbourne, Kent where Mr Dunbar lived at the time. The victim, who was eighteen, was blindfolded and unable to identify the attacker.

Mrs Dunbar is believed to be staying with friends and was unavailable for comment.

Friends and members of the congregation at the Church, where Mr Dunbar was a curate have expressed disbelief and shock at the news. One told us 'Charles was a highly respected member of our church and our prayers are with his wife at this awful time.'

It is believed the parish priest, has already been in contact with Mrs Dunbar to offer his condolences and stated he is happy to assist police with any ongoing investigation but declined to comment further at this time.

Bee read the article out loud in the front room, and acknowledged inwardly to herself that justice had, in some small way, been done for Kitty, but she was maddened that Charles Dunbar was a coward who had evaded punishment and public humiliation.

Angela's thoughts were for his widow. A woman who had put up and shut up her entire marriage and made do with a man who would continually disappoint her. A woman who had convinced herself she didn't deserve love or even normality. And now, a woman who, having been brave enough to stand up for herself, would no doubt feel she had to carry the disgrace that should have been her husband's to bear.

And Kitty... all she could feel was the terrible hollow still inside her, the dark hole where the love of her father should have been. She didn't want to be alone with that great silent space. She moved her body into Paul, who had been sitting quietly next to her on the sofa. He moved his arm to wrap it around her shoulders and no one spoke for a long time.

Chapter 8
New Years Eve 1989
Majorca, Balaeric Islands

Autumn had extinguished itself in the bustle of howling wind and beating rain. Winter had arrived steely, determined to be cold and icy. Everyone had been glued to the TV, as the East German government announced in November that their citizens could visit West Germany. East Germans had crossed and climbed onto the wall dividing the country, and were joined by West Germans on the other side in a celebratory atmosphere. Angela had quietly rejoiced that a whole nation might now enjoy freedom and choice and Bee had boldly suggested to Bob that there might be some wonderful antiquities up for grabs, squirrelled away since the sixties or even the second world war.

When Bob had announced they should spend New Year in a villa belonging to a work associate on the island of Majorca, Bee hadn't taken much persuading. The weather in London continued to bite and most days fled straight into dusk with hardly a shiver of daylight. The teasing of the others about the age difference between Bee and Bob had become more sporadic and actually

Bee didn't really care what they all thought. She found Bob far more interesting and exciting than men her own age and genuinely felt she was accepted by all in his social circle. It had been a natural progression for her to invite Bob to start staying over. She had never met anyone so driven to succeed and while she suspected it was a knee jerk to his early, less affluent life, she continued to marvel at how at ease he was surrounded by wealth and celebrity. Bob had acquired some fairly famous friends on his upward journey and Bee's dream of being loved, cherished and pampered was now drenched in the idea of becoming a full time socialite. She was keen to move their relationship forward and cement herself a little more fully into his life. He had been his usual charming self and asked her if she was sure, before telling her she was the most exquisite woman he had ever met and how he couldn't imagine another woman by his side. Bee found herself day dreaming more frequently of large entrance halls filled with children and the smell of baking, and of course now she could fit Bob and his fine living into the carefully constructed picture she had created years ago. Discussions with Bob's friends had inadvertently thrown up an ex-wife but no children, however Bob had persuasively assured Bee that all was amicable between them and, in fact, she had remarried several years ago. Bee decided this was a mere blip in her chocolate box future. Why wouldn't he have a little baggage given the age difference she had shrugged to herself. More importantly, she was delighted that Bob left her to chat to his friends when he had business to attend to. She had already received several invitations to lunch and charity functions, which confirmed to Bee that she was more than an accessory when they went out. They were, most definitely, a couple.

'Anyway, as I was saying Paul,' interrupted Bee, as Paul and James discussed a football game they were watching while she tried to invite them to the villa, 'It's about time we all went away together again and I want you to spend more time getting to know Bob.'

'Ah surely that's got to be a penalty,' yelled Paul.

'PAUL!'

'What? Sorry, I wasn't listening, did you say something about a holiday?'

'Yes, for New Year. Let's see in the new decade somewhere a bit warmer. Bob says it won't be too hot there, but just nice.'

Bee still wasn't sure Paul was listening so she tried a different angle.

'Kitty's coming. She says she wants to keep away from her family. Her mum is still phoning all the time, wants to get them all back together but I don't blame Kitty for keeping out of it. Does her dad really think he can carry on like nothing happened with Dunbar?' Bee was starting to rant.

Paul looked across at James who was still staring at the TV, not wanting to join the discussion.

'How about it mate? You need to get away, stop sulking over that girl.'

'What girl?' asked Bee a little surprised, but then she had been rather pre occupied with Bob and Kitty for the last few months.

'I'm not sulking,' challenged James slowly and firmly. 'It was me that finished it remember?'

'Well either way, it was months ago, you coming or not?'

'Is Angie going?' ventured James, looking at Bee.

'Um I don't know. I guess so. I planned to ask her. Why? What difference does that make? You two get on OK don't you?'

Paul shot Bee a look that told her to stop talking and then looked at James again. Paul wondered if he was the only one that had noticed a lack of interaction between James and Angela lately.

In truth James had tried to avoid Angela since the kiss on the doorstep. He had intended to talk to her on the Monday after their night out, but had overheard her in the kitchen telling Kitty that she'd had a great evening with him, but he wasn't her type. Feeling a fool, he had left quickly and quietly and it hadn't been too difficult to make sure he was never alone with her. Work was busy. Customers were returning regularly now when they had building work. He had developed a good reputation and was enjoying the result of his hard work. On top of that, James had taken on an extra day at the youth club and lately the only evening he risked bumping into Angela was Thursday when Bee made supper.

'You're coming mate. End of.' Paul shot James one quick glance, and then resumed watching the game.

Angela had also been actively trying to avoid James and so their paths had not crossed for some time. She now had fifteen junior secretaries reporting to her across four locations in London and, loving every moment of her job, Angela was determined to make sure each of the managers they worked for were delighted with the service her team provided. She worked hard to make sure they were trained to the highest standard, but she also wanted them to feel part of a team. As they were young and mostly single, Angela made sure there were social events organised every week to gel them together and reward them for their hard work. The events were becoming famous within the company. Angela's critics would glibly say that was because men were always thinking up ways to get an invitation to go out with an attractive gaggle of women, but in more senior circles there was a mixture of admiration and a little jealousy that this young woman was commanding the respect of her team and of the directors she worked for. She was distinguishing herself from other managers and rumours floated out of the boardroom that she had the potential to be a director herself one day.

Every other Thursday, sometimes more often if they could manage it, Kitty and Angela visited the shelter where Kitty had found herself after being picked up by the police. Initially Angela had gone at Kitty's request, so she wouldn't have to travel alone, but Angela had soon found herself drawn there. Most times they volunteered to make hot food if there was a new arrival and help settle any children that had come along with them. Kitty felt it grounded her to talk and listen to women who had faced more pain than she thought anyone could bear. It helped her to be reminded that, despite everything, she had a job, friends and a safe place to live. She wanted to tell herself over and over that she was fortunate and had the means to move forward. Some of these women had lived through continual neglect and abuse at the hands of people they chose to love. Kitty couldn't even imagine how she would begin to rebuild her life if that was her. It humbled her, and shamed her at the same time, to witness their strength. Angela, however, had found herself wanting to do more than just make tea and read stories. She had no idea where the anger came from, but it was a quiet, slow rage that was fermenting into a passion. Imagine feeling so beaten and so weighed down by circumstance, that you no longer have aspiration, no choice, no where to go. She could not begin to imagine how that felt and had started to have bad dreams at night where she felt trapped and forced to watch someone else live the life she wanted for herself.

Paul had suggested to Angela that she meet James' Mum.

'If you're serious about doing something more, she can point you in the right direction. She has a huge network from being a foster carer.'

Angela had flinched at the sound of his name. The last thing she wanted to do was look like she was trying to make friends with James mum. He would think she was desperate. He had made it clear he thought it was a mistake to kiss her when he'd run off and the humiliation burned fresh whenever she stood still. To revert to the safe world of work was the best option she decided, at least there she could think clearly and find solace in structure while she wondered how on earth she could avoid him over New Year.

*

Bee was overjoyed with Majorca's Mediterranean climate. She decided you could literally smell the warmth and calm. Their borrowed villa was to the south of Palma, a city and seaport located in the south west of Majorca, bordered by rocky inlets, marinas on the south side and villas to the east side. Bee enjoyed flouncing around the villa, in any one of the elegant outfits she had bought for the trip, making up her own little fantasy that this was their holiday home, bought to complement the expensive Victorian town house they would own in the heart of London.

'So, you two just going to lay by the pool all week? You haven't moved for days except to get more beer.'

Bee was stood with her hands on her hips staring at

Paul and James. While they were dressed in baggy t-shirts and shorts, their bare feet dangling over the water, Bee looked positively smart in a summery blue and white dress and white high heeled sandals. The look was finished with a blue wide brimmed hat and large round sunglasses. She looked totally out of place next to her brother and his equally unkempt friend.

'Who do you think you are?' teased Paul, looking up from his magazine. 'You look like an extra in Dynasty.'

'Oh ha ha,' responded Bee tartly. 'At least I could never be called a slob.'

'Are you going shopping with the others?' asked James, lifting his sunglasses and looking around to see if either Kitty or Angela were about.

'No, they left already to go into Palma,' replied Bee. 'Bob is picking me up in a minute. He has to meet a business associate, some deal on a few Spanish antiques. We are sailing over towards Cabera to meet him on the water, and then he is taking me for a late lunch back in Palma.'

Bee was terribly impressed that Bob was taking her to the meeting today. According to Bob a lot of money was about to change hands and the antiques were very precious with potential buyers already lined up back in England. She had already changed her outfit twice after he called and suggested she look as elegant as possible.

'Business deals on holiday eh,' smirked Paul. 'Sounds

dodgy to me.'

'Well it's not,' interrupted Bee feeling irritated. 'Bob promised it's only one morning working and then it's all holiday again.'

Paul and James weren't really listening any more but Bee felt she had to say it out loud more to herself than them. She started to walk away towards the shingled drive and then turned suddenly and called,
'Make sure you're both ready by nine tonight. We're going to a casino for drinks.'
She walked a bit further and then turned again smirking. 'And make sure you shower and dress up you untidy gits.'

Kitty and Angela returned to the villa around six that evening completely exhausted. As well as boutiques they'd found dozens of market stalls and both young women were laden down with bags as they collapsed in the airy living room. Through the patio doors they could see James and Paul lounging by the pool, drinking beer, still dressed in the same scruffy clothes they'd been in first thing that morning.

'Paul, you need to get in that shower. Bee will kill you if you're not ready to go out later,' called Kitty, as she slipped off her shoes and sauntered out onto the patio flopping down on a vacant sun lounger. 'Mind you,' she added as she sunk down, 'I can see the appeal of staying right here too.'

'We have plenty of time,' replied Paul lazily grinning at Kitty. 'It won't take me more than ten minutes to get ready.'
He lifted his glasses onto his head and looked across at James.
'You better start soon though, you need to look your best for the ladies.'
Paul rolled up his magazine and flicked James with it as he spoke.

'Paul. Mate. You taken a look at your sister lately? You are going to have to roll yourself in a big pile of posh to keep up with her and rich Uncle Bob.'

Kitty laughed quietly, enjoying the easy banter. She motioned to Angela to come outside and sit with them but Angela pretended not to see her. Kitty thought this strange and then the thought was lost as she turned her attention back to James.

'Anyway, not coming mate,' James was saying very matter of factly. 'I'm off to play footy with those local lads we met yesterday. Might see you a bit later in Palma. Might not.'

'What? That's not fair. I would've liked a footy game. Mind you, rather you than me mate, telling Bee I mean,' laughed Paul.

'She won't miss me,' replied James, casting a quick look to where Angela was sitting in the living room looking out onto the scene. 'And it's you that has to get to know Uncle Bob.'

Before Paul had a chance to answer, James had got up and was walking towards the living room. He had thought about going around the side of the house and back in through the front to get to his room, but realising how immature and foolish that would make him look to Angela he adjusted his glasses, put his head down and refused to look at her as he passed. Angela feeling embarrassed and suddenly conscious of her bare legs and shoulders, pretended to gather up her shopping as James passed her. Both of them were gawky and uncoordinated willing them selves not to look at the other. It was impossible not to look. The pure physical effort of not glancing at Angela made James so uncomfortable he simultaneously swore under his breath and glanced just for a second straight into Angela's horrified eyes. The hurt he saw there pierced through him. He opened his mouth to speak, but Angela cut across him.

'Excuse me,' she muttered softly and walked quickly out of the room ahead of James, wishing she had never met him, wishing her bare arm had not just brushed against his and vowing to find a way to avoid him for the rest of their stay.

*

When James returned to the villa around ten that evening, he was fully expecting the almost soundless tranquillity he found there. Only the rhythm of the crickets quietly broke the silence. White drapes gave the occasional flutter from a French window upstairs as a willowy breeze lifted them. James knew everyone had headed out to the casino an hour or so ago and he sighed with relief that he had the villa to himself. It was an unusually warm evening for the time of year and feeling hot from the run around the local boys had given him, he pulled off his sweaty t-shirt and jumped into the pool, heading straight under the water.

Emerging just head and shoulders at the far end of the pool, James noticed a brown envelope on the floor, under the drinks table. It was small and would have slipped down without anyone noticing. The only light on the patio was from the moon throwing itself across the water, which now rippled around James torso as he reached out for the envelope.   It wasn't until he looked a little closer that he noticed it had already been opened. It wasn't addressed to anyone but it was stuffed with money, along with one piece of paper containing a villa address located on the other side of Palma. He muttered nothing in particular to himself and threw the envelope on the table planning to pick it up once he got out of the pool. As he turned to dive back under the water he noticed more movement from one of the long white drapes upstairs. Shored up by the buzz from exercising and the local liqueur he'd been drinking, James decided to make sure all was safe in the house and headed up the stairs that spiralled from the patio to the balcony.

He hesitated when he reached an open french window. There was no sound coming from inside but he shivered slightly as his hand touched the soft muslin drape that was hiding the threshold. Berating himself for his sudden foolishness, James swept the curtain aside and stepped onto the cream deep pile rug just inside the door.

A burning desire to leave the room swept over him as immediately as the complete inability to move his feet.

Angie.

Her long, glossy dark hair fell in soft waves across a pillow. She was lying stretched across the bed facing away from the window with a single sheet twisted over her. James caught his breath. The sheet was clutched up around her neck but her back was bare. He couldn't breathe out. Angela stirred and turned over in bed, bringing her leg up over the sheet as she turned. A tingling sensation sped down James as he deliberately moved his eyes down to her lightly tanned shoulder and across her back. His heart started to thump against his ribs. The thin fabric barely concealed her and James felt his body tighten as he fought to take a breathe.

He watched her for a moment, lost in longing. Terrified of being there but unable to leave, James found himself moving forward towards the bed. Should he wake her? He certainly couldn't be caught trying to leave the room. Too late. Angela stirred and opened her eyes, immediately sitting upright. Her hair tumbled over her face and both her legs curled up in front of her. The sheet crumpled up between her legs as she clutched it towards her neck and James felt panic screaming from every pore.

'Wh..What are you doing?' she demanded in shock, to a still speechless James.
She stared at him waiting for an answer but found herself distracted as water dripped down the muscles etched in his bare stomach. She willed herself to stay focussed on his face, but found she could follow the lines of molten gold as they made their way from James temple down his sharp cheekbones and rested on his top lip.

'I..thought there was an intruder. I can explain. This is not how it must look.' James fumbled over the words, a yearning for the woman in front of him paralysing his legs and his brain.
'I. I thought everyone was out...at the casino,' was all he could manage.

'Why didn't you go? I would've thought it would have been the perfect place for you to find the type of woman that appeals to you,' taunted Angela, feeling annoyed that she found James so attractive.

Immediately she realised she had verbalised the thought and moreover it had come out more spitefully than she'd intended. She regretted the comment instantly. It occurred to her that being deliberately argumentative would delay James leaving her room. Is that what she wanted she wondered? Angela shifted slightly on the bed, but made no move to cover herself. James could still see the line of her back. Injured by her comment and tone, he moved towards the bed, towering above her, a solid wall of muscle level with her face.

'And what type of woman would that be Angie? That appeals to me?' James asked, the annoyance clear in his question.

He lingered in front of her, deliberately intimidating, before dropping his body to sit on the bed. He faced her, one knee bent up, faintly touching her leg in challenge. James had no idea why he wanted this woman so much. How dare she judge him. But still, he wanted her.

'Not me, I guess,' countered Angela assertively, pushing her knee out so it continued to touch the wet hair on James leg. She shivered deep in her belly. Although she wished she hadn't started the line of questioning, she wanted James to argue back, the palpable current between their bodies was unmistakeable.

James lent in closer to Angela's face, so close he could count the freckles on her nose.
'Why would you say that?' he asked, frowning but breathing in the smell of violets coming from Angela's skin.

'You had the chance to stay, but you didn't. I kissed you back, but you left,' whispered Angela, hardly able to breathe.

James stomach turned over as she spoke and he looked into eyes crowded with hurt and confusion. Angela's grip on the sheet loosened and the swell of her breasts became partly exposed. James whole body was burning. Leaning forward, their faces barely apart he touched the top of her shoulder with the tips of his fingers. Angela's breathing became more rapid. James allowed his fingers to trace completely down her back and onto her hip. Both shivered, acutely aware of the fragile piece of fabric between them.

'I wanted to stay,' James whispered, 'But, I'd been seeing someone.'
He paused for a second and then added, 'I'm not who you think I am Angie. Paul likes to talk me up, but I wanted to end it with her before I, before I kissed you again.'

Angela closed her eyes as James spoke. His hand came up and rested gently around her throat, his thumb reaching round to stroke her lips. She felt a new flurry of excitement and challenge.

'Paul likes to tell people I'm a player, because girls talk to me a lot. It doesn't mean I want them all.'

Before Angela could reply, James hands were in her hair. His lips brushed over hers, lightly at first and then, as she returned his kiss he pressed dangerously against her. His mouth covered hers and he felt the familiar yearning as Angela responded. Angela pulled James closer still and the depth of her own reaction. as he kissed her harder, unnerved her.

'But I want you,' murmured James into the wetness of her mouth.

He moved his lips down towards her neck and traced her skin gently. Then, with his hands tenderly pulling her hair, Angela felt his lips move to her ear.

'Do you want me to leave? I'll stop, if I'm not what you want.'

Angela opened her eyes, abruptly remembering what she had said in haste last June to cover her own humiliation. She responded to his mouth now, and placing her hands lightly on James face, she let the sheet fall into their laps. James already had his answer as he felt her smooth skin against his.

Angela pulled his face up, wanting to feel his lips on her mouth again.

'I want you to stay.'

*

The following morning was bright with virtually no breeze. The winter sun had heated up the kitchen by nine. The light was dancing from the window sill to the table as Paul, Kitty, Bee and Bob chatted lightly about the previous night at the casino.

'Anyone else for coffee?' asked James brightly, to no one in particular, as he walked into the kitchen.

'Yes please mate,' answered Paul. 'Where did you get to last night? Thought you said you might get into town after the game.'

'Um, yeah, changed my mind,' ventured James, trying not to smile. He could still smell Angela on his skin and the memory of last night was sharp and exquisite. 'Which reminds me,' he suddenly remembered his swim in the pool which now felt like weeks ago, 'Any of you lost any money? I found an envelope out by the pool when I got back last night, stuffed with cash.'

Both Paul and Bob looked up.

'Yeah, got to be mine,' smiled Paul sarcastically at James.

'Was there anything else there? Or just the money?' Bob had stood up and come over to the counter where James was making three cups of coffee. His tone was very formal and perhaps a little abrupt, but James wasn't really paying attention.

'Nope just the cash, oh and an address for a villa here on the island,' replied James absently.

'Thank you. I'm grateful it's safe,' said Bob visibly relaxing. 'I hadn't noticed I'd dropped it but it sounds like the money I had ready to pay for some antiques later today. I'll gladly tell you the address, if you want to verify it's mine.'

Bob patted James on the back as one would a comrade. James decided Bob acted far too middle-aged and hoped he wouldn't be like that in twenty years time but kept the thought to himself. Instead, he looked at Bee and then back at Bob, 'Um no problem, I believe you. Anyway with that much cash it had to be yours,' he joked.

Bob looked a little embarrassed and sat down again next to Bee.

'I thought all the business was done for this week?' she said lightly but looked directly at Bob as she spoke, expecting an answer.

'I know I said that and I am truly sorry sweetheart,' replied Bob smoothly, kissing Bee lightly on the nose, 'But something else came up that was too good to miss and as we leave the day after tomorrow, I wanted to close it out.'

Bee caught Paul raising his eyebrows while looking at James.

'No, of course I don't mind,' she lied, determined not to look at Paul again.
'You didn't build your business with good intentions alone did you?' she boasted, and then she added, 'It won't stop us watching the procession to the cathedral later will it?'

'Absolutely not,' insisted Bob, 'New Years Eve in Palma is fabulous and I want everyone to see it.'

Bee looked around table to make sure everyone was nodding in agreement and noticed James already on his way out of the kitchen with two cups of coffee. James caught the look on Bee's face.

'Sorry Bee, I nearly took your coffee with me,' he lied and handed her the coffee. Bee noted that Paul already had his fresh coffee and was about to comment that she hadn't asked for any, but James had already turned and headed off upstairs.

*

'Psst. Angie. Quick. This way,' James whispered rapidly as he grabbed Angela's hand and jutted to the left in the crowd, so they were hidden from the others. 'Let's get out of here before they notice they've lost us.'

It was New Years Eve and the streets were full of music and costumed people. The Festa de l'Estendard is held each year in Palma to commemorate King Jaumes conquest of the city centuries before. The exultant noises of the crowd wafted and lingered in the still evening air. It didn't take long for James and Angela to lose themselves in the crowds making their way to the stunning La Seu Cathedral for mass and ten minutes later Angela was on the back of a moped, arms enclosing James, winding their way to the beautiful prehistoric Dragon's Caves, on the East coast.

*

'I don't want any secrets between us Bee.'

Back at the procession, Bob had also taken Bee to one side and was now offering her a glass of local wine from one of the many bars open in the main street. Bee felt a tiny jolt of panic in anticipation of what Bob might be about to say. He had been more than distracted this week.

'I know I've worked more than I said I would,' Bob continued. 'The thing is, I am desperately trying to expand the business but am short on cash flow. Nothing terrible, nothing to worry about really. I just wish I could make the most of all the opportunity I have coming my way. I want so much to give you the world Bee, give you all the lovely things you deserve, and I just need to find a way to open up the damn cash flow.'

Bee felt her anxiety drain away and she smiled up at Bob.

'I have everything I could want Bob,' she soothed, stroking Bob's face. 'As long as I am with you.'

'I know darling, but I want to make sure we have a wonderful future. I want to be able to offer you so much.' Bob paused and kissed Bee gently on the lips, and then smiling and pressing his forehead into Bee's he whispered, 'I never thought I would find love again Bee and the chance for a family.'

Bee hesitated for a moment as an idea bubbled. Surfing on a wave of promise for the future she had dreamed of with her own Prince Charming she pulled back excitedly from Bob and gushed, 'I have cash.'

'What?' asked Bob smiling, his eyes twinkling at Bee.

'Remember, I told you last month. My grandmother left us money and her house, but we had to wait until we were twenty five. Well, I am twenty five next month. So, it's mine.'

Bee's excitement was growing as she realised she had another strand to bind her to Bob, something else to cement their relationship and a future intertwined.

'I couldn't possibly,' started Bob.

'Yes you can,' interrupted Bee. 'It's our money now. I can do what I like with it and we are a couple.'

'I don't know....,' started Bob again.
'If you don't want to take the cash as a gift, make me part of the business,' suggested Bee, 'Make it formal.'

Bob held Bee's face in his hands for a long time, looking concerned and serious. Eventually he smiled and said, 'OK partner, if you are really really sure? And when we get home we can start by putting a large diamond on your finger.'

Bee had never felt so complete. She sank into Bobs arms, letting the music and laughter from the crowd swim over her head, completely consumed by perfect happiness.

*

A few miles away on yielding velvet sand, hidden by rocks, James and Angela lay coupled with the water quietly and gently caressing their feet. The glow from the moon softly illuminated them and Angela trembled with exhilaration that they could be discovered there naked and entwined. Every time her body quivered against James she felt his lips curve into a smile against her wet skin. All she knew was this moment and all that she could taste was James. She didn't want to think about the night ending. If someone had told her this was the closest to heaven she would ever be, she would have been satisfied with that.

*

The procession in Palma had slowed and converted to one huge street party. As the night danced forward into the new year and the drink flowed freely, the celebration grew and spilled up into the sky, filling every space with laughter, song and hopes for the coming year. Bee and Bob had finally found Paul sitting outside a bistro nursing some local beer and staring intently into the crowd.

'There you are,' trilled Bee excitedly. 'Where's James? Why are you on your own?'

'I wonder,' scoffed Paul kicking a chair out with his foot and gesturing Bee to sit down.
'You mean you didn't notice him and Angie sneaking off earlier?'

'What?' questioned Bee, looking completely surprised.

'Too loved up to notice.' interjected Paul, without giving Bee a chance to add anything else.
'And from the huge smile on her face when he took her hand and pulled her away, I would say it's pretty clear what they are up to.'

Bee was speechless. Not just because of the news she'd just heard. She was also taken aback at how badly her usually laid back, calm brother was dealing with the development.

'Well, whatever is happening, it won't last,' stated Bee very matter of factly, as if this was absolute fact. 'They don't have much in common and I don't think big relationships are in Angie's plans. She seems married to her job. And on top of that, you know how different they are. Fire and Ice. They'll argue the whole time. You've seen what they are like together.'

Bee was trying to placate Paul and waited for him to reply but he continued to stare into the crowd without looking at his sister.

'Why are you so riled anyway?' asked Bee but with no sympathy in her voice. 'You don't normally throw a hissy fit when James has a girlfriend, and it's not like he's after Kitty...'

Paul cut Bee off mid sentence, with a loud scoffing noise but continued to hold his gaze into the street. Bee followed his eyes and saw the real root of Paul's bad mood. In the thick of the crowd, was Kitty. She was dancing with a handsome local man and giggling flirtatiously each time he whispered in her ear.

'Oh come on Paul, she's just having a little fun,' scolded Bee.

'It's never me though is it?' argued Paul a little aggressively. 'There is always someone louder or pushier to come in and sweep her off her feet.'

Bee, realising her brother was serious pulled her chair closer to his and touched his arm.

'I can't do this any more Bee,' whispered Paul. 'I'm wasting my time waiting for her.'

Bee was about to take a gamble with a counter argument that perhaps Kitty was dancing in front of Paul to get his attention and provoke a reaction, but as she drew breath to speak Kitty pulled up another chair looking concerned.

'Is anything wrong?' she asked with genuine apprehension.

'All fine here, just wondering where Bob is,' lied Bee and she kissed Paul lightly on the top of the head as she swiftly left the table.

'Paul?' asked Kitty, fixing Paul with a stare but ruffling his hair. 'What's up?'

'Nothing,' murmured Paul, smiling weakly at Kitty. 'You know, just the time of year to sit and think about the future and make some resolutions.'

'Oh, right. Me too,' replied Kitty and she took a deep breath. She wanted Paul to know how she felt. 'I was thinking...that...well it would be great to be with someone, you know a real relationship.'

Kitty felt like she was drowning. Three years ago she would never have done the talking. She had never had a serious relationship but she had never been short of men asking her out. She was terrified now of telling Paul how much she wanted to be with him. He was handsome as well as funny, kind too, and he had a calmness that she'd never felt with any other man. All in all she thought he was far to good for her, especially with all the baggage she now carried. Kitty wasn't sure she was brave enough for the humiliation of Paul turning her down.

'Yeah, well good luck with that,' he smouldered, finding it incredulous that Kitty was going to discuss future boyfriends with him. His mood instantly worsened and he wondered if he and Kitty were actually going to fall out tonight, something he had never envisaged happening. Sensing Paul's belligerent mood Kitty felt her own level of anxiety increase and her courage evaporate. Wanting the reassurance that would come from Paul meeting her halfway she lent towards him seductively and asked,

'So, where would a girl have to go to meet a man who

would take care of her and love her forever?'

Paul slowly raised his eyes to meet Kitty's. Kitty had barely registered their watery, tortured appearance before she was drawn down to Paul's trembling lips contorted by his desire to hide resentment.

'How the hell should I know Kitty,' he stormed as he stood up and pushed his chair back angrily, completely misunderstanding Kitty.
 'But don't expect me to keep picking up the pieces!'

Chapter 9
April 1993

Camberwell, London

'Stop bullshitting me Jimmy. You're lucky I haven't had your legs broken.'

An early spring had given way to a relentless onslaught of rain and hail that seemed to have soaked through and sapped the patience from James. It was midnight and he was sitting in one of his van's outside the flat that his apprentice Jimmy shared with his girlfriend. They both stared at the rain, ruthlessly pounding the windscreen through the darkness.

Jimmy started with a new but equally untrue story of how James' other van, the one he allowed Jimmy to drive out of hours, was currently abandoned near Epping Forest impaled on top of two wooden stubs used as roadblocks by the district council. James felt the heaviness in his heart sink even lower and meet the wave of anger riding up in the pit of his stomach.

He turned and cut his apprentice off mid lie, raging,

'Enough! I have heard Enough. Two rules Jimmy. When you came to work for me, I gave you two rules.'

Jimmy fell silent and looked away from James. He wasn't that much younger than James and he didn't see why he should take any grief from him.

James continued his rant, no longer shouting but with a menace to his voice that Jimmy couldn't ignore.

'Don't drink or take drugs while using my van, and never park my van in a pub car park. That was it Jimmy. Just those two rules. I don't even make you pay for your own petrol. I could lose my reputation and my customers. I worked hard. From nothing. *Nothing.* You have no idea how pissed off I am right now.'

James slapped his hands down so hard on the steering wheel the whole van shook.

'I took you on when everyone told me I was mad. I gave you a second chance. I paid for your training and I gave you free use of the van. Have you any idea how lucky you are that someone gave you another chance? You have no idea. No. Idea!'

'I need this job mate, please don't sack me. We're mates you and me James. You know I can be a bit of a prat.' Jimmy spoke matter of factly, assuming James would calm down eventually.

'Always about you!' raged James, throwing his hands up to his head and rubbing his hair. 'You just don't get it, do you? You haven't even got the decency, even now, to tell me that you drove that van from the pub on Friday night and crashed it. Don't even think about lying again - about the van being stolen from outside the flat. The police rang me this morning. You've had a whole weekend to tell me the truth. I know they followed you from the pub, I know you were drunk and I know you are back on the drugs Jimmy. God – do you know how lucky you were that no one got hurt?'

'Mate, give me another chance, I won't let you down again. Come on, we've known each other for years. I can try and pay you back for the damage. It's just a van.'

James sighed heavily and shut his eyes in resignation. No one had been willing to give Jimmy a job twelve months ago, his record for petty crime and drug use flashing like a beacon to would be employers. James had taken him on as an apprentice as a favour to his own mum who had fostered Jimmy for a short time, after his first caution for shoplifting at thirteen. It was true, James had a soft spot for the lad who had grown up moving from foster home to foster home, and whilst James knew Jimmy would need a tight rein to keep him off drugs he also saw the potential in this lad who charmed his customers and was actually a fast learner and a steady worker.

'Jimmy, the vans a write-off. It won't be insured for what you did. And, it's still stuck there advertising my company in the worst possible way. Word gets about, you should know that. And let's not even think about my business and my reputation being dragged through the mud when you end up in court.'

James opened his eyes and looked straight at Jimmy, looking for a reason, any reason to give this lad another chance. He berated himself almost immediately, knowing there was no way he should trust him again.

'James, you gotta get me off mate, I can't end up back in court,' demanded Jimmy, looking horrified as it dawned on him James was not going to be a push over this time.

James clenched his fists to control a pure fury he had never experienced. He needed to get away right now or he really would make things worse. Still no apology from Jimmy and not the slightest sign of remorse or comprehension that he had ripped apart the trust James had invested in him. James thought about the lads he coached every week, some would never get the chances that Jimmy had simply trashed.

James was steady but there was an undercurrent that he struggled to control.
'Here's what's gonna happen Jimmy. You clearly have no self control when it comes to making choices, so let me be crystal clear. You are going to get out of my van, right now and walk away. If you say another word, one word, I will take you on myself. You no longer work for me. Don't ever come to me for a job again. Don't ever ask for a favour. I don't ever want to see your face again. Get out! Now!'

*

James sat for a long time outside the house in Palmers Green before feeling composed enough to go inside. Ever since Bee had moved out to be with Bob, James had virtually moved in, but, after three years with Angela, he wanted more. The idea of anyone else loving Angela filled James with equal measures of deep passion and haunting grief. He hated that he sometimes felt like a visitor. Even with his own key, there was something not quite permanent about their relationship. James sighed heavily as he thought about the money he had saved over the last twelve months. He'd planned to surprise Angela for her twenty fifth birthday this year, take her somewhere exotic and present her with a ring. Now that money might be needed to replace the van that Jimmy had written off for him over the weekend. Angela never made a big deal about earning more than him, and James was infinitely proud of her achievements, but he secretly worried that Angela might tire of him and his slow burning business. In moments of chilling clarity, he wondered how long they could exist in their bubble of frivolous passion. Outwardly Angela showed no signs of wanting anything more, but all of them had agreed, Bee's marriage to Bob last year had been the most showy, elaborate affair they had ever seen. It had gone on for days. Paul had called it ostentatious and made fun of Bee, but Angela had been resolutely supportive that Bee should have the wedding she had always wanted. Only Kitty had been without an opinion and had disappeared off, as soon as acceptable, to one of her now frequent engagements with old university friends.

James shifted to pick up some paper stuck a little way down the back of the passenger seat. He uncurled it absently, just to check it wasn't something important and frowned. The piece of paper was small and clearly ripped from the corner of an old letter, but it had Bob's name and a phone number scribbled across it. It didn't look like he, or Angela, had written it. He scrunched the paper in his hand and stuffed it in his pocket, to throw away later.

*

May 1993
Hampstead Heath, London

'I just can't get my head around this Bee. I mean, why would Kitty marry him? And I can't believe this is the wedding she wanted. No one had even heard of this Greg until recently.'

Three weeks had passed since James told Angela about Jimmy and she was still reeling in the disappointment as much as James was. Jimmy had been a regular at the house and Angela had really thought there was a bond between the two men. She had been in a sour mood ever since.

'I mean, just look at the pictures! There's hardly anyone there and Kitty's dress doesn't even fit properly,' continued Angela, before dropping the snap shots on the table and picking up the glass of wine that Bee had just refilled.

They were sitting at the large table in Bee's extended kitchen. The room had a cosy feel to it and was Angela's favourite of all the rooms in Bee and Bob's lavishly re-modelled house.

'I know, I know,' replied Bee sighing. 'But she said it was what she wanted. I did try and press her, you know, to give her the chance to back out but she said she was happy. I didn't want to go on at her too much in case she thought I was comparing our weddings.'

Bee took a very small sip of wine and shifted in her chair. She had desperately wanted to push Kitty harder but she was too conscious that she and Bob had the most money out of all the group and the last thing she wanted was to come across as condescending or boastful. Bee felt blessed and lucky to have Bob. She sometimes found herself feeling a little out of control never knowing where sums of money had come from, or suddenly gone, but Bob assured her that was the nature of his business. She was trying to stop meddling in what was essentially a pampered, excessive lifestyle which, due to some of Bob's latest connections, now hovered on the fringe of celebrity.

Bee sighed and looked at Angela sadly.
'She kept pulling at the dress the whole day. She knew it looked short on her, but she told me it was his family heirloom and a shame not to use it. It just didn't sit the way it should have and you could see her ankles. She is so beautiful, she was supposed to look stunning.'

'And what about Paul? Imagine how he felt about not

being invited. What a kick in the teeth!' exclaimed Angela.

James and Paul still saw each other at least once a week and Angela felt possibly closer to Paul these days than Bee did.

'Yeah, I guess it was. They haven't been close for a while now, and I can't help thinking if she hadn't started seeing all her old university friends again, things may have got better for them. He couldn't have just stopped loving her and he wouldn't say this, but he must feel like he picked her up and helped put her together again and then someone else just comes and claims the prize from right under his nose. Makes it very hard for me to like Greg, when I spent years wanting Kitty and Paul to end up together.'

Bee paused and looked perplexed.

'She just seems so obsessed with Greg, like everything he says and everything he does is superior to everyone else. She defers to him on everything and that's not the Kitty I knew.   Lucky for Paul he's not seen what she's like these days.'

Bee started to smile gently as she thought about Paul.

'I'm glad he gave up his job and retrained. He always wanted to join the police, when he was little and it's given him a diversion. Seems to be the first thing he's done in a long time that didn't have Kitty as a goal at the end of it.'

Bee trailed off at the end and seemed deep in thought and then springing back she added, 'Mind you, going back to Paul not going to the wedding...I think it helped that none of you were invited to the wedding. Would have been worse if it had just been Paul that didn't go. Bob and I were only invited because Bob offered to give Kitty away.'

Angela scoffed loudly and took another gulp of wine. 'What was that all about? Never heard her say anything more ridiculous! Greg hasn't got family and he doesn't know any of you that well. I don't want my side of the church to be swamped and embarrass him!'

Angela shook her head as she repeated what Kitty had told them. She'd been cross when she heard it the first time and it still annoyed her now that Kitty had bowed to everything Greg had dictated since the moment Kitty had mentioned him.

'Such a rushed wedding. I just would have wanted more than that for Kitty,' sighed Angela, 'And no honeymoon either from what she told me? Is she pregnant?' Angela finished her sentence more animatedly than she had started it. Why hadn't she thought of that before.

'No, not that I know of,' smiled Bee and she rubbed her own beautifully rounded belly.
'You want to hear the best bit though,' she added, raising her eyebrows, knowing that Angela would not be happy with the latest news.

'Greg says we are Kitty's friends and wouldn't it be better to make new friends together. Friends that they can have as a couple. Basically, she doesn't plan on seeing much of us any more, or at least not with Greg in tow anyway.'

'What!' exclaimed Angela. 'Surely Kitty isn't going to go along with that is she?'

'Well, we'll see,' replied Bee. 'Let's be honest, she has gone along with most of what he says so far and I have to say from the few times we've had them for dinner he is...well...intense.'

'Did he get on with Bob?' wondered Angela. Bob got on well with Paul and James, but they had never developed a real bond that saw them go out on boy's nights without Bee or Angela. Bob always seemed to remain politely aloof.

'At first I hoped they would,' explained Bee, 'Because at least that way we would see more of Kitty, but the second time Kitty came over I suggested a girls weekend away and Greg became gradually more and more agitated. It was as if he didn't want Kitty away from him. He kept stroking her hair and reminding her of how homesick she might be. I guess Bob noticed that Kitty seemed to be seeking his permission.'

Bee smiled as she thought about Bob.

'It was quite impressive actually, the way he quietly stood up for her,' she mused. 'He laughed and said there was no way on earth he would be able to stop me going once I got the idea into my head. He tried to point out that Kitty was young and should be allowed to breathe.'

Bee paused and sipped at her wine, a sombre mask coming down.

'That's when it kicked off,' she sighed. 'Not in a loud way. It was something altogether more oppressive, suffocating. Greg said Kitty didn't need to breathe, she needed to behave like a wife. Well to cut a long story short Greg, with the help of two wine bottles, informed Bob that if he wasn't careful his wife would become more famous than he was in local circles, but for all the wrong reasons.'

Angela was speechless. 'What did Bob do? Tell me he slapped him. No, actually, tell me you slapped him.'

'I was amazed Bob didn't ask him to leave. I wanted to, but, Bob being Bob, remained dignified. Actually he found it amusing. He said it spoke volumes about Greg that he thought he was slinging insults. Bob makes no secret of the fact he hates the parties and functions. He would have me front the whole thing if he could.'

'And of course you would hate that Bee. How dreadful that would be for you,' laughed Angela.

Bob was right, it did speak volumes about Greg. It also spoke volumes about Bob, and James, she thought, that they didn't feel in the least intimidated by the women they choose to be with.

'He didn't want to go to the wedding after that, but he didn't want to let Kitty down. So, it's just as well Greg doesn't want us in his circle of friends,' concluded Bee a little more lightly, 'cos, we sure as hell don't want him in ours either.'

*

South Bank, London

The rain had finally relented by the end of May and left a soggy mess for June and July to breathe on and warm.

Angela sat in her air conditioned office feeling slightly chilly, wishing she was out walking along the river bank. She could see people down below with their jackets off and sleeves rolled up and she breathed deeply, conscious of the divide between their tranquil mood and the tense strained afternoon ahead of her.

'You ready Angela?' The voice of her manager coming into the office broke her from her trance.

'Yes. Yes of course,' she lied.

Thirty minutes later she had finished presenting to her senior management team on how she planned to achieve the savings they had requested from her area. Angela sat down ready to take questions with a heavy heart. If it wasn't bad enough that they had to lose people, she would ultimately be making her own job dispensable. Her solution to the problem was certainly viable and fundamentally the way forward for secretarial support but the fact that implementing a change that would see her probable promotion while others had to find new jobs, was not making her feel great about herself. The promotion was important to her and certainly the increased money it would give her would allow them to pay the rent for the house easily, without Kitty living there. So, why did she hate the very idea that she herself had developed and spent the last thirty minutes pitching?

'Does anyone have any questions?' she asked matter of factly.

'So how quickly do the numbers go down?' asked the portly finance director sitting at the back of room. 'When do we start to realise the labour savings in real terms?'

Angela flinched slightly, another reminder that this was about saving money and the quickest way to save money always seemed to be to get rid of people, with everyone who remained picking up the excess. It was never about sorting out root problems.

'It depends on how aggressively we want to move forward,' replied Angela, straightening her back as she always did to sit up taller and create a presence in the room. Angela had long ago noted that women tended to sit back and cross their legs, inadvertently sinking in their chair, not taking up much room and appearing small and dainty.

'For example, I have identified the managers senior

enough to warrant keeping their current secretarial support and which managers could lose dedicated company support and be supported by the agency. If we assume that eighty percent of our current support across the country could become an outsourced service via an agency, rather than being on our permanent headcount, we next need to decide the most viable and acceptable way to move those people out of their roles.'

Sometimes when Angela spoke she could almost pretend she was merely listening to someone else. It amazed her and amused her that she was holding the attention of the room. She decided in that instant to brave it out and try to salvage something from the wreckage.

'Of course, although it would be quicker and more finite to run an exit programme, I believe that would be short sighted. We have so much ability and enthusiasm in the team we have today. I would want to at least try and re-deploy our best talent into other support areas of the company, rather than lose them.'

Angela had not rehearsed that comment with her manager, and she could tell by the way he shifted and coughed that he would rather just pay people off to leave as quickly as possible. Angela suspected he thought she was being feeble, but having trained and coached her team to be a well respected group of women, she was not about to crumble and play their numbers game.

The remainder of the meeting was spent discussing

various options with Personnel, who Angela was relieved to find supported her need to treat both the announcement of this change and the transition of people respectfully.

The next day Angela found herself sitting in her boss's office to discuss the previous days events. She felt drained, not least from the fact that news of the change had leaked to her team in less than twenty four hours and Angela felt like Judas at the last supper.

'You did well Angela, the MD was impressed.'

'Thank you, although I can't say I enjoyed it,' replied Angela, without smiling.

'None the less, all things change and you rose to the challenge. Which brings me to why I asked you to come and see me. Now would be a good time for you to capitalise on your strong reputation and take a career jump. I want to discuss an opportunity with you. There are a couple of others in the frame for this move, and some of the directors are worried about sending someone so young and because you're a ...'

Angela let him drone on. She had never felt less like discussing her career but she listened while her boss wove an opportunity around her that she realised would never come again.

Hampstead Heath, London

One week later Bee found herself alone and in labour. Bob had bought them both mobile phones in case this should happen while neither was near a telephone. Bee had hardly switched hers on and now found herself struggling to reach Bob. This wasn't how it was supposed to be. Bob wasn't due back for days. Since the release of Mandela from prison three years ago, many South Africans had gradually drifted away from their native home as the post Apartheid landscape formed. Bob had enthused that with them came treasures and money. He had persuasively argued that this was business too good to miss. Bee had been less pleased that he needed to be away from home but with Bob's usual charming influence, and Bee's increasingly distracting condition, she had stoically waved him off two days ago. As the hours passed, and Bee tried frantically to reach Bob she felt strangely lost and a little afraid. And then, finally, as her body painfully readied itself for birth, she started to cry. Quietly at first just to herself and then more forcefully, as she realised Bob was not coming and she couldn't do this alone.

*

Palmers Green, London

Across town unaware of Bee's predicament, James stared at Angela. He watched as she pulled her hair back from her face and took a mouthful of spaghetti from the bowl in her lap. Tomato ran down her chin and she laughed when James quickly moved forward and kissed her, licking the sauce before he sat back. The house had become their private sanctuary since Kitty had got married and the front room floor had become a retreat covered in cushions and blankets. Their clothes could often be found strewn over the hallway floor, usually abandoned once the front door locked out the rest of the world. Angela stared at the hard lines on James chest and stomach and for the second time that evening wanted to pull him to her. She lazily wondered if they could stay like this forever, making love in the front room, only pausing to eat and only go to work when the money ran out. James watched her looking at him and the same familiar longing stirred. He watched the movement of her lips as she closed them over another forkful of food. When she was done, Angela put down the bowl and stretched her arms and legs in satisfaction. James moved silently towards her and pulled off the shirt that had been barely covering her. Angela felt the delightful frisson run through her as James breath caressed her neck and his arms enclosed her, stroking her skin as he pulled her in.

As they lay on their backs some time later, Angela knew she needed to tell James about work. James could feel the heat radiating from Angela and although he also had something he wanted to say he was muted by the familiar panic she roused in him.

Angela propped herself up on one elbow and lovingly stroked James head as she explained about the work opportunity in Romania. The shocked reaction of the world when the reality of conditions in Romanian orphanages had emerged had caused many major corporations to team together and offer support to the numerous charities being established. Angela felt privileged and animated at the prospect of putting a new 'community team' together and organising fund raising. The company had promised a major financial contribution to the effort and in return they would set themselves a reputation for giving back to the community and the world around them.

'And the most amazing part of all, is that I get to travel with a team to some of the orphanages and oversee the spending of the money. Lots of them still have no medicine or even adequate washing facilities. Even after two years of world attention. I know we can't fix it overnight but can you imagine being able to make at least some difference to the lives of those children?'

James heart sank deeper and deeper as he listened to Angela's enthusiastic discourse. He looked at his jeans heaped on the floor by the living room door and thought about the ring box in the pocket. He let Angela continue to talk, watching the face he loved in all its exquisite detail.

Finally, when his head felt full, he interrupted.

'What about the people here?' he struggled to stop his voice trembling. 'Yes, I can imagine being able to make a difference, that's what Mum does every day Angie. That's what I have been trying to do since I was sixteen, give something back. There are plenty of people here that need help.'

'I...I didn't mean it like that. I'm sorry. That's not what I meant,' stumbled Angela.
She had got so caught up in her own excitement and now she saw James looking hurt and bewildered.

'It's got to be now though. All the news talks about is the lack of progress,' continued Angela, thinking she was explaining herself but in actual fact she was just winding James up further.

'Wow, Angie, a trendy cause. Never mind the thousands of people that do something great every single day, some of them twenty four hours a day, with no thanks. Are the kids with drug head parents and the women being beaten up in this city not good enough for you any more? I thought you would have realised by now that not everyone here is living the same life as you. Perhaps lately you've just not been looking hard enough from your ivory tower. Is that why you need to rush out there and break us up along the way?'

James felt his skin burning and he closed his mouth abruptly, shocked at the strength of his outburst. He turned away in an attempt to calm himself down. He felt childish, of course that's not what Angela had meant. He just didn't want her to leave and be away for so long. Feeling suddenly foolish in his state of undress, he got off the floor and started to pull on his clothes, pacing around the room looking for each garment.

'James, I don't want to break up with you, what are you talking about?'

Angela was stunned.

'Why can't you come with me? It's voluntary. We could do it together.'

What Angela had envisioned in her head, as an invitation, now sounded like a plea.

'How can I go Ange? Your company is paying for you. I run my own company. No one is going to pay for me. I would come back with no business to run. What would Mum do? She wouldn't have taken on Holly's new sister if I hadn't offered to help her financially.'

His voice rose steadily, as he contemplated all that Angela had clearly not considered in her haste to save the world.

'Besides, I have commitments here with the youth group, and quite frankly I'm not sure I want to go just because your company clicks their fingers...'

James trailed off aware he was ranting. He buttoned his trousers and felt the ring box dig into him as if reminding him, prompting him to make his move now before it was too late.

Angela cut him off before he had formed the words in his head.

'Do you know what annoys me the most?' she snarled, starting to rage quietly inside. 'If I was a man, I would get all the support I needed. There are other people clamouring for this opportunity and I bet they go home and their wives are really proud of them. But not you!'

As she finished her voice rose to a shout and the tears that had been threatening to spill ran with abandon down her face.

'*What*!' yelled James. 'Don't play that card with me. Don't you ever do that. I have never treated you or your career with less than respect. I get a little tired of you assuming all men are the same Angie. How dare you punish me for someone else's sins. Of course I think it's a worthy cause and I wish none of those children were suffering, but I can see the problems in my own back yard that need fixing. And I want us to be together.' James ended his rant with a plea, trying desperately to bring some order back. He looked around their front room refuge and now saw chaos instead of calm.

Angela fell silent and stared out the window, her back to James. She felt cornered and wretched. This was not how she had intended the discussion to go. How could everything had spiralled out of control so quickly? It was like they had fallen from the highest star into the deepest pit of clay and Angela had no idea how to get out of it.

'Stay here Angie.' James spoke first.

He turned the ring box over in his hand, still in his pocket.

'Marry me? We could take on the world together. Try and fix it...here, together.'

James waited and watched, but all he could see was the rise and fall of Angela's breathing. All he could taste and feel was this moment and he closed his eyes, willing Angela to turn round and answer him.

'No,' she finally said. Simply and quietly and without turning round. 'I love you James, but I don't want to marry you. I don't want that expectation over me that I should be a wife and then a mother. It was never what I wanted. I can't marry you. I have to see this through.'

James let go of the ring box abruptly and ran his hand over his head. Everything felt broken. In that moment he would have given up everything and everyone just to hold this one woman. Tell her he didn't need a wife, but he needed her. And now that he could see her shaking body he wanted to wipe away her tears. He didn't move. If he reached out for her now, he would never let go. He knew he wasn't strong enough to walk away and there was no more fight to be had. He felt lost. Watching her, he relived their desire and hunger for each other, but there was nothing for him beyond it and nothing behind him. Just her...and it was ruined. They were both buried, but alone, trapped in tunnels of anger, unspoken words hidden.

When the telephone rang initially, it went unheard. Bee,

unaware of the ruin in her old home and now desperate for someone to be with her as the baby pushed its way towards the world, resolutely held on refusing to hang up.

As the persistent ringing brought James and Angela back to the same space in time, James caught his breath, hopeful just for the briefest second that their world could rewind. But as Angela ran past him he glimpsed the way her face was contorted in misery and her swollen eyes, heaving with tears, were steadfastly refusing to meet his, and he knew they were a thousand miles apart already.

Anger and love clashed around inside Angela as she responded to Bee's call and it was hours before she finally realised what she had done. Only then, that she felt her heart break.

Chapter 10
July 1997

Hyde Park – London

'Mummy, can I go and play?'

'Of course Amanda sweetie, don't go further than the swings though. I need to be able to see you,' replied Bee, gently pulling the long fair hair, held up in a pony tail with lilac ribbons.

Bee pulled her sunglasses down from her head to shield her eyes from the sun's persistent glare. It was the most glorious day for a picnic with Kitty, who she hadn't seen for several months, and they had been lucky to find a vacant bench near the children's park. Many of the parents had opted for dabbled shade under the trees but Bee couldn't bear the idea of Amanda being out of her line of sight.

'You must feel so blessed Bee, she is beautiful. You have everything you dreamed of,' sighed Kitty, as she watched Amanda skip towards the swings.

'I do feel blessed,' replied Bee steadily, still watching Amanda. But she didn't speak with with the conviction that Kitty would have expected.

'Amanda is my world, she's the most easy going child and I adore her. But sometimes I feel a little lost. I know I have it all and I know it's vulgar to complain. Bob lets me spend money on anything I want. He lets me run the house the way I want and Amanda has everything she needs, but I wish we were more of a partnership. Bob works so hard and really strange hours but I've learnt not to ask questions. I suppose, now my parents and I have so much invested in his shops, I expected us to work more as a partnership but Bob doesn't want me involved in what he calls his back office.'

Bee paused to pour some wine and scolded herself, conscious that she might sound very sullen and whining for someone who really had everything she had ever wanted. Someone who had nothing to complain about.

'So if being lady of the manor is my job, then that's what I shall be,' she smiled at Kitty and raised her glass in a toast

Kitty raised her own glass, filled with lemonade, to meet Bee's, but remained silent.

'Tell me about you,' prompted Bee. 'The last few months, how have they been?'

'A strain to be honest,' acknowledged Kitty. 'We are in the middle of our fifth attempt now and you never get used to it. Starting cycles, squandering cycles, embryos that don't survive, fixating on when you will ovulate, on and on and on. It's all so invasive and sterile. But then you get the highs of knowing that some have taken and you don't mind the transfer back in...and then there's the wait,' Kitty paused and sighed, 'The longest time. Each time you force yourself to be positive, wondering if you can bear bad news again. I don't think Greg will go through it again, if it doesn't work this time.'

Kitty had tears in her eyes as she spoke. Four years of wanting a baby and getting nowhere. There wasn't a word she could think of to describe how she felt.

'It's not just Greg that's going through it though Kitty, it's you too.'

Bee tried to sound supportive and not too judgemental, but she liked Greg even less than she had four years ago and was growing ever more impatient at Kitty's passive acceptance. She alternated between admiration for Kitty and a growing contempt for Greg. He appeared to oversee all of Kitty's spending, even though Bee knew he was out at bars and clubs at the weekend. Bob often met business contacts in the evenings and had come home on numerous occasions and fuelled Bee with stories of Greg's excesses.

'Do you think he'll be supportive once you are at home with a baby?'

Bee knew she was wandering into dangerous territory but she was genuinely concerned about Kitty giving up teaching and relying solely on Greg for money and support. These days Kitty seemed to make so many excuses for Greg that he never needed to come up with his own.

'I know you think I'm weak,' muttered Kitty, without meeting Bee's eyes, 'But you don't know him like I do. I know he'll take care of me. When it really matters, he will come through. Just the other day he said I needn't bother about my pension as his would take care of us both.'

Bee tried not to show the irritation scratching away at her.

'Do you think that's wise Kitty? I mean, what if...what if you want to leave him or something?' It was quite unlike Bee, normally she would have been more direct, but she didn't know how Kitty would react.

'Why would I leave him?' asked Kitty. She looked directly at Bee now, answering the question that Bee hadn't asked.

'You think he might have an affair?'

Bee noted to herself that Kitty didn't seem as shocked or outraged as perhaps she should have been. She lowered her gaze, feeling rotten for Kitty.

'Well if he did, it would sort of be my fault,' continued

Kitty, before Bee had the chance to formulate a response. 'I let myself get so obsessed with getting pregnant. I want a baby so badly. I really do. Something to tie us together you know, something that means we're linked. It takes over everything and I guess Greg might feel a little unloved and not special any more. I forget and think about myself sometimes. Couldn't really blame him if he started to look elsewhere could I?'

Bee was glad her eyes were covered by sun glasses. She couldn't believe what she was hearing. So Greg shouts jump and you ask how high, she wanted to shout at Kitty. She could not believe how deftly Kitty could twist the idea of an affair to make it her own fault.

'No, I don't think he'll ever do that,' finished Kitty, 'And I would never dream of stopping him going out with his friends, to get a break from me. I have to trust him and I know it's me he loves.'

Kitty paused for a second and looked down before adding quietly, 'I'm not sure I should even discuss the IVF with you. Might be better for Greg and me if we keep private stuff to ourselves, you know, it will make us stronger if we rely just on each other. I know he feels left out when I share with you and not him.' And then after a short pause, Kitty whispered, 'I can understand that.'

Bee swigged more wine. She couldn't believe it. She knew that had come from Greg and not Kitty. The audacity of the man. Bee decided this relationship was controlling and toxic. Did Kitty have no opinions left of her own? What about what Kitty wanted? She was about to round on Kitty when her thoughts were splintered by Amanda shouting.

'Daddy'.

Bee looked up and saw Bob talking to a couple of younger men on the other side of the children's play area. He didn't hear Amanda and had his back to Bee and Kitty. Bee watched as the men continued deep in conversation and then saw them shake hands and walk away in different directions. She felt an unease but had no idea why. Her need to be in control and at the centre of everyone's affairs was at odds with Bob's charm and beguile to keep her on the outside of his business dealings.

'Did Bob know you were here today? Do you think he's looking for you?' asked Kitty having watched the scene unfold with Bee.

'No, and it's a bit of a strange place to do business,' replied Bee more to herself. 'Let me go talk to Amanda, in case she wonders why he didn't answer her. I don't want her to be disappointed.'

Before Bee had the chance to get up, Amanda was already rushing towards her but looking straight past Bee with a huge smile on her face.

'Hello Mandy Pandy,' sang Paul loudly, as he swung the little girl up into the air and held her upside down.

'Uncle Paul, put me down,' giggled Amanda, clearly enjoying being up in the air.

'Hello Amanda. Don't wiggle too much or Uncle Paul might drop you,' said an unsmiling voice from behind Paul.

Kitty froze. Panic crawled up her throat. It had been a long time since she had seen Paul and she felt totally unprepared to bump into either him or his girlfriend.

'Paul! What a lovely surprise,' enthused Bee as she hugged him and tickled Amanda at the same time, so that the three of them were cuddled together in a chaotic embrace.

'Hello Kimberly, nice to see you again,' said Bee a little more tensely. She had dropped it into a conversation with Paul that she often lunched at the Park on Tuesdays and that this Tuesday Kitty might be with her, but she hadn't intended Kimberly to be part of the plan.

'Hello Kitty. How are you?' ventured Paul, deciding to smash through the awkward atmosphere already building. He sat down next to Kitty and stared right at her, willing her to speak to him.

Kitty looked up and shivered, despite the sun's warmth on the back of her neck. Paul still had the same beautiful blue eyes and comfortable handsome features that made him so easy to look at. He was smiling at her as if they had never been apart and the reality of how long it had been since they saw each other made her insides ache for a time that no longer existed.

'So, this is Kitty. I wondered if I would ever meet you.' Kitty was pulled away from Paul's gaze by the unsmiling voice of Kimberly.

Kitty looked up to find a perfectly manicured hand with long nail extensions waiting formally at her line of sight. It was awkward to shake Kimberly's hand from the angle she was sitting at, and the sight of Kimberly's ice straight bleached hair and lime green lensed eyes made her feel inferior and totally intimidated.

'Hello,' stated Kitty, limply shaking the offered hand and trying to dig deep for some panache that was surely inside her somewhere.

'You know, you don't look at all the way I imagined you would,' noted Kimberly, pulling her sunglasses rudely back over her eyes, 'But then I guess...' She stopped short, catching the glare coming from Paul.

The sun started to chill Kitty and she would have fled but didn't want to give Paul and Kimberly the satisfaction. She sat rigid behind her mask of calm.

'Look, it's really lovely to see you Kitty,' ventured Paul again, wishing he could touch her arm, connect in some way that wasn't so formal and starched. 'Wouldn't it be great to catch up properly one day?' He looked at Bee as he said it, hoping she would agree and rescue him.

'Definitely. Great idea!' announced Bee. 'I think it's time we all got together. I know it won't be the same if Ange isn't in the country but who knows, maybe we'll catch her at the right time.' Bee sounded bright and enthused and completely ignored Kimberly staring at Kitty.

'Not sure James would come with Angela there anyway,' interjected Kimberly, pushing herself into the discussion.

Not sure anyone asked for your opinion, thought Bee, but she didn't even reply with a glance.

'Has James not seen Ange at all?' asked Kitty, with real concern, steadfastly looking at Bee.

'She doesn't stay long when she comes home,' replied Paul and he looked at Kitty, drinking her in, just in case it was a while before he saw her again. He thought she looked tired, with strain pencilled around her eyes and mouth, but she was still beautiful. 'I don't think they even speak on the telephone,' he finished, 'Both too stubborn.'

'Our James is too gorgeous and successful for his own good. He's never lonely for long,' interrupted Kimberly, intent on securing her place in the pecking order.

'I might just have to go and keep him company myself if you don't hurry up and buy me lunch,' she added sweetly and she intertwined her fingers through Paul's and shot Kitty a superior look, before pulling Paul's face around and kissing him squarely on the lips.

Kitty and Bee exchanged looks.

When Paul and Kimberly had left, all Kitty could find to say was, 'Hmm. She was charming.' But the sarcasm was not lost on Bee.

Bee pondered on how Kimberly and Paul had only met because Paul happened to be at her house when the crew for 'London Life' had arrived to interview Bee and take pictures of her home for their magazine. Kimberly, it transpired, knew Bob from her childhood. Her family being one of the foster families he'd stayed in touch with as a young man. Now working for the magazine, she had mentioned his success and wealth to her editor and a piece had been commissioned. Bee had been thrown into the limelight. Follow up pieces ensured that Kimberly spent more time at their house than Bee felt was necessary. Bob's memories of Kimberley, although fond, were clearly less fixated and Bee had been wary and disappointed when Paul and Kimberly had become close.

'You just know,' commented Bee, 'I mean as a woman, you just know when you meet another woman, if she's the type you can trust.' Bee drained her wine.

'But you know what? I wouldn't trust her. Not with my secrets, not with my friends, and not with my husband. I can see right through her. If she could get her claws into Bob she would. I know I should try and like her. For Paul's sake, I should at least try, but I can't.'

And that was all Bee had to say on the subject of Kimberly.

*

West End, London

Two weeks later Paul and James were enjoying a boys night out. They had found a pub nestled in the heart of the West End where you could still sit on an oak bench and enjoy real ale, away from the throbbing music and trendy metal furniture of the bars scattered through theatre land.

Deep in conversation and well into their third pint, they could have had their pick of women that night. Heads turned at the two strikingly different but equally handsome men sitting near the door. Sometimes they laughed, but mostly they listened to each other, nodding occasionally and reinforcing the bonds of their friendship and affirming the history they shared.

'She still looks so fragile,' observed Paul, telling James about meeting Kitty in the park.
'I mean, she still looks as beautiful as she always was, still has those long unruly curls, and huge eyes, but I couldn't tell you that she looked happy.'

'You're happy with Kim though aren't you?' questioned James. 'Would you want Kitty if she was free now?'

Paul paused and thought about that.

'Don't get me wrong, Kim isn't second best, she's not like the consolation prize. They are just different. Maybe that's why I fell for Kim. She likes to boss me about.' Paul laughed as he said this.

James laughed too. 'Yep, she is definitely feisty and likes to get her own way.'

Paul looked thoughtful again. 'Being with Kitty would've been high maintenance, don't you reckon? I know Kim is high maintenance too but with Kim it's just do it her way and all is well. But Kitty, she always looked like she needed someone and I guess I thought I was that someone. I wanted to be that someone.'

Paul trailed off. He wondered just for a second if, given the chance, he would leave Kim for Kitty. He pushed the thought away and buried it quickly. It had taken him so long to move on, there was no way he wanted to revisit his feelings for Kitty. Not tonight, perhaps not ever.

'So,' said James, trying to lighten the mood, 'Kim doesn't need you, she just wants you?'

'Ha! Yes, that would be it,' smiled Paul and raised his glass to meet James.

'Still no news from Ange?' asked Paul, while James was draining the end of his pint.

James shook his head and swallowed his beer.

'Nope. I know she wants another stint in Romania but setting up personnel teams in the New York office has taken her a while and she told Bee there were rumours of new offices in Europe, so she is the obvious choice to set up the admin and secretarial support for those too. She wants to concentrate more on the community work but clearly the company want her to do something that earns them money as well. She's doing really well from what Bee says and I'm glad for her.'

James got up and motioned to Paul that he would get the next round in.

Paul wondered if James knew how lonely Angela had admitted to Bee she was. She had friends, people she'd met as she travelled, but she hadn't settled anywhere. She'd told Bee that the poverty and misery she had seen at the orphanages, when she first went to Romania, had almost been too much to bear. She had wanted to close her eyes to it and turn away. It had almost ripped her soul away to see those children's eyes full of love as they sat in filthy cots. Her heart had crumbled when she'd held a little girl called Mia. Mia had rubbed her back when Angela had cried. This little lost girl who had nothing and had never experienced affection from anyone but could still find compassion and share it so easily with a stranger. There was something in that little girl's eyes that pulled Angela's heart up till it burned in her throat. And she saw it wherever she turned. The lives of those children completely wretched, but for hope. Bee had cried when she'd first listened to Angela and she'd cried again as she retold it to Paul.

None of them knew, Angela was working harder than she had ever worked before. She thought of nothing else except getting back to the orphanage. She knew Mia wasn't there any longer, she had been one of the lucky ones. Another volunteer was going through the paperwork to adopt Mia and take her home to France. Angela tried to absorb comfort from a happy ending, but the alarming truth was the little girl was one of the few.

James set the drinks down on the table and took a long gulp from his. Paul was still thinking about Angela and what Bee had told him and he couldn't decide if he should tell James what he knew, or leave the wound alone.

But it was James that spoke first. Deciding that Paul would forgive him a moment of sentimentality, he played with his glass a little and then spoke quietly.

'I go over and over it in my head. About me and Angie.'

He didn't look up at Paul but he knew he had his attention.

'What if I'd never let her go. I don't mean kept her here, I mean what if I had gone with her?' James paused. 'We might still be together.' he added shortly and then when Paul said nothing he added again, 'Guess I'll never know.'

James and Paul sat in silence for a minute, taking

another gulp of beer every now and again.

'Wonder if she ever thinks about me, being there with her, by her side.' started James again. 'Does she think about what it would have been like? I think about it all the time. It won't go away. Sometimes I wonder if she'll ever come back. Do you think she is still the Angie we know? Do you think she could still want me? Or do you think she's moved on? Sometimes I wish I could go right back to the start and take that chance and go with her.'

Paul had never heard James talk so openly about Angela and he felt simultaneously out of his depth as to what to say and envious that James was so clear about his feelings for the woman he'd lost.

*

Half a mile away on a much trendier street full of bars and bright lights, the music thundered through entrances out onto the pavement. Inside a particularly fashionable bar called 'The Loft', bodies jostled for space at the bar and groups of young women eyed the available men like packs of hyenas waiting for a chance to move in on the kill.

'C'mon mate, if your girlfriend doesn't have the money, I can't give you nothing. The boss'll kill me if I give it away.'

Jimmy emphasised the word 'kill' with a hand gesture, to make his point over the throbbing music. He took a swig from his glass and threw a glance around the room to make sure he looked like a regular customer.

Greg stood with his arm around a skinny blonde who, even in a poor light, did not possess any of Kitty's beauty or softness. They swayed together slightly, completely unaware they were moving.

'Oh Greg, come on. Buy me some, you'll like it. I promise,' she whined, tracing her finger down his chest.

'OK,' began Greg, putting his hand in his pocket to find his wallet. 'But lets not make a habit of this. I'm a school teacher, and this is not the way we're supposed to behave.' He smirked at the blonde as he said it, and she hung off him ever more needy for support as she greedily kissed him.

As Greg came up for air, he saw a familiar face walking towards him and panic shot through his body as he straightened up and tried to extract himself from his blonde sidekick.

'Well, well, well,' sneered Bob, extending his hand to shake Greg's. The contrast between the civil hand etiquette and the contemptuous tone confused Greg and he stumbled over what to do next.

'W..What are you doing here?' he mumbled, searching for something intelligent to say that would excuse his current state and the blonde who was refusing to be pried off.

'Just a little business,' replied Bob grinning and focussing on the blonde, who was now trying to get the wallet from Greg's hand to pay Jimmy. If she was trying to be inconspicuous, she was failing.

'Bob. Look. Um, can we keep this between ourselves? I mean, no need for this to go any further. I don't usually. I mean, I have never done this …'

Greg continued to stumble over his words and wished he'd not had so much to drink. He was growing tired of the blonde now pawing at him and he was convinced from the way Bob looked at Jimmy that he knew Jimmy was selling drugs.

Bob drew himself up to full height and Greg hated him at that moment. He looked so self possessed and elegant, whilst Greg felt dishevelled and self conscious. Moments seem to pass in silence. Long, heavy seconds full of loathing, apprehension and dominance.

Then Bob smiled, 'Of course, of course, wouldn't want a momentary indiscretion to ruin someone forever,' he agreed, and even though Greg felt his muscles visibly relax, there was a seedling of doubt already sown somewhere deep in him that he may not have had the lucky escape it seemed on the surface.

Bob shook Greg's hand and then patted Jimmy on the back, before striding off to shake hands with some suited business types that had just walked in.

It took Greg about twenty minutes to make his excuses to the party he was with and after visiting the toilets to clean himself up he headed for the exit alone. He kept his head down as he worked his way through the crowd, lest he should see Bob again before he could get away. His head was spinning, weaving excuses should the need arise when he got home. He only stopped for a moment to wait for a new crowd to come in and clear his exit path when he saw Jimmy again, tucked into a corner and with him, with his back to the crowd, was Bob. Greg hung back, shielded by the tide of people coming through the door. His eyes widened as he saw Bob smile at Jimmy and pat him on the back again, but this time Jimmy was handing a huge wad of money to Bob. Bob took the money willingly and after counting away some of the notes placed them back in Jimmy's hand, in the pretence of a handshake. Greg reeled as he watched. Well, well, he thought to himself. Bob was the boss. Bob, was a liar. Greg stood mesmerised as Bob exchanged money twice more with different young lads before heading off to use the toilet. Deciding to slip out ahead of Bob rather than risk being noticed, Greg hurried out into the cool night air.

'Touché Bob,' he said under his breath as he hailed a black cab. 'Touché.'

Chapter 11
New Year Eve's 1999

Hampstead Heath

Hi Ange.
I am just loving all this computer mail malarkey. Being able to write to you and know you can see it so quickly is amazing. So here I am, wanting to wish you a Happy New Year! Seems like a life time ago we had those New Years together and I so wish we could do it again. I feel quite lonely today and I wish you were here with us.

Bob had to go away just after Christmas. More antiques. We will have them coming out of our pores soon. This time it's Ibiza and he wanted to go and check it out himself before he organises shipment. He should be back by tomorrow morning though. I wish I could have gone with him but Joseph has been unwell over Christmas (typical) and it seemed best to stay home with him and Amanda. Can't believe he will be two in February. You'd better still be coming home to see us for the party.

I miss talking to you whenever I want. That never goes away. I still don't have any involvement with the business and the dressing up and going to parties gets tedious now. Bet you never thought you'd hear me say that? It's really time I stopped moaning though. Lovely husband, a beautiful home and two gorgeous children. It just seems so far removed sometimes from the girl I was when we met. Perhaps I'll just never be satisfied. Bob says I spend so much money he won't ever be able to stop working. What a cheek.

Anyway, as I am on my own tonight for New Year, Kitty and Greg are coming over plus a couple of people I got to know when Amanda started school. Don't know if you have spoken to Kitty lately, but it's still no go on the IVF. Kitty seems so desperate about it and says she can't give up. I did try and put the idea in her head that they might adopt but she seems hell bent on having a baby with Greg. Takes all sorts I suppose! Greg still doesn't like her talking to me about it, he says she is under enough stress without me adding to it. What a charmer. I swear he just wants to isolate her from us all and it seems to be working. It will be lovely to spend the evening with Kitty but part of me (well a lot of me) wishes Greg wasn't coming.

But to get to something I really need to tell you. You better be sitting down as it's not good. I don't even want to tell you but if I don't and you bump into Paul when you are over next...I am not even sure how to start, so I'm just going to come out with it.

It seems at some point James got it together with Kimberly. I'm so sorry Ange, I hate having to write this. Paul says he'll never speak to James again. It breaks my heart to think of those two not being friends. I don't know if it's once or been going on a while, but it all seems to have kicked off at a party we had at Paul's just before Christmas. I'm not trying to defend James, but he hasn't been right since he heard his Dad had died. He pretends he is and goes on about how his father wasn't there for most of his life so why would he care now, but he's seemed so lost lately.

It was awful when Paul found out. He launched himself at James from across the room and pinned him to the wall. Their faces were almost touching and I don't ever remember seeing Paul with so much rage. James looked stunned more than anything and I was just relieved he didn't retaliate, as I know he can handle himself. When Paul let go, he just walked away without looking back and they both had the same strange heart wrenching expression, sort of like grief.

I blame her. You know I never liked her and I never liked the way she hung around James and flirted with him. Paul would just ignore it. He said it was just James always getting the female attention so nothing new there – which is true – but you'd think she would have had a little more respect for Paul. She wound him up a treat.

Anyway, Paul is blaming James but has also thrown Kimberly out because she seems to think that James loves her and they're going to be together now. That's what she told Paul. But I had a chat with James (well I cornered him one evening actually) and he said the whole thing had been a huge mistake and he never promised her anything. He says it was just too much drink. I bet she came on to him.

Paul is in a real state. On the one hand he can't quite believe James would try and take Kimberly off him but, on the other hand, he is devastated. If it's true, I mean, that James could just sleep with her and destroy Paul's relationship when he doesn't even want her. It's a real mess.

I feel a little like I'm betraying Paul but I don't want to lose James. I've always had a soft spot for him and this is just not like him. He seems completely out of his depth with that woman calling him all the time and turning up to see him. She is acting so desperate and I don't know who James has to turn to about it. His business is really successful now so I suppose with that and his dark smouldering looks he is quite a prize.

Sorry I guess you don't want to hear that bit, but I want you back so I am being totally selfish and telling you everything.

Do you speak with James at all? I know its been a long time since you two were together but of everyone I know, you might be the one to get through to him and see what's going on. That's a big ask isn't it? Sorry Ange. You don't have to if you don't want to, but if there is anything you can do to salvage their friendship, I would love you forever. You always had a way of getting through to James like no one else could. I don't care about Kimberly by the way – she can run off and stalk some other poor fool. I know that's harsh for Paul but I just think he is way too good for her.

Anyway, better go and make myself beautiful for my guests. Still hopeful only Kitty will turn up. I miss you so much and so so wish you were here with me now. You had better write or call soon and you had better not ditch me in February. I expect you here.

Much love always
Bee
(and Bob, Amanda and Joe)
xxxx

*

<u>Vienna - Austria</u>

Angela sat in her apartment with her laptop in front of her. She hadn't expected an email from Bee tonight and when she saw the name come up in her mail file, she poured herself a drink and settled on the sofa to enjoy it. She had been startled by the empty feeling that surrounded her as she looked out onto the street below, awash with tourists and locals all busy getting to where they wanted to be this evening. She sighed as she realised she was relishing reading the email and making the moments last until she opened it, dreading the inevitable second to come when the email would be finished. She was lonely. She instantly rammed the notion to the back of her mind. So unoriginal she thought, to be lonely in a beautiful, romantic city full of people. She had invitations, but she suddenly knew this was not where she wanted to be. Her life was full to brimming and yet empty. She smiled as she made yet another trite observation to herself. It occurred to her that she had come so far and yet here tonight she was still that eighteen year old girl running away, or was it hiding, from life. Ridiculous she thought. What exactly did she think she was destined for that kept her moving and searching and too scared to stand still? Would she even recognise it if she ever found it?

She read the email smiling, enjoying the way Bee wrote just as if she was speaking to her. She smiled that is until she got to the part about James. James. Just reading about him made her homesick and Bee hadn't pulled any punches. The scars of heart break tore just a little at the mention of his name. It was a feeling she had got so good at suppressing she could usually ignore it completely. Angela knew she couldn't expect him not to have moved on, but a sadness in her knew that if he had, it was her fault. He could have been hers. Completely hers. She had heard about his Dad from Paul but had decided against contacting him at the time. It had been so long since she had spoken to him she wondered if she ever could again. The irony was not lost on her that on a daily basis she collaborated, compromised and argued with some of the most senior executives in her company, but she was terrified to pick up the phone and speak to the man she had never stopped loving.

*

Cobham – Surrey

Kitty put the finishing touches to her make-up and scrutinised herself in the mirror. She wondered if Greg would mind her wearing make-up, he normally liked her more natural but she wanted to make a special effort tonight. It wasn't often Greg agreed to come out with her to see her friends and she was really looking forward to the party at Bee's house.

As she slipped on the high heeled shoes she had bought last week, she thought back to when she was eighteen and would have been able to run down a street in towering heels. She was still only thirty three but felt so much older. Greg walked into the room and she pulled herself up straight and smiled at him.

'How do I look?' she enquired sweetly. 'Do I look lovely enough?'

'You don't need dresses and daft shoes to look lovely Kitty,' he replied silkily and persuasively. 'You don't need to do that for me, you know that.'

In Kitty's head she mumbled that perhaps she wanted to do it for herself actually, just for a change, but the words didn't come far enough forward to make an impression or make the leap onto her lips. He hadn't given her a proper answer. She felt herself deflate inside.

'We should get going soon, I know it's only twenty miles or so, but I can't wait to see Bee.' Kitty forced a smile onto her lips as she spoke and tried to breath away the ache in her chest. She really wanted to see Bee and she really wanted Greg to share her excitement.

'And you say Bob won't be there? He's away?'

'Yes, you know how he likes to travel far and wide to pick up the unusual stuff. He works really hard to keep Bee in the manner befitting a queen.'

Kitty smiled a genuine smile to herself as she spoke. She loved Bee and although she had wealth and luxury Bee never made anyone feel uncomfortable or any less than welcome to share in it. Kitty also hoped Greg wouldn't be too disappointed that Bob was not there. There was bound to be other men for Greg to chat with she thought. Kitty suddenly realised she was hoping Bee's female friends were not too attractive.

'Hmm,' replied Greg distractedly. 'Yes, he certainly works hard.'
He turned away so Kitty didn't see his eyebrows rise or his lips twist.

The ring of the doorbell followed immediately by the knocker being banged very hard against the front door made them stare inexplicably at each other for several seconds. They weren't expecting anyone. Greg moved to the bedroom window and peered down onto the small driveway.

'Lets leave that love,' he suggested smoothly, his face soft.
'It's one of the girls from my school. She'll make us late if we stand there chatting.'

'W..what. What girl?'

'Sarah. Sarah Donnelly. Not sure you've met her. One of the newer teachers.' Greg closed the curtains and smiled disarmingly at Kitty.

'Well don't be rude Greg, we should at least say hello. She'll understand if we explain we can't chat for long. That we're going out.'

Kitty moved for the stairs as the loud hammering came again.

'Kitty!' Greg almost shouted. 'For once why don't you do what you're asked!' His tone was forceful with a slightly nasty edge.

Kitty felt scolded, and wondered how this had suddenly become about her.

'Don't go down there Kitty darling.'

Greg's expression had softened. Now he moved towards Kitty and placed one hand on her arm, the other he ran down her hair. He stared into her eyes, as if trying to hypnotise her. She loved his eyes and at this moment they were dark and alluring.

'After all,' he whispered intently at her, 'You're the one always saying we should do more together, so why let someone else hold up our New Year. You'll moan if we're late to the party and it'll be your own fault.'

Then his grip seemed to tighten, holding her to the spot. Something didn't feel right to Kitty. Familiar feelings of uncertainty and paranoia flooded her. Feelings she usually managed to brush away once Greg had reminded her of how daft she could be.

The knocking became heavier and insistent.

'Greg, what's the matter with you? By the way she's knocking I'd say she needs to speak with you. Go and let her in.'

Kitty took a step back trying to assess and fathom why she felt suddenly odd.

'You're right, of course.' Greg backed off from Kitty completely.
'I'll go down. Let me go down. I'll get rid of her,' Greg offered, resuming his smooth, glossy tone.

He kissed Kitty before he breezed down the stairs. A strange forceful kiss full of passion but lasting only seconds.

Kitty noted, but didn't recall the detail until much later, that the woman who stood on their doorstep was young. She looked tired but was clearly very attractive. She wore a pale grey tracksuit over her trim figure. A shivering heat shot through Kitty as her gaze targeted and locked onto the tiny baby tucked inside a pale blue blanket in the woman's arms.

Initially as she watched Greg from the top of the stairs, talking quietly at first and then with a raised voice, confusion roared in her ears. And then as both Greg and the woman started to shout and the woman tried to step into the house and push the baby into Greg's folded arms, Kitty felt a flash in her head. A soundless, colourless surge but with the power of thunder. Kitty was falling even though she was standing as still as she could be. She wanted to speak but fear and a sick dismay had started to swell in her chest and crawl up her throat cutting off any words. But she didn't need to speak, and even if she had, she didn't need Greg to answer. As he turned around and looked back at her, Kitty sank defeated to the floor. It was there in his eyes; everything she needed to know.

Harrow – London

James nearly didn't answer his mobile. He was trying to escape all interaction tonight despite being in a house full of people. His phone didn't register that it recognised the number so he took a chance answering it, assuming it was a wrong number which was typical at this time of year.

His heart stopped dead in his chest when he heard her voice.

Angela had paced backwards and forwards around her apartment for forty minutes before switching off all the thoughts zooming messily around her head and pushing the buttons on the phone. Paul had given her this number a while ago and she'd kept it safe in her purse, without realising the significance of not throwing it away.

For ten minutes they walked between land mines.

Angela desperately tried to sound cheerful and light as she fiddled with her necklace. It had been a gift from all the friends before she'd left England the first time. A long chain, with a maze charm hanging at the end, spun delicately in sterling silver. In the centre was one small diamond. She had cried when Kitty had told her they hoped she would eventually reach the centre and find a place she would call home. A place she would put roots. Angela was still waiting for that to happen.

James took the phone into the garden, hoping the crisp night would keep him grounded and the darkness around him would hide his feelings. How could it be that her voice was the last one he needed to hear, but at the same time the only one he wanted to hear.

As they danced around superfluous and flimsy subjects James tried his best not to unleash the images of Angela that were swirling around him, too painful to bear but too beautiful to push away. He remembered the first time he had kissed her after the dinner dance and the times at the beginning of their relationship when no one else had known about them. Their passion and desire for each other exquisitely unbearable.

Every now and again, as they spoke, they would sail dangerously close to the subject of Paul and each time James would navigate swiftly away. What could he possibly say to Angela that would not make him the bad guy? He was the bad guy. It was his fault – he knew that. He had allowed flattery and vanity to chip away at his moral code. He should have pushed Kimberly away sooner. The longing for Angela and a realisation that she would never be replaced in his heart had already beaten into his integrity and weakened him. And there it was, the heart of the matter, weakness. It didn't matter what excuse he used or who else he might want to blame when he was feeling sorry for himself, at the bottom of all this was his weakness, his need for some attention, all mixed with a large serving of alcohol. He didn't blame Paul for hating him, he loathed himself. He had lost control of the situation. So what if she had come on to him. He would not try and justify the impossible to Angela if she asked, he didn't deserve forgiveness and Paul certainly didn't need to hear on the grapevine that James was looking for sympathy.

But then she said something that reached down to his core, touching feelings he had expertly hidden away and worked hard at burying completely.

'I was sorry to hear that your Dad died. How are you bearing up?'

James stumbled and his mind went blank. Angela sat quietly and waited, worried she had made a mistake bringing it up but praying that James wouldn't hang up on her.

'How do you expect me to react?' he began, having tucked himself further into the darkness at the end of the long garden. 'I loved him once and he let me down.'

James felt the familiar wave of anger and sadness woven in a confusing mess but he was immediately sorry for the sharp tone he'd used with Angela. He wondered if she might think he was having a stab at her. His face softened and he closed his eyes.

'Do you know before he left us, Mum had never worked. She had so much to take on, and she did it without complaining. I can't imagine what those first few years must have been like.'

James spoke more quietly now and kindly but Angela knew he was still angry with his father.

'She's such an incredible lady,' acknowledged Angela. 'Such calm and grace. Was she very sad when she heard the news?'

James sighed into the night air and spoke almost to himself. 'It was all a long time ago for her too,' He paused. 'But she's often wanted me to see that the things he did didn't make him terrible. Just weak and flawed. But I don't want to talk about him or remember him. I have no memories worth mourning.'

Angela's heart ached for James. On the one hand he was angry and needed to believe his father was a bad person to justify that anger, but Angela could hear the pain in his voice, the pain that showed he wished his father had been a better man. If she had been with James now she would have held him, kissed his face, stroked his hair and not cared one bit that she no longer had the right to touch him.

'You are allowed to feel the way you do James,' began

Angela carefully.

James felt the nerves in his body unravel. His practised resistance, used to keep people at arms length was disintegrating. Angela had pulled at scabbed wounds and in his moment of panic a decision was made. James found himself wanting Angela to see him defenceless, he wanted her to know it all.

'I guess I thought I would feel closure and relief, but all I feel is a bunch of loose ends,' he said calmly, feeling as if he and Angela had never stopped speaking. A feint smile played at the corner of his mouth when he realised how easy it had been to say.

'But there must have been something good?' Angela could hear his voice relaxing and decided to push further. 'One perfect day perhaps that you had together. You know that memory deserves to stay alive in your mind, just as much as some of the bad stuff. Just because it was a long time ago doesn't make it less real.'

James didn't reply at first and then quietly, soaked in years of sadness he whispered, 'I was young when he left. I don't think I can remember anything good.'

Angela wondered what else she could say and then suddenly she smiled gently at an old memory,

'You know some very wise person once told me to write a letter. Doesn't matter if no one else ever reads it but it does matter that you have a place to write all your feelings in total honesty, find a way to move forward.

Write down all the anger and disappointment, tell him how much he hurt you, if you want to.'

Angela paused and heard James breathing and then what sounded like a muffled chuckle at the mention of writing a letter. So, she put a smile in her voice and finished with, 'On my travels I've met people who believe anger is a poison and if you hang on to it you're just giving it a home to live and grow. It will only hurt you, not him.'

'Is that all you've learnt?' he gently joked with her, the corners of his mouth raised in a very real smile. In his mind he was thinking, please come home and let me love you.

As they said the usual New year salutations a little of the awkwardness returned, neither one of them wanting the call to end. Angela wanted to tell him that he was already everything his father wasn't. Already a better man, perhaps because of his father, but she felt that would be better done face to face where she could kiss his lips and look after him. She immediately caught herself and pushed away the picture of James chiselled face.

Both sat for a long time after the call, deep in thought and still clutching their phones. Angela stared out of the window, down into the crowd watching fireworks screaming into the empty sky.

James was only barely aware of the countdown. He sat perfectly still and stared into the darkness realising he couldn't reach the one thing that mattered to him and made all the other stuff important. He looked at the phone as if Angela was inside. He had never felt so alone in his life.

Hampstead Heath – London

Bee had never wanted a party to end as much as she did this one. As the clock plodded towards mid night Bee realised that making sure a group of friends had a good time had never been so painful or engineered. Surrounded by magnificent food and dignified dinner discussion, all Bee wanted to do was throw off her heels and hear a good joke. Kitty hadn't turned up and to be honest right now she couldn't blame her. These people were so formal and stiff and quite frankly, fake. She looked around her dining room as if she had just arrived from another planet and was invisible to the occupants. The children had fallen silent upstairs about thirty minutes ago and provided perhaps her only possible excuse for a temporary escape.

Suddenly, as if it had been perversely choreographed, several things happened simultaneously. Bee would never be able to recall which had come first, even though she would live the next few moments over and over again for the rest of her life. She saw the window come herding in towards her dinner guests, showering them with glistening shards. She heard the sound of the glass shattering. She also heard the crystal lamp fall off the side table by the window and smash onto the wooden floor, as the room was dropped into darkness. Then came a whole series of sounds, but they were so close together they blended into a terrible wave of noise. More breaking glass in the hallway. People's raised and confused voices around her. The scraping back of chairs from the table and above all of that a scream of pure terror from upstairs. Bee was shaken back to reality as she heard Amanda calling for her. She heard feet pounding up the stairs. More screaming. An adult sound, awful, raw and angry.

Bee had never been much for church, but from a place deep inside her terror was welling up as she climbed the stairs. She whispered frantic pleas to a God she wasn't sure existed, feeling every sickening thud in her chest.

The house plunged into a heart stopping silence as everyone stared.

On the floor in the spare bedroom sat two small children, one of them Joe. Around them was a white dust. No, not dust, powder. It was in their laps, on their hands, in their hair and it floated magically around the room as they dug their small fingers into the pile they had created and threw it up towards each other engrossed in the most wonderful messy game. They were not just surrounded by it, they were in it.

'Mummy I'm scared,' whispered Amanda, barely audible as she stood frozen in equal amounts of confusion and terror.

As Amanda stepped to one side chaos and noise rose within the room, ending the silence as abruptly as it had started. Behind Amanda was another boy, motionless, sprawled across the carpet and breathing too rapidly to be asleep. White bubbles were foaming at the edge of his mouth which was tinged with a pinky blue that caused Bee simultaneous confusion, recognition and horror.

Bee knew she was going to be sick. She knew it. She knew it without embarrassment or time to consider what else was going on around her. She hurled herself towards a waste paper basket and became only vaguely aware of time passing.

Finally the yelling lessened. An ambulance came and went. People left her. Had she asked them to leave? She didn't remember. They had left anyway. Bee waited in darkness and silence for the police to arrive. She held her children close and rocked them, telling them everything was going to be fine. By her side were the rocks that had shattered her dining room window and everywhere she looked she saw glass. Oh please, she thought, please please help me someone. She didn't know what help she wanted, or who she was reaching out to, she couldn't gather her thoughts that far ahead, only - please please help me.

Most people will be able to tell you where they were on the eve of the new century, who they were with and what they did. Memories they will treasure, meticulously planned or spontaneously relished. For some though despair and misery will forever mark the date.

Angela spent a long time staring down into the swell of the party on the street below. Tears trickled slowly down her cheeks as she realised she had no idea where home was but she knew she needed to get back there.

Kitty, walked through the entire night towards Bee. All she knew for certain was that every man she had ever cared about had let her down. Actually, not just let her down, but led her to believe they would always be there for her, look after her and then drop her from the highest pedestal to simply watch her fall.

And Bee. She continued to rock her children while strangers in uniform filled her house and took away her possessions. She looked through the staring neighbours out on the pavement. Time slowed and the voices of the strangers became stretched and dull until there was nothing but silence in Bee's head. Silence, except for the strange sensation of her memories swirling into a frenzied hurricane, only to disintegrate, leaving nothing except a void filled with nausea and disorientation.

Chapter 12
March 2000

Berry Bay Nr Fairmouth, Dorset

Bee sat outside the Smugglers Rest watching her parents down on the beach with their grandchildren. She wrapped her silk shawl more tightly around her shoulders and breathed in the crisp, untainted morning breeze. On her right she could see the gulls flapping over the cliff face, foraging noisily and to her left she realised that spring was quietly covering the landscape with early lambs and daffodils. Bee sighed as she lamented that the world had kept turning. She was about descend into the now familiar wallow of her loss and torment but was brought up short by the sound of her children yelling and waving from the water's edge. Bee's parents had waded just a little way into the cold sea and were dangling Joe and Amanda above the water, all four of them laughing and becoming unsteady against the swirling foam crashing against wellington boots.

She looked up and smiled lovingly as Kitty placed more coffee in front of her, but she was too lost in thought to start a conversation. It was one of the most comforting ways their friendship had evolved over the last three months, that they could sit in silence. Wonderful, secure, comfortable silence. Knowing there was no pressure to speak but reassured they were never alone.

The last few months had been corrosive and hard to bear. Bee often wondered if she would still be here, if it were not for those that surrounded her and held her up. Kitty always dismissed this and remarked that Bee was always the one with guts, but Bee had felt those guts ripped from her slowly, painfully and with maximum humiliation as each sordid fact had unveiled itself to her and to an eager, hungry pack of journalists and hangers on.

Drugs. Illegal. Destructive. Addictive drugs.

Bob had built all their dreams, all their memories and all their wealth on a mountain of illegal drugs. Everything they owned, the respect they had in the community, the future they were building - all by moving and selling drugs. Bob's speciality had become transporting drugs around holiday islands and working with his own network of dealers living permanently close to the most popular resorts, ensuring the teenage holiday market was never short of supply. He was known in the right circles from Dorset to Devon and into Cornwall and his move to London had been his most ambitious yet, gradually building a web of lies to distract and ingratiate himself with fashionable suburb society. Bee had been horrified to discover how many of their elegant, sophisticated friends had private, seedy habits at the weekend. Bee now agonised if Bob had ever really loved her, or if she had been the perfect cover for suburban life. A perverse form of arm candy. Was that how he viewed the children? As cover? Bee had spent hours torturing herself over this fact. Did he ever love the children? What should she tell them about their father now he was in prison waiting for trial? How could she cope with the humiliation of it all? Was it possible to still love him? Should she visit him? Why should she visit him? Loss always turned to grief and then to anger, which in turn led to feeling humiliated and scared for the future and then back to loss. Over and over the cycle had rolled week after week until she had been exhausted, retreating further into herself. Being here, away from London, and with her family had kept her sane and perhaps alive. Alive. Bee would sob quietly at night for the lives that Bob's repulsive career choice may have destroyed or even taken. Families wrecked, smashed, just to fund her three holidays abroad each year, private education and her convertible. But of course that was all gone now. Bob's antiques shops had been seized by the authorities, as evidence. They had turned out to be just a front for the real transactions. Bee recoiled in a wave of nausea every time she thought about the amount of money she and her parents had lost investing in Bob's 'antique' business. Their money had been used to destroy lives, and they had given it willingly, albeit unwittingly. Repulsion flooded her senses again. Even if she did get to keep the house, Bee knew she would sell it. She needed to repay her parents and she could never return to live there. The disgrace was too great. The wealth it represented disgusted her now. She had no idea where she would go or how she would fund it and she didn't have the strength to plan ahead. For now it was enough that she could stay at Ivy cottage, Amanda could attend the local school in Charmouth and no one had made a connection. It allowed Bee to conduct herself with her last shred of dignity and grace. She'd become paranoid enough to imagine that people here were staring at her, but no one had raised even their voice to her. She was grateful for that. The house in London had continued to be targeted and although Bee hadn't returned there, her parents had told her all the windows were now boarded up. Bee didn't blame whoever was responsible for taking the law into their own hands. She could only imagine, with yet another wave of nausea, the lengths a family might go to seeking revenge for a life ruined. Ruined by a man she loved.

Bee sighed and turned to smile at Kitty, who had been sitting quietly by her side lost in her own thoughts. She placed her hand on kitty's arm and rubbed it gently. No words were needed to offer simple, pure and absolute support. Besides, something primitive had been building in Bee for the last two weeks, almost imperceptible at first but growing stronger towards the end of each bout of soul searching and angst. Some days Bee was amazed to find herself brilliantly clear on the future and she felt positive that she could see a path ahead of her. She knew who she had to protect, she knew that wasn't Bob. Regardless of whether she still loved him or not, she knew where her priority was and nothing else should matter. And there they were.

Laughing on the beach, waving back at her and radiating love. The small seedlings of strength Bee felt when she looked at her children warmed her and she had begun to nurture hope, and a belief that there was a future.

'Do you think we'll get through this Bee?' Kitty looked at Bee, with eyes full of loss and betrayal.

'Yes,' answered Bee quietly, and then more firmly, 'Yes, I do think we'll get through this. Because those days when we can't stand up, that's when I'll bloody well pull us up.'

Kitty felt a feint smile form on her lips as she looked into the pinched, worn out face of her friend. She wore the strain around her mouth and through her hair, but, behind the pain and despite her wilted posture was the distinct beginnings of resolve and determination. The Bee she knew.

'We'll pull each other up,' Bee asserted softly but unyielding.

After a moments pause she continued, 'Because you know what? So what? That's what we should say. So what?'

Kitty looked at Bee quizzically. How could she even say that after what they had been through. Bee noticed her expression.

'So what Kit?' she repeated. 'What now? So what are we

going to do? With everything bad that has happened to us, around us, what are we going to do with that? About that? Are we going to lay down and stop living? We've done that already. That's what we're doing now. Is that it? I'm not going to do that Kitty, and I'm not going to let you either.'

Bee's face softened and she looked almost shy, something Kitty had never seen.

'Kit, you saved my life you know. If you hadn't turned up when you did. If you hadn't walked into my house, through all the destruction and taken us all into your arms....'

Bee's voice tailed off. She didn't want to contemplate where she might be right now, if not for Kitty. And then she snapped her head up, her voice strong again,

'And that's what friends are for Kitty. So, there is no way you're not getting through this.'

Kitty felt buoyed by Bee's words, at least for a minute or so but as she looked down onto the beach at Joe and Amanda she was starkly reminded of what she didn't have. As she thought about Greg's affairs and the baby he had fathered, her relentless, exhausting attempts at IVF and her passion to have children of their own, she felt ridiculous and pathetic. Her humiliation and heartache may have been more private than Bee's but it was just as real and sharp and she felt that now familiar sensation of ice water dripping down her spine as she re-lived New Year. It was a feeling that reminded her how close she was to shutting down and letting the misery smother her. Sometimes the irony of what Bob had hidden in Bee's house crossed her mind and the idea of buying something to take the edge off her gloom seemed the answer. The thought of running back to a world with no responsibility made her dizzy and then frightened and she longed to just sleep the feelings away, hoping to wake up magically more positive. What she really wanted was to wake up and find none of it was true. She missed Greg. She missed his charm and the power he had over people. She felt lost without him and she just couldn't imagine not loving him but if the last few weeks had shown her anything it was how much control Greg had over her world. She had ignored his affairs, submitted to his increasingly controlling behaviour and obsessed over babies as a means to keep him. Kitty wondered how she had got here. Was this really what she wanted? How could it have ever ended well? How could it end anything better than toxic?

Kitty stared down at the pile of mail she'd brought with her from the cottage. It was a safe ritual for Bee and Kitty that they opened the mail together each day. Most of it was junk, but not always and they had learnt to seek strength by dealing with each new revelation together.

On top of the pile was a hand written envelope addressed to Kitty. She fingered the address and the stamp, but made no attempt to open the letter.

'Is it from Greg?' asked Bee, although she had already guessed it was.

Kitty sighed.

'Yes,' was all she said for a moment and then she added, 'He knows I'm here, I told him. I also told him I didn't want him to visit. Just a little surprised that he listened.'

After a moment, Kitty looked out to the gulls, circling and swooping near a hog roast the pub landlord had just started up. She chewed her lip nervously.

'I hope this letter doesn't change my mind.'

Bee was about to ask Kitty what she meant, what decisions she had made but decided to stay quiet as Kitty suddenly ripped open the letter as if she was afraid of another seconds delay.

Darling Kit,

I don't know what else to say to you. I'm sorry you are upset. I know that sounds hollow and if I was there with you, you could look at my face and see I'm telling the truth. I wish you would let me see you. I don't get why you won't see me. I am sorry I have been such a disappointment. Do you really want this to be the end of our marriage? Do you know how much I want to hold you? I really need you. This is killing me. I know I was weak, I see that now. I guess I was under more stress than I realised. Only you can fix this. You can't leave me. I know we have something special and I can't lose you. You know we have something special too, I know you do. We can get through this. We can't live without each other Kit.

Please believe I didn't plan the baby. I made a mistake and one I know I will have to pay for forever. I know it will be hard for you to live with, but I know you're strong. I don't see why this should spoil what we have. Come home. Stop listening to your friends and talk to me. Let's stop this madness of IVF and the stress it's putting us under. I can see now that I could be happy with just you. I don't need a baby. We don't need a baby. We have each other. I can't function without you. You are my world Kitty. I love you, please talk to me and please please come home and love me.

Greg x

Kitty remained silent for some time after reading the letter. In fact, she read it over again and again searching for – for what? As she read the letter for the fourth time she imagined Greg's boyish pleading smile when he wanted his own way and how he could turn it on and off instantly. A smile that she had adored for its charm and power. Kitty lifted her head back and let the weak warmth from the sun bathe her face. She combed her fingers through her hair and pondered on how she would like it cut next time she was in town. Greg had always liked it up and tidy, so she would have it layered so the curls would bounce up wild and free. She felt like a naughty child, out on her own for the day and she smiled. While she was in town she might buy herself some perfume. It had been a long time since she had chosen her own she realised. She felt herself step over an invisible line and she knew without any sadness that she didn't want to step back.

'Are you considering taking him back?' asked Bee, trying hard to control the judgemental tone of her voice. 'I bet he's fed you loads of lies Kit, don't be fooled by him. You have to think about what you want, how you want your life to be. Do you think he can really change?'

Looking up at Bee for the first time in a while, Kitty laughed. She felt strangely calm and powerful.

'No, he didn't tell any lies in the letter. Everything he says about himself in this letter is all true,' she smiled and waved the letter at Bee.

'Read it.' Kitty pushed the letter down on the table and towards Bee. 'Read the self-serving crap all about poor Greg and how he feels. All about him and what he wants and what he needs.' Kitty was smiling. 'Do you know what I've just realised. That it's partly my fault,' she said, allowing herself the smallest of laughs at the irony that Greg would probably agree with her, that it was always her fault in the end.

Bee look confused and said nothing. Kitty was losing the plot.

'You know how all our lives we're fed the notion of the alpha male?' Kitty was looking intently at Bee now and shifted in her seat, as if she couldn't wait to share the revelation.
'And we all want him don't we? Our own alpha male to show off. That's who we want. The loudest, the most colourful, the most powerful so he must be the best. You'll please him and he'll make your life complete. Make you the woman all other women wish they could be.'

Bee was still staring as Kitty spoke loudly, clearly and with a tone immersed in irony.

'Well what a load of crap!' Kitty exclaimed, waving her arms in the air, as she gathered pace, happy for everyone to listen.

'What ..a.. load ..of.. crap.' She spoke slowly and loudly this time, attracting a few more stares.

'A real alpha doesn't need to sing and dance. He's the one that glues the pack together. Doesn't need to shout about how good he is, he just *is* good and soundlessly goes on being that glue that holds it all together. He leaves the posturing and preening to the wannabes.'

Kitty looked down at the floor as if suddenly disappointed in herself.

'I just never saw it that way before. I didn't stop to think about it or about what was right there in front of me.'

'So, Kitty...I'm kind of confused. Are you going back to Greg or not?'

Kitty got up from the table and kissed the top of Bee's head.

'No, I'm damn well not. But I'll tell you what. I'm starving. Fancy some hog roast?'

Chapter 13
August 2000

The Guardian Newspaper
August 10th 2000

In the sensational and historical court case that has exposed the seedy drug trafficking trade funding the lives of our middle classes, Robert Brooks has been dramatically found guilty and sentenced to twenty years imprisonment.

Brooks 55, was arrested re-entering the country on New Years Day, after police raided his London home following a tip off. Class A drugs including heroin and cocaine were found on the premises and at all of the upmarket and exclusive antique shops that Brooks has run for 30 years, at least 20 of those as a front for his sordid, drug business. The jury heard how Brooks had managed the purchase, movement and selling of drugs across London and the South East with teams built up over the last 20 years.

During the investigation, police raids into homes and

hangouts of suspected and accused associates of Brooks, across many popular holiday island destinations, exposed a substantial and growing business in illegal recreational drugs, targeted at the increasing number of young people travelling on holiday each summer. Over forty arrests have been made to date with police sources claiming this will be the biggest operation exposed in the UK to date.

Friends of Brooks seemed astonished with the overwhelming evidence as it mounted and, notably, his wife was not present during the trial or while the verdict and sentencing were delivered. Bee Brooks, 36, has steadfastly declined to comment on her husband's arrest and has not been seen by the couple's friends since the New Year. Police have confirmed that they are satisfied Mrs Brooks was not implicated in her husband's crimes, although she continues to assist them with their enquiries.

Turn to Page 7 for full story on all the dramatic events. Also....
Offshore drug parties in the Balearic and Canary Islands – Page 9
Dining with Mr & Mrs Brooks – a friend gives their account – Page 10
Were the children exposed to Class A drugs? – Page 11

Bee sighed and put the paper down. Paul looked up from one of the tabloids and smiled kindly at his sister.

'You're famous. You made all the papers again.'

Bee sighed again, louder this time and thought about how hard it had been over the last six months to protect her children and keep intrusive journalists away.

'Come on Bee,' Paul remained kind but added some authority to his voice, 'You knew this day was coming. You knew it would attract this much attention and your lives would get dragged through the mud.'

Paul tossed his paper on the floor.

'It's a shame some of your so called friends decided to speak to the press. But to hell with them Bee. You don't need them. In the bigger picture they mean nothing to you. Let them all gossip.'

Bee hadn't said a word and Paul was not going to let her slip backwards. She had come so far in the last few months and had so much about to go right for her.

'That little lad, in your house, you know he's OK. You know he survived Bee.'

'But what about all the others? What about those I never met?' interrupted Bee. She knew she would never shake the guilt that fermented and bubbled in her stomach.

'Stop beating yourself up Bee, how is this your fault? Come on, please, keep moving forward.'

Bee took a deep breath. There was one last thing she

needed to say before she could free herself. Something that had nagged at her for years while she was married and if she said it to Paul now, out loud, and he still loved her, if he didn't run away or look at her with disgust then maybe she could learn to live with the guilt.

'I think I knew all along Paul.'

Paul froze and stared at his sister.

'I think I knew something wasn't right. I mean, I often wondered how we had so much money. How were we earning so much, so often, from antiques? I could understand why Bob knew so many people and why he was out all the time. That all made sense to me and he was – is - such a charismatic man, I could understand why people liked him and why everyone wanted to do business with him. But always at the back of my mind was the money. I often wondered if Bob was doing something illegal, although I never considered drugs for one second. I'm not sure what I thought he might be doing. I never questioned it though. I'd hit life's jackpot. A gorgeous man to fall in love with, being swept away to different countries all the time, gorgeous house, gorgeous clothes, gorgeous kids. It was all I ever dreamed of as a child and there it was, all my dreams came true. So I pushed the bad feeling away. I lived with a gnawing doubt deep inside until I didn't pay it much attention any more. I got to the point where I didn't want to know why we had money. We just had it, and that was all I needed to know. I didn't want anything to shatter my fairy tale ending. It was my dream life, mine Paul, and nothing was going to spoil it for me.'

Bee stared at no where in particular.

'I didn't care,' she muttered to herself as if summarising her distasteful opinion.

And then facing up to Paul, to gauge his reaction she sighed, 'So I guess this is payback time.'

Paul's face hardened and Bee swallowed stiffly.

'Don't you dare give up.' He shook his head as he spoke, his pale eyes hard and focussed. 'You are not to blame here. Why don't you get that. Bob needs to pay, not you. Find a way Bee. Find a way. Move on from this and build a future. Don't you dare give up on those kids.'

Paul continued to stare at Bee, refusing to let her look away. Then his face softened and he stroked her arm.

'You are so close to a new life Bee. People here have loved your baking. You've loved your baking. Mum and Dad will back you, they've told you that already. So go out there and open that business we talked about. Dye your hair if it helps, cut it all off, change your name back, do whatever you have to but above all, you make sure you fight.'

Giant tears splashed down Bee's face as she looked at her brother and nodded her agreement. He wore his hair cropped quite short now but she could see the unruly waves desperate to grow again. His eyes, always the same quiet blue, were now framed by crinkles reminding Bee of the horrors he must see every day, but when he smiled the crinkles deepened into compassionate creases that only served to emphasise the humanity in his smile. He really is a very handsome man she thought. Her thoughts then turned to Kitty and the game of cat and mouse the two of them seemed to have played over the last six months. Their visits to stay with Bee never seemed to overlap by more than a few hours and Bee pondered on whether she was the only one that could feel the sea air sizzle in any room they both occupied.

Her thoughts were interrupted by the sound of her mobile phone.

'It's Ange,' she exclaimed, looking at the screen and quickly wiping her face and forcing on a smile.

'Hey, high flying buddy. Are you allowed to speak to me now I am no longer a lady that lunches?'

Bee realised with irony that she was about to become the lady who makes lunch for ladies that lunch.

'Come off it Bee, you'll always be the poshest person I know and I guarantee people will soon be paying mega bucks for one of your cakes,' answered a happy, carefree voice.

'Listen Bee. Not got long, I just read the paper over here

and wanted to see how you are and let you know I am thinking of you all.'

Bee heard voices in the background, a lot of noise and commotion.

'And to let you know, I've nearly finished here, and guess what? My next move is home. I'm coming home Bee, for good, and I'm bringing someone with me...a man I can't wait for you to meet.'

Chapter 14
April 2001

Lyme Regis – Dorset

An early, glorious spring had come hurtling towards Bee and Kitty. In fact, standing in the narrow cobbled street which wound down to the promenade, they could feel an unusually intense sun on their faces. The normally busy Jurassic tide was breathing calmly in the distance. Bee was fidgety and fussing over every detail for their big evening, but Kitty retained a new calmness she'd found and embraced over the last few months. She breathed in the quiet Easter breeze and smiled at her own peace. Nothing to feel paranoid about, no one quietly enforcing she was wrong, no feelings of being unworthy, no one slowly bleeding her into submission. This must be how normal people live she thought, amused but at the same time rueful that she had let herself become so manipulated.

'Hey ladies, what's a girl got to do to get coffee around here?'

Kitty and Bee pulled their gaze away from the shop front and smiled towards the voice calling down the street.

'You my darling will get free coffee forever,' sighed Bee, holding out her arms.

Kitty, Bee and Angela stood and hugged together, squeezing each other lovingly.

'Looking good ladies, looking good,' said Angela, pulling herself out of their embrace and pushing her sunglasses up through her hair.

Kitty smiled. 'Yep, I think we may just pull this off.'

The last three months had certainly been manic. By the end of the previous year Bee had done all the maths, all the planning and all the preparation, albeit in her head. The only thing left to do was take a leap of faith and find premises. There were still mornings when Bee woke up and felt the familiar thump to her chest, reminding her the past would always shroud her. Some days the nausea burnt at her and made her shiver so completely she wished she could pull the covers tighter and resign from life. Only the continual nagging by Kitty, her parents and the growing network of customers who loved her ideas and her cooking, had made her plunge head first into opening 'Bee's Knees'. The idea had started out as a simple coffee and cake shop and then Kitty had dropped the bombshell that she was leaving teaching and leaving London. The two women, even now, were not sure if Bee asked Kitty to partner her or if Kitty put the idea in Bee's head, all they knew for sure was that one night after several bottles of wine an idea came to them. Why not create a place that's elegant and full of delicious goodies, doesn't exclude parents with their noisy children nor those who want a quiet coffee and piece of cake. And imagine if the kids love it so much they drag their parents there.

And so after months of putting the plan in place, here they were staring up at the large cream and iron-work sign over their shop front and patio. Bee had been in her element organising everyone and keeping them to strict deadlines, while Kitty had happily taken a back seat but made sure the open plan area to the side, where she would run the activities for younger customers, was as comfortable and bright as possible. She loved the look she'd designed with rugs, small squashy sofa's and walls lined with picture books. Kitty's den was as homely and cluttered as Bee's tables were neat and tasteful with crisp white linen cloths and chic wall art.

'Do you know after being here virtually every weekend this year, I won't know what to do with myself after tonight,' sighed Angela.

She had loved ever minute of the project, watching it grow and become real. Being with Bee and Kitty again had made her feel warm and loved and reinforced her decision to stay in England. Bee wondered if the promotion to Director of Administration had helped Angela's decision to come home but then she noticed Angela was toying with the small maze still hanging around her neck.

'You seen James since you've been home Ange?' she asked without any pretence of subtlety.

'Nope,' replied Angela, looking squarely at Bee. She was used to Bee being up front, it was one of many unpretentious qualities she loved about her.

'So, I take it he doesn't know about that gorgeous new man of yours?'

Angela smiled as she thought about Alex.

'No. I'm not sure he needs to know either,' she sighed and dropped the necklace back under her tee-shirt, thereby putting the thought resolutely away.

Bee looked cautiously at Kitty, who started to tidy her hair into a pony tail as a distraction.

'We invited James to the opening party tonight Ange. I hope you don't mind?'

An involuntary thump hammered Angela's stomach.

'Of course we didn't hear back, so he probably won't even turn up,' Bee added as she winked at Kitty and skipped off to meet the lady who had just arrived with more table linen.

*

It had been a long time since Bee had dressed so elegantly and that evening as she found herself greeting friends and strangers alike she hoped she had struck the right balance. While Kitty and Angela had dressed the shop front and topiary with fairy lights earlier that afternoon, Bee had stared at the mirror wondering how to dress her black knee length shift dress, so she looked classy and tasteful without looking tactless and uncaring. She knew some people would turn up to judge her for Bob's actions. Sighing and steeling herself, she had added the smallest diamond studs to her ears and swept her hair up into a pleat. So what if people stared and commented behind her back, she knew she had to focus on the many people who wanted her to succeed and she had a duty to keep moving forward for the sake of her children.

'Long time no see Bee.'

The familiarity of Kimberly's disdain knocked Bee off guard and rammed her back to the present, but she forced a smile quickly in place.

'Kim, how nice,' she lied. 'What brings you away from London?'

Bee knew news of her venture would have reached London. Some of her remaining friends were here today to support her but inevitably there were the gossips who wanted her to fail and they would have alerted the media. Although in Kimberly's case she didn't need much alerting. She seemed to follow any news of Bob or Bee like a bloodhound. Like it or not, Bee knew she had to work the media to her advantage. Bee's Knees needed publicity and Angela had offered her corporate experience to control public relations. Bee smiled politely at Kimberly as she thought about Angela's joke that it would be like trying to tame a thrashing snake.

Kimberly ran her expertly manicured but perfectly fake fingernails through her ice blonde hair, 'I've been asked to do a follow up story. You know, follow you into this new stage of your life. It's a great angle. You're still quite the talking point in some circles Bee darling.'

Angela, who had been standing slightly behind Bee giving an interview to a local paper, swooped in on the stand off.

'If you're writing about Bee's delicious baking then you need to come and taste some,' she said lightly and gestured Kimberly to follow her away from the shops entrance.

Angela felt Kimberly's gaze as they walked. Inspection and being judged came with the territory at work, the higher up the ranks she rose the more durable and unbreakable she had become. Facing scrutiny was the norm, but it was unsettling to come face to face with the woman James had chosen to take to bed, and in doing so break a bond with his best friend.

James was not perfect, and Angela knew he was not blameless but she had always held his moral code up as the one to aspire to. It was hard for Angela to reconcile that alcohol, lust and an encouraging partner had been the weapon of choice to destroy his friendship with Paul. She was surprised to feel the sting of tears behind her eyes but braced herself as she turned to face Kimberly with the offer of a glass of champagne.

'You must be Angie,' smirked Kimberly, taking the glass. 'James had pictures of you around his house.'

Angela forced her composure not to waiver. This was harder than she had expected. For the first time in years, she felt like the new girl again, unsure and awkward. This is not the time, she chastised herself, for a confidence crisis.

'Speaking woman to woman,' Kimberly continued, when she realised Angela was not taking any bait, 'You have to admire the front of her don't you. I mean, most people would run and hide after such a public humiliation. And you know some people in London don't believe her story. I mean, how could she not have known?'

As she spoke Kimberly looked over her shoulder to where Bee stood shaking hands and smiling coyly. Angela also looked across at her old friend and felt a wave of love and pride as she quietly acknowledged the incredible strength of a woman who had wanted to hide, but had instead got up and taken the much harder option, of living.

Anger rose through Angela, smothering the insecurity

she had been harbouring.

'Speaking woman to woman,' she replied calmly and with precision locking eyes, 'I would have thought you of all people would have respect for a woman taking control of her life and doing whatever she needs to do? Personally, I find it sad that it's more often than not women that sabotage each other. Surely an ambitious woman like you would respect another woman who wants to succeed?'

Angela was shocked at her own presence. She sounded unruffled and immoveable but inside a fire was burning in her belly and she breathed deeply to steady the flame.

Kimberly raised one impeccably arched eyebrow and took a step back. As if the next battle move was hers, she slowly ran her gaze down Angela and back up again. Angela stood still, fighting back the urge to say something loud and coarse which would have made her feel so much better but completely turned the advantage over to Kimberly. Jeez, she thought, were they actually having this fight. At least she knew she looked every inch as groomed as Kimberly. Angela's pale gold silk shift was long and split to the thigh. The dragon, embroidered delicately in golds and reds, curved elegantly from the bust to her ankles. With her hair pulled tightly from her face in a chignon at the nape of her neck, Angela knew the dressmaker she had found on her visit to Hong Kong would approve. Black Kohl and red lips finished off the ensemble that Kimberly was now surveying while she contemplated her next move.

'Do you know if Paul is coming tonight?' she asked, a feint smile playing at the edge of her mouth.

Angela glanced at the tight red dress barely covering Kimberly and the matching stiletto sandals. Now it made sense, she acknowledged to herself.

'No,' she answered undaunted, 'No. He had to work. He couldn't get his shift changed.' So your shameless outfit is wasted, she thought.

And then anxious to show how united Paul and Bee were she added, 'Of course, he has spent all his free time here over the last few months. Good to have strong arms around when you need them.'

Angela couldn't believe how brazen she was being and sensing that she had the upper hand she finished with, 'And it's been wonderful watching how creative Kitty is. They've made a great team.'

If Kimberly blanched at this it was impossible to see under her make up and she quickly returned the shot hitting Angela straight in the chest.

'No matter. Just wondering as I don't want any trouble. It's James I really came to see.'

'James?' Angela didn't have time to hide her surprise.

'Yes. Didn't he tell you? We have unfinished business.

So when I was told to come and cover this story for the magazine, I jumped at the chance.'

'James,' muttered Angela under her breath again. She had taken the blow and was unsure what to say next. She stared at Kimberly. Her beautiful blonde hair, her flawless skin, an enviable figure with long, long bronzed legs. Why wouldn't James want her? The thought that James might be here made her shiver and then immediately burn.

'You may not want him Angela, but I do,' she continued boldly and unashamed. 'Let's face it, you did enough damage.'

Kimberly, who loved the frisson of the illicit, was positively glowing with the anticipation of seeing James again. At first, like most of the relationships in her life, the thrill of the clandestine had been the prize but both Bob and James had proved elusive and stubborn. She was not about to watch James walk gift wrapped back into any one's life but hers.

Angela could only stand and stare, as Kimberly delivered another blow.

'I know a good thing when I see it and I know what James wants. Your loss honey. Your loss.'

Angela let the words swim around her. She felt short of breath as humiliation and rage blended and rose in her throat. Her head started to spin and she was vaguely aware of Kimberly turning to walk away from her.

Angela felt no control over what happened next. Grabbing Kimberly's arm and pulling her back sharply, she hissed involuntarily,

'You don't know anything about me. What makes you think I don't want him? What if that's why I came back? I know exactly what kind of man James is and I know for damn sure he wasn't in his right mind when he took you to bed.'

The words grew louder as the indignation and anger came spilling out. Several people had stopped to watch. Ashamed and furious at herself for causing a scene and taking the attention away from her friends, Angela released Kimberly's arm with a forceful shove and made her way out of the shop, towards the promenade, her eyes to the floor.

James, who had arrived quietly some fifteen minutes before, kissed Bee lightly on the cheek, asked to be excused for a while and headed out into the darkness.

*

Despite the earlier warmth of the day the sun had retreated quickly. The evening had become a familiar chilly, although the sea was calm and watchful, breathing steadily and massaging the moon's admiring light.

'So, who would have thought it? You fighting over me. Hard to believe it's the same woman I met in that kitchen all those years ago.' James voice was full of laughter.

Angela froze and dug her bare feet down further into the sand, feeling an excited nausea run down her stomach. She didn't think she could bare to look up and see him standing there. Not after all this time.

'Oh god,' she whispered as she laid down on the sand and crossed her arms over her face. Angela had no idea what she was going to do next.

James took off his jacket and sat down next to her. She could hear him taking off his socks and shoes but she still couldn't look. As the sand moved, she imagined his tanned feet close to hers and as she inhaled deeply, the familiar smell of his cologne filling her with memories and longing.

'Thank you for defending me,' he finally said quietly and seriously. 'Although I'm not sure I deserve it. I wasn't completely blameless.'

And then, after a brief pause where Angela could sense James playing with the sand, he said almost to himself,

'But the truth is, I didn't sleep with Kim. Paul won't give me long enough to explain and he has every right to be that way. The truth is I sent her away that night. I told her I didn't feel that way about her. That my heart belonged to someone else.' James paused. 'But, that's not what she told Paul or anyone else that would listen and I don't know what I can do when it's my word against hers. Why would he believe me over her?'

James let out a heavy sigh and Angela realising his voice was not as close as she'd hoped moved her arms and peeked up.

'It would just stir up the pain,' he finished in a voice held down by its own weight.

'Did you hear everything I said to her?'

'Yes.'

Angela groaned inside. She could see his broad shoulders shake as he fought hard not to laugh at her. Even from the back he still looked striking. James hated to wear suits, so Angela had always found him completely irresistible when he dressed up.

Propping herself up on her elbows, she watched him as he undid the top button of his shirt and slowly removed his tie. The shivers playing in her belly were moving dangerously towards her legs.

'You've got sand stuck on you now,' he breathed as he turned and lent down towards Angela locking his pale green eyes onto her.

Slowly, James reached out and touched her face. Angela closed her eyes and trembled against the brush of his hand.

He started to gently smooth the sand from Angela,

starting with her cheek and then moving his hand into her hair. Each time his fingers danced dangerously close to her mouth Angela's stomach tightened another notch until she couldn't remember how to breathe. She had laid in bed and dreamed this so many times, she didn't want to move and find it wasn't true. James stroked the sand away from her neck, his breath on her face, his lips coming so close to her. The thought that he could so easily kiss her and she would let him made her tremble. When his hands stopped, Angela barely had time to register disappointment before he tugged at the pins holding her hair in place. Angela gasped and tilted her head back into his fingers as he grabbed gently at her hair. In return, he buried his face into the base of her neck and wrapped his arms around her pulling her to him.

As James pressed against her, Angela felt the first drops of rain coming in from the sea. The moon had disappeared and the water was now a smooth black poison. Illuminated by sudden shards of lightening, James pulled back and stared straight into her eyes. He held her there, as he'd always done from that very first day, with the palest green she had ever seen. Angela could see the rise of his chest through his already damp shirt, clinging to a wall of muscle she had tried to forget. She could feel droplets of water running down her bare neck. Her breathing quickened as she stared hopelessly at James. Thunder roared ahead of her as he wiped the water down her throat. Both of them continued to stare into each other, their faces being drawn together with such tiny but determined movement that it shocked them both when their lips finally touched. Then James was kissing her, one hand in her hair, the other holding her face. Kissing her with a new fierceness. Losing herself in his almost violent embrace, all she heard was the roar of the sea stirring itself against the spring storm and all she felt was the warmth of James mouth pressing into her. She could taste the rain and the sand and him. Angela was so completely lost she was unaware of a ringing sound. It was James that finally pulled away and started to look at the sand in the near darkness.

'My phone,' Angela exclaimed, still not quite coming to her senses and scrabbling about on the wet beach.

'Um...Angela Duncan speaking.'

It was like falling abruptly from a cloud. One minute the world had been intimate, warm and surreal and now Angela felt cold, on sticky cloying sand.

'Angie?' James watched as distress seeped through Angela's body, tightening every nerve and severing her link to him.

'I have to go,' she cried softly, 'I have to go now. Right now. It's Jenny. Jenny's dead.'

Chapter 15
May 2001

Bayswater – London

It was late when Angela got home from the funeral. James had dropped her off and she was glad that he didn't ask to come in. She'd appreciated him wanting to come to the funeral, he'd loved Jenny as much as she did. It had felt awkward at first, seeing him so soon after their encounter on the beach but thankfully it was not the place or time to discuss it. Bee and Kitty had wanted to come but Angela knew how busy they were and how crucial it was for them to be in Dorset, so she fronted it out pretending she was fine. Jenny had taught her that. She knew James had seen through the act and she accepted the comfort that gave her.

She pushed herself down under the hot bath water until only her nose and eyes were visible. From here, she could just make out the old photograph frame on the window sill, and she sighed, staring at the little girl in the pink pyjamas. With the lights turned down low she felt safe, soothed and she allowed the fragrance of lavender and bergamot to carry her away from the day. The last two weeks had been harrowing and full of surprises.

Jenny had no immediate family and it had fallen to her two brothers and Angela to make arrangements. Angela had been shocked to learn that Jenny had left lists of people to contact and fairly strict instructions on how the event of her funeral should proceed. Even in death, Angela smiled sadly, she organised us all and thought of every elegant detail.

No one had known Jenny had cancer. She had chosen to carry it by herself. Angela had noticed in the time she'd been back in England that Jenny was slower and more deliberate in some of her movement, but her hair had stayed chestnut brown, and her heels had never been lower than three inches, right up to the end. They'd shared many lovely days and wonderful evenings out. Jenny had remained, and always would in Angela's mind, the woman she aspired to be.

With her usual knack of knowing exactly what to say to make someone feel valued and ready to face the world, Jenny had written letters to be distributed after her death. Everyone had agreed with Angela that it would be a fitting tribute to the memory and essence of Jenny if the letters were read out at the service. And so it was that Angela had her next shock. She assumed that over the years she'd learnt everything there was to know about her friend and, although mildly amusing, it was not unexpected that Jenny had a line of admirers that arrived in suits and beautiful cars to say goodbye. What was astounding though was listening to their letters. Jenny gently teased each of them for holding such affection. It became apparent by the end of the day that Jenny had turned each of their marriage proposals down more than once and in some cases they knew of each other and had fought for her attentions many times. Intertwined with years of pursuing Jenny, were stories of the lavish holidays they'd taken her on, not to mention the gifts willingly bestowed on her by suitors desperate to secure her commitment.

It didn't surprise Angela that so many men would want Jenny by their side. She was curious though, that Jenny hadn't wanted to make a commitment to even one of these sharply dressed, handsome men who, as far as she could see, had the most impeccable manners. She had made just that comment to one of Jenny's brothers.

'Scratch the surface and you'll often find something altogether more sordid underneath.'

Angela had been horrified. What was he suggesting? That Jenny took advantage of all these men? That Jenny led them on? Or was it altogether seedier? Did Jenny escort them in exchange for gifts? Perhaps it was just a brother's destructive envy towards a woman who made a success of her life.

James had seemed amused by the notion and almost impressed.

'Well done Jenny,' he announced to Angela, but then

sensing that she was truly upset he argued kindly, 'What if she did Angie? Doesn't change the woman you knew, the woman she was in your life.'

Angela couldn't and wouldn't tolerate the idea and, not for the first time, she pushed it sharply away. Laying here now with the warmth accelerating her need for sleep, her mind drifted to *her* letter.

Angela,

I wish I could give you many more years. But I have to let go of your hand now. Please don't cry. You must be tired of all my advice by now surely? And, there is little left I can give you.
If someone had to describe you, my darling girl, I can think of so many words. Beauty and Grace would be there. And a kind, kind heart. But most of all my treasured friend, you radiate warmth like a blazing fire. Never have I met anyone who inspires the way you do. You sparkle like a diamond. I don't want these words to make you cry and, of everyone, it's you I don't want to say goodbye to. So forgive me not telling you that I would be leaving you. I want you to remember every day how many lives you touch. You are loved so much. And when you need me, just look inside yourself, I won't ever really be gone.
My one wish for you now darling girl is this. You know the old saying that in the hope of reaching the moon men often fail to see the flowers that blossom at their feet. This was never truer than it is for you right now. Look at the flowers Angela. That's all I have to say.

With my love forever, Jenny

After the service Angela had read the letter over and over. The same thought lingered now, as it had done all day. This letter described Jenny, not her.

And so it was, as Angela closed her eyes and felt the tears spill soundlessly down her cheeks, that she realised she was finally the adult. She had become what she had set out to. She knew Jenny would chastise her for doubting that she was worthy to carry the baton, but Jenny wasn't here and if Angela knew one thing, it was that there was still a world of other Angela's out there.

A quiet knock on the front door hastened Angela to wrap a robe quickly over herself and creep down the stairs. She switched on the lamp in the hallway not wanting to flood the stairs with light and risk waking Alex who had gone to bed hours ago.

She knew before she opened the door who was standing on her steps. That jaw line and tall lean silhouette was burnt into her memory. Familiar shivers ran down her stomach and she felt immediately guilty. Rushes of heat tingled across her skin as she pulled the door back.

Angela had no idea what happened first. She heard the door shut. She felt James hands push roughly into her soaking wet hair. She was aware of moving backwards rapidly, being pinned against the wall. An urgency of alarm and passion filled every space.

'What's it gonna be Angie,' he breathed into her neck, his face nearly touching hers, but deliberately restrained. 'Do you love me?'

'Yes.' The word came out of Angela's mouth before she had even thought it. 'But please, James you have to listen.'

He pushed his hands up the wall, trapping Angela and trying to control his need to touch her.

'Then let's fix this. Before it's too late. Tell me to go and I won't ever come back, but I have to know.'

His mouth was so close to hers she could feel his breath inside her. Neither of them moved. Angela knew she had to say something. She loved James and she couldn't live without him a day longer, but would he feel the same, once she told him.

She lifted his face to hers and held it between her hands, so close he could have possessed her mouth without a seconds warning. She was shocked to see James had been crying.

'James, I need to tell you something.'

'Angie, I can't pretend I don't love you any more.' He wasn't listening. His eyes looked pained.

'But there's someone you need to know about...'

'I can't be your friend. I need to have all of you. Please tell me you want me.'

And then James was whispering against her face, fierce

involuntary things about how he loved her and how they needed to be together. With every word his mouth grazed her skin with memories of their life together and Angela closed her eyes to pretend this might really be forever.

'Hello.'

Angela lurched away from James and looked towards the voice.

James seemed to stopped breathing and he stared uncomprehendingly at Angela before slowly turning his head to look in the same direction as her.

On the stairs was a three year old boy with a mop of curly brown hair. He had the brightest, greenest eyes. Angela had commented to Bee they were, perhaps, second only to James himself.

'James,' said Angela, pulling herself free and straightening her robe. 'I would like you to meet Alexandru. He likes to be called Alex. He used to live in Romania and he's my son now.'

Chapter 16
May 2001 – ten minutes later

'James. I'm sorry, that must have been a shock?'

James was sitting on the kitchen cabinet nursing a whisky.

'He seems a great kid Angie.'

Angela poured herself a glass of wine. She owed James an explanation but she had no intention of making an apology for Alex. Children had never been on her agenda and she had been utterly unprepared for the torrent of feelings she'd encountered at the orphanage. Shame being the most painful. She'd loved Alex from the moment she had seen him and bringing him here to London was one of the few decisions Angela knew she would never regret.

She sat down at the table and looked down into her glass.

'Alex was abandoned when he was three months old,

left at a state hospital in Romania. He spent two years in institutions, horrendously neglected. He couldn't walk and was speaking less than ten words when I met him.'

Angela paused before adding, 'There was no one to love him.'

She closed her eyes. 'There was no one to love any of them,' she whispered.

Seconds ticked by and James would have given anything to rip the anguish from her face.

'By the time he was two, no-one there wanted to adopt him. New babies come along every day. He became one of the fortunate ones, placed in foster care while I struggled with the red tape. I couldn't leave him James. Every time I went back I loved him more. I denied it at first. Told myself I wasn't the mothering type. And anyway, I was far too busy being me. You know I never wanted kids. But I wanted this one. I ached to see him run and jump, like a normal child. I wanted him to laugh and play but he had such sorrow in his face, like he didn't dare to try.'

Angela looked up at James and let her tears spill. 'Do you know what's seared on my heart forever?'

James almost looked away. Hearing Angela talk about her love for a child with such passion and realising she had taken this on alone, without him, plunged him into an unintelligible pit of admiration, anxiety and self pity.

Angela barely contained a sob as she spoke. 'Despite their sorrow and the fact they'd never been shown love, those children eye's would burst with hope when they looked at you. And when you reached out, they knew how to hold you. They knew instinctively how to love you back. How would they know that? After the life they've had. Does that seem wonderful or all the more wretched for them?'

Loving Alex had torn her open and now she could only sit motionless while James penetrating gaze reached across the kitchen and cut a path through her soul. She wanted him to hold her again, and suddenly more than anything else she wanted them to be a family. The thought hung between them suspended, paralysed, waiting for an answer.

Straightening up and wiping her eyes quickly, Angela regained her composure.

'I know I've been selfish and done exactly what I wanted for a long time.'

She needed to move, she felt slightly sick and uncertain of what James was thinking.

'I haven't always got it right. So busy making plans. But meeting Alex made me realise I've wasted years believing I didn't need anyone. All those years spent thinking the only person who really understood me or that I could depend on, was me. I've missed out on so much. He's shown me I need him, as much as he needs me.'

Angela reached past James towards the fridge for more wine. It took James two seconds to jump off the worktop, grab her elbow and spin her round to face him. Time slowed so that Angela took in every millimetre of his face, his cheekbones, his eyes, his hair, before his mouth bent to hers and kissed her with a passion that overwhelmed her. She pressed against him and let his hands wind through her hair.

Angela didn't open her eyes as James kissed her, preferring to drink in the scent of his body and feel his lips capture her skin. She lost herself in his voice as he spoke with an intensity contrary to the gentle tracing of his lips.

'I am so in love with you. I can't make sense of anything without you. I'm yours Angie, I'm yours.'

James held Angela's face in his hands and she could feel his lancing stare through closed eyelids as she wrapped his words around her.

'Say something Angie,' he demanded, with an almost crazed anguish.

Angela opened her eyes and was immediately trapped and held by James, his stare blazing.

She smiled. 'Take me to bed.'

Chapter 17
June - 2002

Lyme Regis, Dorset

Bee took another batch of cakes out of the oven and set them down with a satisfied thump on the worktop. She heard Kitty saying goodbye to the last of their customers for the day and decided to put the kettle on rather than face the mountain of paperwork in her office.

'Oh god, yes please,' came an exhausted plea from Kitty, hearing the kettle and flopping herself down at one of the tables. Bee smiled. It had been this way for weeks and the summer was still gearing up, showing no signs of any respite.

'Do you think we can do it Bee? I mean really, really do you think we could branch out? It's one thing for everyone else to tell us we should.'

Bee didn't answer immediately. It was the question she

had been asking herself ever since she had taken the brazen step six weeks ago of approaching a couple of big named supermarkets in the local area and pitching her own brand of cakes and pastries. One had loved Bee's baking and having looked at the preliminary business plan Bee had presented to them, they were keen to meet again. There was no doubting that on paper and to Bee's customers the business was becoming a huge success that, with more hard work, could spiral unreservedly upwards. Bee had a passion for creating delicious food and the panache to make her customers feel spoilt and elegant. There was no doubt, professionally, Bee was flying. Paul worried for her whenever he visited. He watched her attempting to cover every detail and serve the most perfect food and knew she bore the hard work like a punishment.

'Don't be ridiculous,' she would snap and then smile fondly. 'I love what I do. Why shouldn't it be hard work? Nothing comes to those who sit around. If I do nothing, I should expect nothing in return.'

Same no nonsense Bee, he thought to himself, at least that would never change.

Bee refused to wallow but, when a quiet moment crept in unwanted, she would feel the shadow of shame and guilt. In front of the customers, in the light, she could almost forget it was there and she convinced herself when she looked in the mirror that it was right she never forget the past. She should always remember, it could all disappear again overnight.

'You deserve the success Bee,' pointed out Kitty, who had noticed a cloud pass over Bee's face.

'*We* deserve the success,' reminded Bee, trying to avoid a discussion on feelings and wanting to remind Kitty of just how important she was to the business... and to Bee.

'So what's stopping you?' Kitty was undaunted.

Bee sighed and cut two large slices of walnut cake.

Kitty waited, stretched her feet out onto a nearby chair, let out a mock yawn and made it obvious she wasn't going anywhere.

'What happens if we supply the supermarkets here?' began Bee.

'Everybody will love you and want more, and then the supermarkets will want to take you national.' Kitty sounded vital and strong, truly excited at the prospect.

'Yes and then let's suppose one, just one, person that remembers me digs the knife in. It will take twenty four hours for the press to destroy us.'

Kitty reached across the table and touched Bee's hand.

'Why not just stick with what we have?' said Bee. 'It works, people love it, we love it. Perhaps it's just greedy to want more.' She felt like an expert as she shuddered, remembering the excess of her old life.

'Because Bee,' assured Kitty gently, 'You and I both know this isn't about greed. You deserve to take this further and see it be a success. You deserve to be happy and feel good about yourself. It's time to stop punishing yourself.'

Bee looked across at Kitty and smiled. Kitty seemed so together and content at the moment and had never looked more beautiful. It suddenly occurred to her that she might be holding Kitty back. It seemed hard to remember the girls they were when they first met. Bee so determined that she would marry big and never have to work but now, through perverse circumstance, exhausted and fulfilled at the end of every day. And Kitty, so uninhibited and naive, now by her side with such poise and flair with their customers.

'Anyway, you know what Paul thinks?' Kitty's voice almost made Bee jump. 'He says you should milk the notoriety and turn it to your advantage, rather than run from it.'

'Well it's not Paul that has to live with knowing there are lives ruined out there. I think enough money has been made out of innocent people.'

Bee was about to get cross and moan about Paul but an idea sprung into her head.

'Why don't you do it Kits?'

'Do what?'

'Why don't we make you the face of the baking?'

Kitty opened her eyes in horror and stared at Bee.

'We don't have to change the name of the products, but we put your gorgeous face on any publicity shots.'

Kitty continued to stare horrified.

'You run the shop floor most of the time anyway and everyone loves you. Come on Kit, why use me, when we have the blonde, exquisite you!'

Kitty threw her hands up at Bee and laughed. It was true that over the last few months she was finally starting to feel like the girl she once thought she was. Ironically, that was in no small part due to Greg, who's repeated attempts to convince Kitty that she needed him and would never be happy without him seemed to reinforce Kitty's resolve to avoid him and any man like him. That's not to say she didn't have admirers, in fact, she had several. Bee was always teasing her about the amount of coffee and cake they sold to men and Bee was also convinced that some of the men coming to the shop were borrowing children from family and friends to allow them to sit and listen to Kitty in the reading corner. Kitty had started to enjoy going out again and although you wouldn't find her at wild parties or dancing till dawn, she was definitely the belle of the ball. Bee knew Kitty had turned down at least two proposals in the last year. Kitty had never confided that she thought about Paul all the time. There was nothing wrong with any of the men she went out with but they would never be Paul.

Lurking and picking at her just below the surface of conscious thought was the knowledge that Paul knew so much about her. How could he ever love her, when she found it so hard to love herself? Kitty found it easier to be the girl she used to be with people who knew nothing about her. It was too scary to be with someone who knew everything about you and still loved you. Having to face, every day, who you really are. It would be like having a permanent stone in your shoe. She would rather start over with a stranger. Except none of them matched up to Paul. Bee never mentioned Paul's love life and Kitty didn't ask, she assumed he had someone and that was that. They had found their former easy manner of being together when Paul visited and Kitty hoped she didn't sit too close or laugh too much. She worked hard to force the disappointment away, when his visits ended and he returned to London.

Bee was about to respond to Kitty's disdain when the phone rang.

'Good evening, Bee's Knees,' sang Kitty, in a bright professional voice.

'Oh hi Paul. How's things?'

Bee watched as the colour drained from Kitty's face. She saw all her muscles fall simultaneously down, like watching the batteries die in a toy. She rushed around to the other side of the table just as the phone fell from

Kitty's hand.

*

'I'm coming with you Kitty.' Bee was forthright, but spoke gently.

'What about the kids?' answered Kitty, dazed and shoving clothes into a bag with no real regard for which items she was picking up.

'I'll drop them off with Mum. She's at the cottage.' There was no way Bee was going to be dissuaded. 'Besides, you are in no fit state to drive.'

Bee placed her hand over Kitty's and held it there. She had never mastered the touchy feely midas touch of her friend but she knew their friendship was deep enough now that the simple gesture would be understood.

'I'm fine,' lied Kitty, every word she spoke an effort that made her nauseous. 'It's Holly we need to worry about.' She turned Bee's hand over and squeezed it, before turning away calmly and walking out the room with an empty look in her eyes.

*

Bee tried desperately to pull Kitty into a conversation throughout the drive to London, but Kitty remained detached and silent. Any subject would have sufficed, just to make sure she was being rational. She had no idea how Kitty would react when they arrived and she was frightened that Kitty was returning somewhere dark and unreachable.

'You might need a referee Kits,' Bee mentioned lightly. 'It's been a while since Paul and James were in the same room.'

'Hmm,' mumbled Kitty.

'Paul only rang because he cares about you, you know that don't you? He's probably going to get into trouble now, if they find out at work that he told you.'

Bee immediately winced to herself as she realised what she'd said. Talk about insensitive.

Kitty sighed heavily, shivering and closing her eyes at the same time. It had been incredibly kind of Paul to think about her straight away, and he had sounded so gentle and considerate but that didn't stop Kitty feeling saturated with humiliation and confusion. She re-lived snatches of his words over and over during the four hour journey.

'I wanted you to hear it from me Kitty.'

'Your father told us Holly stabbed him. At the surgery. She's not been arrested yet, but we will have to ... talk to her.'

'He's likely to be in hospital for at least a week.'

'I'm sorry you have to hear this Kitty.'

'Holly was trying to protect her sister. From ...your father.'

'It may not be the first time.'

Bee had to wait until she had paid for fuel before Kitty spoke again.

'Where is Holly right now? Is she at home with Angie and James?'

Kitty spoke quietly but with a determination that frightened Bee. Bee had assumed she would want to go to her father's bedside and see how bad his injuries were. She herself would not have gone to see him, if she were in Kitty's place, not after so many years and the appalling way he'd behaved when Kitty had needed him, but Bee was starting to realise she had misjudged her friend. She'd texted Angela, from the queue at the petrol station, to give an arrival time and found herself typing that she had no idea what Kitty planned to do. She now considered the possibility that Kitty would show no sympathy towards her father. After all, she'd not spoken to him for so long why should he expect an open arm reunion. What Bee hadn't considered or even registered was Kitty and Holly in the same room.

'Um Yes. But...'

'Then take me there please Bee. I want to see Holly and Freya.'

Freya, Holly's sister, thought Bee. She had not seen her for some time. She was only eleven. Bee felt queasy.

'Are you listening Bee? That's where I need to be.' Kitty's tone was resolute and, Bee decided, not to be argued with.

The miles passed in silence. But whilst it seemed to be deafening for Bee, weighing heavy against her chest, each mile seemed to clear Kitty's head and straighten her spine. By the time they reached London, Kitty looked indomitable and Bee exhausted.

*

Bayswater, London

'Are you sure this is a good idea Kitty? Don't you think you should take a step back and find out some more facts from Paul first?'

Bee was annoyed with herself for not speaking up sooner and the resolute expression Kitty wore was now so watertight Bee was convinced this would not end well.

They were standing at the front door to the house Angela and James had bought together in the Spring. James had been reluctant to get something so big but had conceded that with Alex, Holly and Freya now living with them, they needed space. In another life Bee would have admired the clean, leafy streets and perfect paintwork but instead she grabbed Kitty's arm gently and pleaded with her.

'Kits. What are you going to do? Please. Let's just stop and think about this.'

As the door opened and James stepped aside to invite them in, Kitty tugged her arm free from Bee.

'There's nothing to think about Bee. Nothing. I know exactly what needs to be done.'

*

The living room fell silent. The scene in front of Kitty should have been a sudden shock of deja-vu, but instead, it was merely a spectacle that had replayed a thousand times behind her closed eyes. Kitty stood motionless and watched James return to where Angela sat holding Holly's hands. James looked hollow, distant eyes framed with darkness. Angela glanced helplessly around the room and then up at Kitty, looking for words to reveal themselves.

There was an air of desperation, grief and anger swirling towards Kitty but she pulled a deep breath in, unafraid and undaunted. Holly leapt to her feet when she saw Kitty and pushed Angela's hand away when she tried to stop her. She looked frail and scared but oddly strong and defiant at the same time.

'Kitty. I'm sorry. I'm so sorry about all this. But I couldn't stand it. It's my fault..'

Mascaraed tears were speeding down Holly's face, but Kitty cut her dead before she could finish.

'Don't you dare.' The words fell out of Kitty's mouth, in a rush to silence Holly.

As she spoke, loudly and clearly, she rushed at Holly and a shiver went through the entire group watching.

'Don't you dare say sorry. Don't ever, ever say this is your fault.'

As her arms enveloped Holly and folded the sobbing body against her own, she felt the weight not only of Holly's tired bones but of humiliation and guilt. Nobody could change the way Kitty's father had reacted to her own attack but now, as Holly balanced on the edge of the rest of her life, Kitty knew she could pull her away from a cliff edge of self destruction. And for the first time in years, Kitty felt free.

It must have been ten minutes before Kitty or Holly spoke again and when they did neither let go of the other.

'But this is my fault,' started Holly.

'No, it is most definitely not Holly,' reprimanded Kitty.

'But he got away with it before, so why wouldn't he move on to someone else when I got older? How could I have been so stupid? Not to realise he would move on to Freya.' Holly struggled to catch her breath, as she stifled sobs through her determination to get the words out.

'There is nothing to excuse him Holly,' soothed Kitty. She was astounded at how complete her detachment from her father was. 'He was the doctor all the parents loved. Always had time for the kids and never minded house calls. There weren't many parents when I was growing up that didn't consider him a friend.' A shiver of horror ran down Kitty's back.

Holly looked over to James, a new stab of guilt that she had never found the courage to tell her foster mum about the doctor.

'He betrayed everyone's trust,' reassured Kitty, finally pulling back from Holly but staying close and holding her hands. 'What happened to me spoilt my view of myself and ruined my relationships with everyone around me. The attack filled me with shame. Don't let that happen to you Holly.'

Holly stared at the floor.

'You were young, an easy target to manipulate. People like that make you think everything is your doing.' Kitty spoke softly, and felt a calmness not suited to the situation, as she took comfort in believing her own words.

Holly took a deep breath. 'When I was little I liked the people who would pay me compliments and say what I wanted to hear. I craved attention. But I didn't ask him to touch me, I promise. I felt grateful for the love of my foster family but,' she looked over at James guiltily, 'I wondered why my own mum couldn't love me.'

'You didn't ask for this to happen to you Holly. You need to understand that he is the sick one.' Kitty paused, as she realised how easy this was to say and how undeniably true it was. This man was no longer her father.

'He seemed kind and interested in me,' whispered Holly. 'I liked that. So how could I tell anyone what he was doing when I had craved some attention.' Holly's mouth was twisted with shame and despair.

'But Holly you were so little. Don't let this define you,' begged Kitty. 'Don't waste years of your life searching for the why, blaming yourself and being a victim in every relationship.' Kitty looked into Holly's face and smiled, 'In a nutshell Holly...don't be me,' she offered kindly and with a trace of humour that made Holly stop crying and look earnestly at Kitty.

'I don't think I was the only one. It's just a feeling I have. He was too nice to all the girls, so involved in our lives, so interested. With me it was just touching and he told me it wasn't wrong and I should just let him. As I got older, well...I just knew it wasn't right.'

Kitty's heart sank as she realised Holly was almost certainly right. Her father's friendship with Charles Dunbar, his reluctance to believe or support her when she was attacked. Depressingly, Kitty and Angela both knew from listening to women in the shelter that repulsive patterns and vile covert activity were a reality that most people would be grateful to stay completely ignorant of. Nobody wanted it in their back yard.

'But it was me Kitty. I stabbed him. I am going to tell Paul the truth or whoever turns up here for me. I couldn't let him touch Freya. You see that don't you? She's just eleven.'

Kitty winced. Fond memories, long forgotten of gentle father daughter moments interrupted her vision. Had she ever been safe she suddenly wondered, around him, around his friends. The final threads of hope to ever call him father again dissolved.

Everyone's attention was violently forced to James. as

his fist punched through the living room door.

'James,' cried Angela, rushing from the sofa towards him.

'Why did I not see this happening?' yelled James at the newly formed hole. 'For Christ sake, we were supposed to be keeping her safe. Taking her away from a life like that.'

An undulating rage was visible on James face.

'It was my idea to change doctors, to someone we knew,' he stormed before wincing and adding, 'Someone we trusted.'

Angela pressed her hand on James back and rubbed gently.

'If we are going to place blame then look at me too,' she offered, trying to calm the untamed power she could feel running through him.

'I left Freya in the surgery with him. I needed to make an appointment with the nurse and he told me to just pop out and leave Freya with him. I trusted him too.'

Angela felt sick as she recalled in her mind the moment Holly had come into the surgery.

'Sorry I'm late Ange. Where's Freya? What doctor is she with? Did you leave her in there on her own?'

Holly's voice had escalated steadily towards banshee. Not at Angela, at everyone, anyone. Angela had not had the chance to answer as Holly had burned through reception and thrown herself into the room bearing the name of her own tormentor. What Holly had found there had been enough to make her pick up scissors from the desk and plunge them with utter and complete vindication into the side of Kitty's father.

A knock on the door jolted everyone away from their thoughts. Paul walked into the living room, dressed for Police business and wearing an expression of professional aloof spread thinly over sadness. Everyone breathed again, before the now familiar feeling of nausea resumed its position.

It was Kitty that spoke first, clear-cut and fierce, addressing not just the room but herself.

'Let us all be very clear here. You can roll this over and over, you can pick out the way each of us is to blame. Holly could have told someone. Angela could have been less trusting. James could have been more observant, but really there is only one person to blame. And you all know who that man is.'

Kitty took a moment to look at each of them and nod her acceptance. Strangely, and despite subconsciously searching for it, she didn't feel anger but she was resolute and unwavering. They couldn't change what Holly had been through but they could give her the one thing Kitty never had from her parents.

'There is only one thing you can do right now, if you really want to help Holly. Stop thinking about yourselves and make sure the right person is punished. Make sure the right person *feels* punished.'

The friends all stared at Kitty. Angela felt ashamed that she had never respected the driving force Kitty had within her. Ridiculous really, thought Angela, when you consider what she has faced. She felt humbled at the reminder that not all victories have to be grandiose or dramatic. Bee beamed at Kitty and blew her a silent kiss.

It was Bee that spoke next.

'Paul, I guess you want to have a chat with Holly and you don't need me here, so how about I make us all a drink?' she ventured supportively.

'Thanks Bee, that'd be great,' replied Paul, smiling reassuringly at Holly.

Suddenly remembering James, Paul turned and regained his official stance.

'Would it be acceptable to you and Angie if I come in and speak with Holly? You will, of course, be here with her and whilst I'm sure she may have to come to the station that will be with my female colleagues.'

James remained silent.

'Let me also say in cases like these, as word gets out,

more victims,' Paul winced inside at his choice of words, 'Um more people, tend to come forward with their own experiences, which will naturally make it easier to get a conviction for ..,' Paul stole a glance at Kitty, who didn't waver. 'Well just to say Holly, your bravery over the next few days by telling us as much as you can, will give strength and hope to other people who haven't yet found the same courage.'

Angela knew Paul was probably reciting, but she also knew he would have meant every word. She wanted to hug him but his uniform and the palpable pressure and unease between him and James kept her stationary. Instead she sought out James hand and said decisively,

'Thank you Paul. You are really welcome here and please, please let us know whatever you need, whatever Holly needs. Right James?'

Angela squeezed James hand tightly and bored a hole in the side of his face with her gaze.

'Sure.' he said, looking Paul squarely in the eyes for the first time.

*

Two hours passed before Paul's colleagues arrived to take Holly to the police station. Holly had spent the time motionless on the sofa flanked by Angela and Kitty, while Bee had taken refuge in cooking and making coffee. Paul had busied himself making phone calls and reassuring Holly that she wasn't under arrest and she would receive a supportive ear when she was questioned. Paul had no idea where James had gone and assumed he was somewhere in the house avoiding having to talk to him.

'Paul, can you stay here and wait for Freya? She's due back soon.' asked Angela, putting on a coat ready to follow Holly and two police women out the door. 'She wanted to go to a friends sleepover last night. I was torn between keeping her with me and trying to keep her world normal. I hope I did the right thing.'

'What about James?' answered Paul, with a hint of boldness. 'I'm not sure he wants me in his house and I'm certainly not ready to spend time bonding with him.'

Angela paused and Paul could feel her sigh from across the room.

'He's gone to see his mum,' she explained carefully, covering her hurt. 'She's a bit frail these days and he wanted to check on her, make sure she hears the truth and not gossip or lies about Holly. The reality of what's happened is horrendous enough without dumping more injury and regret on top. To be frank, he's worried about what this will do to her. He'll meet me at the station in a bit.'

Angela closed her eyes and exhaled, trying desperately to catch and pull back rising anger. An overload of emotions she knew but, none the less, real and about to run untethered from her mouth.

When she opened them she saw Kitty was standing next to Paul barely touching him but close enough to feel the safety he radiated. Angela was reminded of how Paul had found Kitty all those years ago in a hallway, not dissimilar to this one and held her for hours. Watching the two of them standing together, older but still somehow fused, softened Angela and she longed for the days when all you could hear was James and Paul poking and prodding each other with insults and laughter.

'Talking of gossip and lies Paul.' Angela took a deep breath. 'James didn't sleep with Kim.'

Paul was rooted to the spot, wanting to turn around but unable to move. He felt himself lean closer to Kitty.

'I know it's his word against hers and I know James has never tried to explain this to you. But you need to hear this from someone. I don't expect you to thank him for this, but he decided to accept the blame and not tell you the truth. Perhaps he thought you and Kim might get back together and he didn't want you thinking badly of her. I don't know. Look, whatever you think of James, you just need to know he didn't sleep with Kim. She made it up.'

Angela spoke confidently and gave a compassionate, thoughtful smile as she turned to leave.

'Oh and by the way, stay as long as you want and help yourselves to anything you like.'

*

Kitty felt so normal sitting at the kitchen table eating with Paul that it was actually unsettling.

To realise there was no need for impressive chatter was liberating and that understanding seemed to bring them closer, until their minds seemed to be touching. Instead of noisy, awkward silence they had a rich wordless communion.

'Do you ever think about getting married?' It was Kitty that spoke, as Paul cleared their plates and loaded them into the dishwasher.

'Well,' he responded, with a mock serious expression, 'That would require us both to be under the influence of an insane passion, and she would be required to behave in that abnormal, and completely exhausting manner until death do us part!'

Paul looked up and winked at Kitty as her laugh rang around the kitchen.

'Bet you don't feel the need to be married ever again do you Kits?'

It was a question that made her sit up a little straighter.

'Why would you say that?' She was genuinely interested to hear what Paul had to say about her.

'In a good way. I mean look at you. You've had a crap time and come through it. Don't you ever stop and look back at how far you've come. You've got the business to run with Bee and ... well ... Kitty, you are a wonder.' Paul spoke with genuine admiration and Kitty loved him all over again for it. The man who had seen it all, knew the worst of her but chose to honour the best.

Kitty didn't have a suitable response. No, she didn't believe any man would make her want to marry again. But surely that was a reflection on her wounds and barriers rather than her strength and independence. Then again, why would she marry anyone other than Paul? So she said nothing.

'I should get going soon,' he said gently, a few minutes later.

'Or,' he ventured, 'I could sit here with you until they get back, if you want the company?'

Kitty nodded.

Paul watched her sitting with her knees pulled up under her chin. He could see the closure tonight had given her but the scars where there, thin and easily re-opened.

'Come here,' he said plainly but with a fierce edge that made Kitty want to be in his arms just to feel his body against her.

He took the hand she'd extended and pulled her against him. And then he simply held her.

His body felt different than before. It was still secure and warm but the hard lines in his arms and back caused a shiver to cavort wildly down Kitty.

Assuming the shiver to be events of the last twelve hours catching up with Kitty, Paul whispered against her hair, 'I know.'

Just that. Not 'don't worry,' or 'everything's going to be all right', just 'I know.' His voice was warm, inviting her to drown.

Neither knew how long they stayed like this but it was long enough for them both to feel one chapter of their lives ending and a new one begin.

Kitty pressed herself against him, winding one hand across his back. Paul pulled back, brushing cheeks with Kitty and taking her face in his hands. She stared unapologetically at him, searching his eyes. She could see pain and longing, so intense that whilst she could hardly bear to look at him she was locked in and couldn't look away.

Seconds passed and Kitty edged her chin forward in his hands, reaching out. She started to feel the friction from his bottom lip as he breathed. She twisted the back of his shirt in her hand, a futile attempt to steady her breathing. Then his lips were on hers, gently at first, pulling at her mouth until he was sure this was what she wanted. Kitty responded and lost herself completely with the man who had loved her for a very long time.

Chapter 18
April - 2003

Bayswater, London

Bee and Kitty shivered at the same time as they settled into the back of the cab and headed towards Hyde Park and on to Angela and James house. Months of planning and grafting had led up to today; the official national launch of their home baked cakes, scones and pies. Despite their elation and pride at how well the press meeting and unveiling of their first advertisement had gone, both smiled secretly at each other knowing they couldn't wait to get to Angela's and kick off their shoes.

'You were both incredible back there,' laughed Paul as he lurched into the cab rubbing his hands together. It had felt like winter for months. Bee had grown used to living by fairy light in her cocoon of oven warmth and steamy windows.

'See I knew it would work Kits. Me wielding the palette knife and you charming the suits.'

Bee winked at Paul and sat back. She was happy with her life and very proud of what she'd achieved, not least her two gorgeous children waiting for her at Angela's. She rolled her eyes in mock despair as Paul and Kitty cuddled up and kissed across from her. Bee wondered if it was Paul feeding Kitty's confidence or their challenging venture. Not that it really mattered, the important part was, it was there and Kitty was embracing it. Bee felt her own ghost of self doubt creep around her. It usually caught up with her in moments where she'd forgotten how far she had come but this morning she'd felt it there right beside her when she walked into the conference room, a cold judgemental presence reminding her how easily life can change.

'Bee, can you talk to your brother? He's being an idiot again,' Kitty's voice demanded a response and Bee pushed the demons back into their hidey hole.

Paul raised his hands in mock submission but his voice held assertion and frustration.

'I just don't want there to be any trouble today. It's a day of happiness and celebration and I expect Angie has told James he has to tolerate me in the house.'

'Paul, when is this going to stop?' questioned Bee, looking wearily at her brother.

'OK. OK!' His hands went up again in surrender. 'There's enough of us there, I can probably avoid being on my own with him anyway, and I promise no trouble from me.'

Paul kissed Kitty lightly on the nose, as if to seal the deal and then turned and looked out at the park. The sun was moving slowly in the sky and throwing a weak but determined warmth on the frost bitten buds of spring.

*

Fifteen minutes later, Bee was exactly where she wanted to be. High heels off, enveloped by friends and hugging her precious babies. Actually, she found she was being bundled by not just Amanda and Joseph, but by Alex and Freya too and she screeched in mock horror as they climbed all over her and argued about which one of her cakes was the best.

'Not long now, till the big day Kits,' smiled Angela, handing Kitty a glass of champagne. She couldn't wait to hear all about the planning but also wanted to distract Kitty, who she noticed was looking at the gaggle of children with a trace of sadness.

'I know!' squealed Kitty, decisively moving her gaze towards Angela. 'We can't wait. It will be perfect. And this time I get all of you there with me.'

'Has Paul got a best man yet?' Angela made sure Paul was out of ear shot before she asked.

'No,' complained Kitty, 'I wish those two would make up. I don't think either of them can remember who started it now and I don't know what's worse; when they couldn't be left in the same room together or this stand off in plain sight?'

An afternoon of eating and drinking floated away lazily, with the children practising for the wedding in front of the casually strewn adults. Amanda was in her element, organising the younger children and making sure they didn't miss a line or forget a step.

'Look, she even has a list,' whispered James to Angela, his eyes dancing with amusement, 'Wonder where she gets that from?' he said more loudly, winking at Bee as he drained his glass.

'Thank you James,' chastised Bee fondly, not sure whether to be offended at his comment or secretly pleased at her daughter's budding organisational skills. 'Your comments have been noted and there will be no cakes with lemon frosting and yellow fluffy chicks delivered here this Easter.'

James' bottom lip pouted and then arched into a wide smile as Alex stood with his hands on his hips pretending to look cross with James.

'Sorry buddy,' laughed James as Alex jumped closer and playfully grabbed James ears.

Angela slapped James lightly across the arm and moved to pick up the bottle of champagne.

'Time to refill glasses people, I have a toast to make.'

'It's not going to be one of your long corporate

presentations is it Ange?' called out Paul, 'Kits and I have a wedding to get to in December.'

Angela shot Paul a glare and then poked her tongue out. Kitty was transported back to a time when Paul and James would have been sparring off each other like brothers. Private conspirators oblivious to the outside world. Now, she thought sadly, they were throwing their comments into the room like little lost olive branches.

'Hang on. Wait for me.' The plea came singing brightly from the hallway above the sound of the door slamming.

'Sorry I'm late.' Holly threw herself down on a sofa next to Kitty and lent deliberately into her. Kitty gazed with warmth and understanding at the young woman and felt a rush of tears gathering at the simple gesture.

'To our lovely, beautiful ladies Bee and Kitty,' started Angela, and Kitty bolted back to the present at the mention of her name,

'I hope you are as proud of yourselves, as we are of you.'

Bee looked anxiously at the floor and then back at Angela, who raised her glass and one eyebrow at Bee.

'Sometimes you breeze through life. But most times you don't. It's the decision to get up and triumph and never look back that defines you. And I don't know two worthier women to celebrate triumph with right now.'

Cheers filled the room.

'I would not be the woman I am today, without your love,' continued Angela, 'I don't want either of you to ever underestimate how important you are to every person in this room. What you have achieved, against the odds, is incredible and who you are is inspirational. Not just to me, but to these gorgeous children. Never, never forget how loved you are.' Angela paused to compose herself, and then finished, 'So please, raise your glasses to our gorgeous ladies, Bee and Kitty. And to each other...always.'

More cheers sung around the room, before James cut in with perfect comic timing,

'I think I'm gonna cry.'

Even Paul laughed, despite himself.

Eventually, everyone settled down with their drink to watch Amanda's planned entertainment for the wedding reception. Bee allowed herself a moment of pity, watching her confident, funny daughter orchestrate the singing and dancing, knowing Bob was missing each moment of joy. She wondered if he ever contemplated his own loss, or Bee's sadness at never having anyone to share each triumph and hurdle with.

As the light faded outside, Angela went across to the window to close the curtains. The atmosphere inside was warm and secure and seeing the dusk creeping in made her feel vulnerable and exposed. She noticed movement just beyond the front garden.

'James, can you pop over here a minute?' she tried to make her voice sound light and calm but her stomach was already shifting uncomfortably.

'Look at the end of the path,' she tried to whisper. 'There's someone out there, hanging about by the gate.'

'Stay here. I'll deal with it,' James replied knowingly and he turned and paced towards the hallway.

Fuelled by an afternoon of slow, steady drinking, it only took the ten second walk from the living room to the front door for James to ready himself for conflict. He opened the door and stepped boldly towards the visitor.

'What the hell do you think you're doing here?' he spat, somewhere between a whisper and a threat. 'Don't you know when enough is enough?'

Kimberly swung round to find herself just inches from James face. She lifted her chin in challenge, flicked back her blonde hair and smiled just a little too sweetly.

'We didn't get the kind of story our readers really want at the press conference this morning, much too foody and friendly and,' she pouted slightly and blinked slowly, 'I hoped as we're old friends, that Bee would give us an exclusive interview. Our readers love a story of riches to rags to riches.' Kimberly could barely contain her jealousy and the last single sentence carried all her resentment. 'I've got plenty of Bob's friends lined up ready to talk about Bee's new life.'

James could feel the acid dripping from her voice and as Kimberly lent in towards him he got a whiff of her perfume. Dark, sweet and heavy, reserved for seductive evenings.

'You really are a prize...' Paul flew down the path but didn't get to finish the sentence. Faces had appeared at the open front door and at the window.

'Look. The kids!' shouted a photographer, coming to life at the foot of the garden, throwing down his cigarette and lurching with his camera towards the open door, where four children jostled to see what was happening outside.

In that split second before the camera flashed, James shoved the photographer so hard he stumbled and crashed against a wall. Sprawled on the ground, James stared at him, the menace and intent clear.

'You.. leave.. our.. children.. alone,' he raged into the face in front of him, holding the crumpled man down with his arm under his chin. The crushed face started to contort and change colour as James' anger weaved erratically towards the summit.

'James, let him up. I think they've got the message.' It was the first time James could recall Paul addressing him directly in such a long time, that his face snapped round, his eyes still full of anger. Paul held his gaze and nodded reassuringly, understanding, and finally James loosened his grip.

'Besides,' said Paul, pulling a badge from his pocket, 'I'm sure there is something I can arrest him for.' He turned to face Kimberly, 'I don't want to see you here ever again. In fact, if any of us see you again, you'll be the next one arrested.'

Kimberly ran her hand through her hair and sneered towards Bee, Kitty and Angela, who had watched the circus unfurl through the window.

'What have any of them got that I haven't? They can stare all they want at me. Wait till I tell Bob about this. Bob won't let you, or any of them, treat me like this.'

The air smouldered with envy and a fury weighed down by its own density.

James stared with contempt at Kimberly as she climbed defiantly into her car. He didn't even glance at Paul as he took off back into the house but smiled secretly at their teamwork as he heard the crunch of the camera under Paul's boot. He hadn't needed Paul to stop him or at least he didn't think he had, but he was not unhappy that Paul had done it.

Paul stood at the gate and watched the car leave perplexed and with an uneasy outbreak of panic in his stomach. What did she mean about telling Bob? Telling

Bob what exactly? That she was mad at James for being with Angela? Yes he got why she would be mad about that. Mad at him for being with Kitty? Possible but unlikely. And what exactly would she be mad at Bee for? And why did she feel the need to tell Bob?

*

It was several weeks later that Kitty found herself unable to keep quiet any longer about the situation between Paul and James. The wedding was approaching in a little over six months and she couldn't bear to think that James might not be there. She wanted to believe that, deep in his heart, Paul felt the same way. The incident outside Angela's house had convinced her they could move forward, it was just a question of when she should bring the subject up.

That moment presented itself after a wonderful day of viewing cottages around Lyme Regis. Paul was waiting for a transfer to one of the larger towns in Dorset and seemed very upbeat about the future. He was visibly relaxed, lying on top of the bed in Kitty's small cottage, counting down the days until the end of commuting. Kitty laid down and twined her legs around Paul, as they made plans for the future and laughed that there was once a time they could never have lived without London's non stop breathing and glare. Now Kitty wasn't sure she could live without the dark.

'Did Ange mention to you, there is one more international job they want her to do?'

'Yes, but only briefly,' muttered Kitty, realising this was the moment, 'Wonder how James will take it? Do you think he will go with her? They're a family now.'

'He'll go,' said Paul firmly but with no trace of anger or resentment in his voice. 'He once told me how much he regretted losing Ange. He won't lose her again.'

It was now or never.

'You were so close Paul. What's stopping you calling him? Everyone misses you both, the way you used to be and I think you do too.'

She lent up on her elbow and fixed a loving but steely gaze on Paul. She ruffled his sandy hair with her free hand but remained otherwise still and poised. Several minutes passed in an intense but comfortable silence.

When Paul finally spoke he gave the only explanation he had.

'It's like it needs to be marked somehow, the betrayal I mean. I don't know but it's like it needs to be remembered, suffered. And there's nothing else there. Just anger. I don't even know why I need to mark it. I thought I loved her, but I was just filling a hole, I was just trying to... trying to not love you.'

Paul stopped, smiled at Kitty and then playfully jumped

on her and started kissing her. It was Kitty that broke away first.

'You know of course that your anger isn't hurting her in the slightest?' ventured Kitty, cautiously at first but she finished the question with a tinge of anger in her tone. The woman enraged her.

'I know,' replied Paul sadly, 'But if you take away my anger, what's left? I mean, what's left to mark how I feel?'

Kitty took Paul's face in her hands and kissed his lips gently.

'A friend. That's what you have left. You have a friend.' She spoke against his lips, 'And your integrity, and the best kind of revenge on Kim. The revenge where you picked yourself up and moved on and got happy, the happiest you could ever imagine.

She kissed him again.

'So let it go Paul, just let it go.'

Chapter 19
December - 2003

City of London

*From the offices of Brown and Lawton Solicitors
Divorce and Family Lawyers
on behalf of Ms Bee Brooks-Jackson*

Bob,
As you can see from the accompanying paperwork, our divorce is now final.
I haven't decided what to do about my name yet. I would like to revert to Jackson, but clearly this affects the children and changing their name requires your consent. Please think about this. I enclose, as requested, some recent photographs of the children.
Bee.

Bee read the words one last time and handed the piece of paper to Lloyd Brown, who smiled kindly.

'Thank you Lloyd. For sending this for me.'

'Bee, you know I'm here for you. Any advice you need.' And then with a gentle formality he added, 'Copies of all the paperwork will be sent first class to Dorset this afternoon. Now get yourself back down there before you miss that wedding and please give our best to Kitty and your brother.'

Bee smiled sadly as she got up. It was such a special day for Paul and Kitty and she wanted to be happy, but writing even those few short words to Bob was exhausting. She had no idea how to address him any more or what to say. She couldn't bring herself to deny him pictures of their children, but couldn't work out why he deserved to have them either. She sometimes thought she still loved Bob, after all, how could you just stop loving someone? But then she'd remember her marriage was a lie and the Bob she loved was an illusion. Just like Charles Dunbar's widow, she often thought to herself. The crushing irony was not lost on her. It would stab her every time, a fresh wound. Today of all days, she wanted peace but somehow she'd denied herself again. Bee was still unsure if Bob felt guilt or remorse or just an injustice at not getting away with it. He seemed to know he deserved his punishment and he accepted Bee's fury. Bee hated that it was hard to stay angry with a man whose destruction was now total.

'By the way, pick up a copy of London Life on your way out of town,' mentioned Lloyd as Bee extended her hand to take his already offered. 'Another great advert for you and Kitty in there this week. Great things are coming your way Bee.'

Greenwich, London

Bob,
Thank you for your last letter, it's so good to hear from you. Mum and Dad send their good wishes to you and want you to know they will always welcome you. So will I. I know I have told you this a million times, but I have always admired you. I haven't always gone the right way about getting close to you, but I want to change that now ...

Kimberly paused, tapping the end of her pen impatiently against her face as she pondered what to write next. She needed to think about how to word this, after all, Bob was a man with class and style. He might not like to hear her disparaging Bee, so perhaps she wouldn't do that, not this time anyway. She could leave that until they were closer. Once he saw he could rely on her, she would show him what a waste of time Bee and her friends were. His money and his lifestyle could have been hers and, she was sure, would have been hers in time - if he hadn't met Bee. It wasn't right that he wouldn't benefit from Bee's new business. They were still married when Bee set the whole thing up, she reasoned to herself. Perhaps she should drive down there and remind Bee that Bob deserved more. After all, she needed to look after their future, hers and Bobs. She looked at the open copy of London Life next to her, looked at a radiant Kitty beaming back at her and twisted her mouth into open loathing.

Whitechapel, London

'Hey Jimmy,' called a gruff voice from behind the bar.

Jimmy looked up from the beer he'd been nursing. 'What?'

'You seen this? Isn't it Brooks' old lady that runs this little number?' He held up the magazine to show Jimmy. 'She done OK out of him, hiding herself away in the country, while you did time.' There was an obvious mocking tone to his voice.

Jimmy drained the end of his pint and pushed it roughly across the sticky bar for a refill. The last thing he needed right now was to be reminded of how well Bob Brooks wife was doing when he had nothing.

'Gotta admire her eh?' scoffed the barman airily, further aggravating Jimmy. He tossed the magazine on the bar and forgot about it instantly.

Jimmy cast a gaze at the front cover and decided in that instant that he deserved more. Much more.

Chapter 20
December - 2003

Grassmere House Hotel near Lulworth, Dorset

'It's time.' James slapped Paul gently on the back as he approached him. Both men were dressed in matching dark grey morning coats with dove grey waistcoats over their white shirts. The rich red of their ties and single buttonhole rose softened their angular, hard lines. Paul, now used to a uniform, looked as at ease as James looked uncomfortable.

The Autumn had given way easily to a sharp, crisp December. Most days started with a frost that stayed effortlessly until lunch time and the sky was ghostly pale, waiting for any excuse to drop snow across the west and ice the landscape.

Paul looked out across the lawns one last time and then turned back to the wood panelled lobby. He eyed the double doors that led to the large sitting room, now decked out in deep red poinsettia flowers, white roses and holly. The fragrance wafting through was subtle and perfect.

'Ready?' he asked James, who looked more nervous than Paul.

James started to smile. 'Let's get it done, so I can undo this tie,' he replied playfully, turning away.

Paul grabbed his arm. 'James. Thank you.' He nodded, acknowledging James, and the edges of his lips lifted in genuine affection. 'I can't imagine you not being here with me.'

'I had to say yes,' smiled James, 'There's a room full of police in there, not to mention your sister, when she arrives, who is quite frankly scarier than the lot of them.'

Paul gave James a playful pat on the cheek and the hand shake that followed turned into a hug, which lasted mere seconds but held so much love, friendship and reconciliation that both men looked overwhelmed.

It had been an airy August evening when Paul had sat waiting for James at their old haunt in the heart of the West End. James had been late and Paul had sat alone, on their familiar oak bench, pondering on being stood up. Holly had taken the message when Paul had called James, so perhaps James had no intention of coming. When James finally hurtled in thirty minutes later he was genuinely surprised and relieved to see Paul still there. He hadn't expected him to wait, but then he had no idea why Paul had asked to meet.

That evening Paul had listened to James side of the story but, contrarily and unexpectedly, the facts held no influence over him. As he'd relaxed into James company and immersed himself in the depth of their friendship, the words themselves were no longer important. The complete and honest respect and affection he could feel radiating from James, both that evening and now standing here, made Paul feel ashamed that he had judged so quickly and so badly.

He was pulled back to the present, realising what James had just said.

'Is Bee still not here?'

'No. I've called her and she is on her way but she's had a nightmare with two blown out tyres.'

Paul frowned and checked his watch.

'I'll call her again in half an hour. She'll be here, don't worry.'

'We can't start yet, she has to be here.' Paul was adamant and James was dispatched upstairs, not for the first time, to check on Kitty, Angela and all the children.

*

A wonderful rich feeling of going home spread through

Bee as she drove towards Dorset. Finding herself with two flat tyres had set her back, so she was thankful the roads were not too busy, particularly as it was one of those winter days that never quite gave way to daylight. She'd only been away for two nights but she couldn't get back fast enough, knowing everyone she loved was there. She smiled, realising she now had the big, wonderful family she always wanted, albeit with no loving husband. What a great subject she would make for one of Angela's presentations on women in the workplace, she mused chuckling out loud. Bee doubted you could find a better candidate for wrong turns ending in happiness. Now Paul was finally marrying Kitty and that was completely perfect. She was, for the first time in years, actually looking forward to dressing up and playing hostess. The time had finally arrived, perhaps, when she could enjoy success without the weight of demons tied to her apron. Bee raised a virtual glass of champagne to the bride and groom as she drove, allowing herself to day dream that she herself might find love again.

*

When Kitty came down the wide staircase to greet Paul two hours later there was still no sign of Bee. It was now four in the afternoon and an already weak light was only being held at bay by snow flurries wafting around the gardens.

Kitty was proceeded by Angela and Holly, elegant and

festive in lean red silk gowns. Next came Amanda with her white velvet arm linked tightly to Alex, practising as the bride and preventing Alex from pulling at his scratchy waistcoat. Finally, just ahead of Kitty came Freya with Joseph. Joseph looked so adorable in his red silk cravat and waistcoat that Kitty had stared in wonder when she'd seen him earlier in the afternoon.

'Thank you for lending me all these beautiful children,' she had said tearfully to Angela. There was one sadness in Kitty's life that she knew she would always struggle to understand and endure.

'We wouldn't have it any other way, any of us,' Holly had interrupted, before Angela had composed an answer.

'Doesn't she look completely beautiful?' Angela was now standing at the bottom of the stairs with James, watching Kitty descend towards them. She was struck by the serene woman in front of her. The girl she'd met dishevelled and unruly was now in white silk, edged with velvet. Her hair was a mass of curls, piled high and fixed with glittering stones. No one, except Angela, knew that earlier Kitty had read and tucked away the letter confirming her father's trial with the hard won expression of suffering and strength. It had been Kitty that had gone straight to Holly, held her hands and warmly searched out her eyes. A wordless, simple act that bound the two women together and gave them both more strength than either would muster alone.

'Yes. Yes she does,' quipped James, looking at Angela

rather than Kitty before taking his place next to Paul. Angela caught his gaze and raised her eyebrows in mock disapproval, whilst a shiver of anticipation coursed through her, as it always did with James' unrestrained, wanton gaze.

James weekly marriage proposals had become an amusing game between them. Although James always held on to hope that one day Angela would agree, in reality he knew they didn't need it. What he had, now, was enough. Angela had, with long deliberation, agreed to a short European assignment but only if James went with her. It had been arranged that Holly would run James business for three months and Freya and Alex would go with them to Europe.

'We go as a family, or not at all,' Angela had stipulated to her bosses.

'The lads won't give me any trouble,' Holly had insisted. She had become used to running James office for him and knew each of them would protect her like their own. Angela marvelled at Holly's resolution to be the victor.

'Bring me back something nice,' she had bantered, 'Maybe a girl this time!' James and Angela had laughed but actually neither had completely discounted the idea of growing their family.

Angela swept her gaze lovingly over the children now whispering and poking each other at the bottom of the stairs and then replaced it with an anxious sweep across the hallway willing Bee to walk through the door.

*

Bee was only fleetingly aware of how close the car behind her was driving, before it rammed the back of her and pushed her off course. She felt it hit her again as she tried to brake. First of all she thought the weather had closed in on her, but now she realised she was spinning. She didn't see the lorry attempting to cross the dual carriageway from the side road. Even if she had, it's doubtful she would have been able to stop in time.

*

The snow came more heavily as Kitty married Paul. She smiled up at him with a complete clarity and peace that she had never felt before. This *is* perfect, she thought. Candles flickered against the still, even dusk and hundreds of fairy lights danced to their own reflection against the windows. More than once, an intangible shiver stole through Paul. It was like the cold darkness was waiting outside the windows, watching and looking for a way in. Just nerves, he thought and he chased the unwelcome notion away as Kitty squeezed his hands and cajoled his gaze back to her own, willing him to immerse with her in this one flawless, unspoiled moment.

Chapter 21

Three a.m

Paul stood, in body only, facing his friends. He seemed to blend with the pale sterile walls of the hospital waiting room. The scent of loss and decay now saturating his senses.

'They say there is no possibility of recovery.' His voice was slow and disconnected.

Kitty sank to her knees completely missing the worn blue seats, as a fresh wave of fire swam around her face. A soundless nausea moved up to her throat and burnt itself a pit, to fester and wait.

'No. No. No. This is not happening. Go and talk to the doctor again Paul. That's not right. There must be something...' Angela babbled loudly at Paul in a voice barely concealing hysteria as she lunged towards him grabbing his arm and shaking it to wake him up. James quietly intervened and tried to move her away, but Angela gripped on more desperately as Paul just stared unblinking at them both.

'Her body is dying. The Bee you know has already gone.' Paul repeated the consultant's words blindly. His body was trembling and held up only with disbelief. 'She won't regain consciousness.'

The moments between the call from the police and here and now were not linear in any of their numb, detached minds. Those silent, deafening, claustrophobic first hours would be remembered forever and yet somehow forgotten when the searing tsunami of grief hit them.

Angela was now sobbing quietly, still clutching and pulling at Paul's arm in a frenzied madness. He made no attempt to move her.

It was James that spoke next.

'You need to be back in there Paul.'

'I can't.' The spell was broken and Paul looked up at James, his eyes terrified.

'Yes. You can. We'll come with you.'

'I can't.'

'I'm not going to leave you. And you can't leave Bee.' James held his voice steady, trying to hold down the panic gripping at his ribs. It felt like nettles tightening around his gut. He could hardly breathe. He looked around the room taking in the antiseptic lines, broken only by calming coastal paintings, trying to focus on anything except the smell of distress and fear. Taking a deep breath against the world, James let go of Angela and pulled Paul against him, holding him tight and steering him slowly back towards his sister.

*

Bee lay without movement, on a bed of crisp white cotton. Her body was covered with only her head, shoulders and arms visible. Tubes and wires seemed to be everywhere and Angela gently moved Bee's hair to fall more gracefully on the pillow; Bee would want to look her best. Knowing that she would never allow shoes on the bed, Paul slipped his off and climbed next to Bee, wrapping his body around hers to keep her warm. He thought he could still feel her heart fluttering and pain pierced through him with a convulsive sob.

Through the one window in the room the world continued to languish in winter darkness. Nothing stirred outside. The ground grew steadily more frozen and the air seemed to hold the snow, silently animated. Time passed in its own tiny universe, everyone lost in the haze of disbelieving confusion. How could the most perfect day descend into this? Was this really happening? What exactly had happened? No one spoke.

Paul held Bee in his arms and closed his eyes. His head throbbed from the million words spinning and colliding with each other, utterly out of control. His heart was ready to burst from fear and the unbearable pain. When he opened his mouth to scream out, no noise came. Just tears. Unchecked, they spilled across Bee and bound them together.

James sought out Angela's fingers and clenched them tightly to remind her he was there. She looked frail leaning against the sterile wall, too tired to stay standing but too horrified to sit down. Dread was thumping through her chest and laying like curdled cream in her stomach. Her mind wildly lurched from the terror of them all losing Bee to erratic wild thoughts about the children. Every time she exhaled, she fought the urge to throw up. She had a wild notion that she should go and shake Bee. This is ridiculous and it needs to stop now, she screamed silently at Bee.

Only Kitty looked alone. Hunched over the other side of the bed from where Paul lay, she scrunched her wedding dress in one hand and wound her fingers lovingly into Bee's hair with the other. Every now and again, Paul would touch Kitty's hand gently but she didn't look up. She was silently, desperately praying. Asking for forgiveness for being selfish. Making trades with God. She would never ask for anything again she promised. She would give up all hope of having children if He would give her Bee back. What could she do to get Bee back? She would do anything. She would endure more pain and heartbreak in return for Bee. She told Him she would do anything, over and over again - silently she told Him.

All of them stayed, like this, for the longest time. Hours passed. The darkness outside gave way to a muted half attempt at day light, which no one noticed. Silence and pain filled the void and resonated off each of them. No one dared to look at the other, lest this nightmare be real.

'I think we should let her go now.' Paul's crumpled, exhausted voice was just a whisper but still everyone jumped at the sound, after hours of heavy silence.

Kitty looked at Paul and saw lines of distress etched in his face.

'No. No... I'm not ready,' she whimpered and she covered Bee with her body, as if that would make Paul stop.

Angela moved to put her arm around Kitty, which caused her head to buckle and a raging wail of grief flooded the room.

'Please Paul. Don't. There must be something.' Kitty continued to howl, finding it impossible to accept the inevitable and almost angry that Paul should.

'Please,' begged Paul quietly, 'Don't make this any harder for me.' The words choked him as he pleaded with his eyes. Kitty felt his impossible choice.

It would have been hopeless to track how quickly or

slowly time passed. As the half-hearted sun, which had barely shown its face, started to set early on another day, Angela briefly wondered if they had been there for only minutes. She looked at Paul and saw a man physically diminished by a grief he would have to live through all over again when they finally let Bee go. She looked at Kitty and saw how thin the voile of sanity could stretch before it tore beyond repair. Only the steady hand of James seemed to hold Angela up in a room that was falling away from her.

Angela watched as the machine that was breathing for Bee was finally switched off. It was a surreal quiet moment, where a last breath should have made way for another, but no one was surprised when it failed to arrive. Angela was pleased the sheets were so crisp and white. She knew that Bee would see the irony of this moment in pristine bedding.

Paul lent forward and whispered to Bee. 'We love you.'

Dizziness and detachment once again overcame Angela as images of Bee slammed into one another. Bee laughing. Bee throwing open a door, long sandy curls tumbling about. She saw the sports skirt, heard the attitude, felt her competitive determination. With a faltering intake of breath Angela wondered what they would do now - without her.

When they knew Bee could no longer hear them, that's

when they let it out. They wept love and loss, hot and fierce until their skin was sore and they only shared one thought. One certain, undeniable thought. Nothing would be the same again.

Epilogue

December - 2009
Smugglers Rest

Berry Bay Nr Fairmouth, Dorset

As Angela drove along the narrow road that hugged the coastline, she glanced out at the sea stretching away from her in an excited frothy madness, and an unexpected feeling of euphoria swept through her. She loved the journey along this road and drove it feeling the cold of the water and the sting of the salt on her skin. Despite her earlier unusually negative mood, the day had been successful with nearly everyone signing up to the JEWEL programme. Angela's mind wandered into memories she hadn't thought about in years. Jenny coaching her on how to get through an interview. Jenny elegantly sat at her desk. JEWEL would never have been possible without the legacy of Jenny living and breathing in every step Angela had ever taken and it had been fitting that Angela had named the programme after her.

She glanced over at her father sitting in the passenger

seat, looking proudly at the paperwork for her creation. The word JEWEL was emblazoned in gold across the front of a red cover, only the small print on the back gave a clue to its origins 'Jenny Empowering Women Everywhere to Live'.

'This is amazing Angela,' he spoke gently, with immense pride in his voice. It was the first time he had really studied the material, although he had followed and encouraged every step of Angela's innovation, from its early beginnings as simple talks at schools and community centres five years ago, through to the trusted advocate for young women he saw today.

'Thanks,' replied Angela lovingly. 'It's not just the workshops for teenagers now either Dad. Although, did I tell you we now have contracts with another four local government groups to provide the programme out to young women in their communities and schools? But now there's something new.' Angela could hear the excitement in her own voice. 'We've just set up a wardrobe loan system at three shelters in London. I borrowed the idea from an interview I read. Sounds daft, but sometimes all that holds a woman back from an interview is not having the right clothes to wear. I was amazed at how many shops were willing to give free clothes for free publicity.'

Angela's father patted her hand, sitting on the gear stick.

'Your mother would be very proud of you running your own company. You do know that don't you?'

'I hope so Dad. I think about her every day...'

'No regrets today Angela. It'll be a hard enough day for everyone as it is.'

'I know, but, so many things I didn't....you're right, of course, you're right.'

Angela smiled, willing back the joy, focussing on the celebration she was heading towards. There was not a day that she didn't think about her mum. Would she have done anything differently with the hindsight of life? She knew there was irony in the fact that her mother would have loved James and the children. Here Angela was, with everything she said she never wanted. She could hear her mother nagging her now to marry James, but it made her smile fondly. There was no anger now, just regret and the sad heavy knowledge that nothing could be reversed by raking it over and over through the dark hours.

She heard her father chuckle.

'What?' she asked quizzically.

'Just the name. JEWEL. Bee would have loved it.'

'So many women to thank. Not just for JEWEL, but for everything I am. I hope Bee will forgive me for selling the jewellery she left me, but I had no need for flashy.'

'She would have loved what you did with the money.

Look at the lasting legacy. School outreach programmes, training for teenagers, work experience, placements. Angela you have been unstoppable over the last five years. The fact it's paying for itself now is proof you're doing something valuable.'

Angela thought back. They had all been numb for months. Through the bitter cold of December and the near arctic temperatures of January and February. March had been swept quickly through by gales. Nothing had prepared them for the impact of Bee's death. When spring had finally shown up late and limping none of them had noticed. It was all they could manage to stumble through another day, and then another, until the weeks reeled by, then the months and the world continued to turn like the trickster it is, until each of them in turn had begun the guilty struggle of finding a new normal.

As Angela wound down the narrow lane towards Berry Bay, she felt hope. There was so much to be grateful for in their lives. This might not be where any of them imagined they would be but Bee, even in death, continued to shape the texture and pattern of their lives and in this fact, they each found their own happiness and comfort.

The cliff sat ancient and majestic as Angela helped her father out of the car. She was delighted and relieved in equal measure that time was being kind to him and, although in his eighties, his only concession to age was a walking stick. In fact, in the last few years with so many children in his life, he seemed to have taken on a new energy and sense of fun that Angela could not remember being there when she was growing up.

As they reached the Smuggler's Rest, it was clear the party was in full swing. Balloons were fastened to tables on the lower patio and outdoor heaters sat blasting out warmth to the world. For the last four years, they had met this way every December. No matter where they were or what they were doing, this date was carved into their lives as the time to celebrate. The time to remember and rejoice in Bee's life, her achievements and her children. Berry Bay was the place that held memories of Bee, and for Bee. It was where Kitty and Paul brought the children most weekends to visit Paul's parents and keep the essence of Bee alive for them.

Angela embraced Kitty tightly and lovingly. She smiled, knowing that within seconds Amanda and Joseph would spot her and bound up to sabotage the hug and claim her as their own. A thick winter chill whipped the sea into a white frenzy behind the group on the beach, who were now waving wildly and running up towards them. Of all of them, Angela thought it was Kitty that had endured the most turmoil after Bee died.

Bee had planned a surprise for Kitty that none of them could ever have imagined. In the void that existed in those early weeks, after her death, had come the news from Bee's solicitor that Bee had signed her business over to Kitty as a wedding gift.

'That's why I needed her in London just before the

wedding. She wanted to continue to run it with you of course, but she wanted it to be in your name Kitty. If only we had waited, she wouldn't have been in London, but she was insistent she wanted it all sorted before the wedding.'

Lloyd Brown had hated to interrupt their grief but he had information that just couldn't wait.
'I don't think she ever truly believed she deserved the second chance and the success it brought. She wanted you to have it Kitty. She told me, without you she wouldn't have survived what Bob did to her and the children. I don't think she ever got over the shame of what he did.'

Kitty had been struck dumb. She didn't want the business, she wanted Bee back. She felt an unreasonable fury that Bee would entrust her with so much and not be around to argue with. Bee did deserve success and certainly more than Kitty herself felt she deserved it. Kitty had agonized for months over the fact she had not only lost a friend she loved with all her heart, but she had gained money and success as a direct result.

But there was more. A entrust that would give Kitty everything she had ever wanted, at the most unthinkable cost.

'Kitty.' Lloyd Brown had insisted she sit down and listen. 'It's all signed and agreed with Bob. If Bee were to die while Bob resided in prison...you and Paul become legal guardians for their children.'

And so it was, Kitty had finally became a mother. A role she embraced with the tenderness, strength and love of a hundred women. Angela watched in awe as Kitty emerged from the fog with a determination that left them floundering, throwing herself into her life as business woman and protector. It took time of course to find new bakers to work with and Kitty fought hard to ensure the brand kept its name and reputation. Naturally, as with all grief, it sits forever by your side. Kitty could be thrown back into the abyss from a single memory, a thump to the chest. It was only in the last two years that she had become adept at accepting the blow and forcing herself back above the waves.

Now Kitty watched as Angela embraced Paul. For so long he had looked so vulnerable. Kitty had been so afraid he would never move forward after he lost Bee. It had terrified her for the longest time, that their love would slip away from them because of it.

As Amanda and Joseph reached them from the beach and bundled into their hug, Kitty smiled at Paul, who returned her gesture with a wink and she knew, completely knew, that their family was safe and solid with love and security.

'Bit of help here, this is heavy.' James had appeared from inside the bar with a tray full of drinks and was smiling broadly as he made his way down to Angela.

As he walked down to the patio, a late afternoon sun pushed through and drenched him in light. The muted winter white of the cliff and the pale cream sky shone behind him and Angela grinned. She would never grow tired of looking at his beautiful face. James put down the tray and took Angela dramatically in his arms.

'We missed you.' He inhaled her neck and smiled seductively to himself, as the familiar sultry violets enveloped him.

'I was only away two days idiot.'

'So...' James murmured as he kissed Angela's neck and worked his fingers into her hair.

Angela's body stirred as it always had done.

'Oi you two, not in front of your children,' shouted Paul, pointing to the figures making their way back up from the beach.

A beautifully pregnant Holly was followed by Alex, now a handsome young man who, James knew without a doubt, was going to cause plentiful headaches in the next few years.
Behind them Freya, now eighteen, was holding hands with a small pale child with straight glossy dark hair and large almond eyes.

'My feet hurt Frey Frey, can you carry me to see mummy?'

'Yes, my little pixie Rou. Come here.'

Freya swept Rou up in to her arms and wrapped her tightly against the sea wind. The pebbles crunched under Freya's feet and caused her to lightly stumble with the shifting weight. Rou squealed in delight as Freya pretended to drop her before setting her down lightly on the path leading up to the patio.

The last of the disenchantment that had clouded Angela's day cleared as she watched the group approach her. As they hugged her, one by one, filling the winter air with the warmth and spice of chatter and laughter her earlier frustration seemed indulgent and a sense of guilt washed over her. As they all embraced her father, Angela knew she was blessed but she also knew that a fire still burned in her belly. A fire that would never allow her to retreat into a cosy existence.

It was well past midnight and the candles had smouldered to extinction. The light from the heaters and the moon kept them company. The sea breathed quietly to one side, leaving the friends to their restful and earnest conversation. The passionate, fiery chat of earlier had given way to an easy, deep gathering of hearts and Angela bathed in the warmth of this and of the gentle snoring from Rou, snuggled on her lap under her favourite blue blanket.

'Do you think we'll ever know the truth? About the car crash I mean.' Paul spoke with no trace of anger and addressed no one in particular. Kitty reached over and squeezed his hand.

'Let's not focus on that,' she whispered quietly, glancing

around. In the absence of answers, the children, however grown up, would remain her priority. The legacy to be protected and nurtured.

'I don't think it was an accident. I never have,' added James and felt the gaze from Angela burn into his cheek without even turning to look at her. 'I'm just saying. There were people out there filled with hate.'

'One final toast before bed,' announced Angela, with a firmness in her voice that made Rou stir slightly.

'We all have so much to be thankful for. So much love and so much friendship. We are blessed to have each other and we will always remember and celebrate those we've lost.'

Angela paused and looked at each face around the table. She stopped when she reached Kitty and gazed tenderly, taking her hand and holding it tightly. She could hardly remember a time without the love of Kitty and Bee. The air suddenly wafted a little more firmly around them and the moon unexpectedly caught each face perfectly. A tang from the sea filled her nose and reminded her of the wild beauty and fragility of life. She knew Bee was close.

'This is a celebration of love, of trust, partnership and tenacity. There is nothing stronger than a bond created by time and sorrow, but the bond is only as strong as the people on either side.'

Angela took a breath to steady her voice.

'Losing someone is not the very worst that can happen. The very worst is not being able to tell them how much they mean to you. We are the lucky ones - Bee knew how loved she was.'

The sea slowed to a gentle rhythmic breathing and the moon seemed to move even higher over cliffs that would guard them for generations to come. Glasses were raised and the deepest smiles shared around the table.

'So I would like you to lift your glass and join me in a toast to Bee, and …to each other... always.'

..End

Also available by the same author:

Daughters of Daron – The Lost Daughter

Annie lived her short life blessed, and cursed, by a powerful love that came to her in the space that exists between awake and sleep. In her woodland cottage, it was intense and beautiful and ... enough. But now someone dares to reach beyond desire and the power of illusion. Ava, consumed by her Aunt Annie's stories of love and longing, starts to uncover the secrets binding them all together. As the world she knows unravels, and the beautiful strangers she meets become more dangerous, she will take you to a place full of fury, passion and vengeance. No one is who you think they are and everything has a price.
Will you follow Ava into the woods?

Daughters Ascending

Once upon a time, at the beginning of her ordinary life, Ava was offered a fairy tale.
A chance to find out who she really was. To grab what she'd always dreamed of.
But sometimes the people you've known forever, don't see things the way you do.
And those you've just met, offer the promise of the universe as easily as they hold your fragile existence.

Ava continues to walk between worlds that are tantalizing and threatening, flawless and treacherous. The fight for power and victory isn't over; The search for passion and knowledge just beginning.

Trying to make sense of the truth drags Ava deeper into battle. In the search for her place in any world, she discovers that life isn't always fair, others will want to hurt you and.... people you love, will die.

Love does not always begin and end in a manner that makes sense.
And Ava must learn it takes courage to grow up and become who you really are.

You can connect with Jane on Facebook - Jane Dare / Wearing Pink Pyjamas or follow her on twitter at www.twitter.com/ladybholaj

Jane's blog can be found at wearingpinkpyjamas.wordpress.com

Special thanks to Stephanie Parcus for her amazing cover design www.stephanieparcus.com

Printed in Great Britain
by Amazon